DEATH IS BUT THE BEGINNING

BY

KEN MYLER

Published by ACME Publications, New York

© Ken Myler, 2007
ISBN 13-digit: 978-0-9774636-1-9
ISBN 10-digit: 0-9774636-1-3

www.KenMyler.com

Cover design © Ken Myler, 2007

This book, *Death is But the Beginning*, is a work of fiction. Names, characters, places, and incidents are either the product of the author's imagination or are used fictitiously, and any resemblance to actual persons, living or dead, events, locales or other works of the same genre is entirely coincidental.

This book is dedicated to abused spouses of both genders, living in a prison they would love to call home.

Although "Death is But the Beginning" is a work of fiction, it is meant to bring to light the suffering and the hidden torture of abused and battered husbands. The fear or the embarrassment of admitting the physical abuse by the opposite sex compels these men to live their entire lives under the control of a domineering spouse.

If you have been the victim of domestic violence, there is help available. Start with www.batteredmen.com for a list of resources, advice, and help.

Danny Dillon is an abused husband who is driven to the brink of madness when he believes his enslaving wife has orchestrated his father's kidnapping. When a futile attempt to forcefully extract information from her goes wrong, he enlists the help of Barry Leonard, a man who communicates with the dead. Together, Danny, Barry, and Schmedly, a dog with a sixth sense, embark on a journey into the Deep South, searching for his missing father. But digging too deep into the afterlife can be dangerous - it could get you killed.

Chapter One

Two fingers pushed between the window blinds, separating them barely an inch. Danny Dillon stood in the dark peering out; his stomach churned. He glanced back at the clock, then at Schmedly, who lay quietly on the living room floor. They both knew the time drew near – the time when *she* came home.

It was almost five o'clock. A car crept toward the house and pulled up the double driveway. Its headlights illuminated a sign between the two garage doors reading "deliveries and customers", underscored by an arrow pointing to the right side of the house.

Danny stepped away from the window. Following the light from downstairs, he walked across the living room and down the first flight to the front door. He reached for the knob but then pulled back and continued down the second stairway to the lower floor of the split-level ranch home.

Once back at his workbench he poked around inside a half-gutted computer. Schmedly, hearing the sound of the car door, let out a low growl. Danny spun his chair around and put his index finger to his mouth.

"Shhh."

Schmedly lay down and put his snout between his paws; his tail swept the floor. Danny smiled – it was hard not to – the small black and white spotted mutt had one ear flopped over in the middle while the other stood up straight.

His smile disappeared quickly as he heard Cheryl fumbling with her keys, finally sliding the right one into the lock.

"Why aren't there any lights on in this house when I get home?" his wife screamed to him – her mild southern accent now more pronounced as she yelled.

"I was working on something and I forgot," he called back meekly.

"Come up here and help with these packages – right now."

"I'm coming, Cheryl."

He bent down and patted Schmedly on the head. "You stay here." The dog almost had a look of pity for his loving master.

Danny walked up the stairs and straight out the front door to the car. The powder blue Mercedes was a sharp contrast to his aging white van that sat adjacent. He leaned into the open trunk, snaking each arm through three plastic grocery bag handles. He attempted to lift them but the years of physical inactivity had taken its toll on his diminutive frame and the grocery bags wouldn't budge. He opted for two instead and wrestled them out of the trunk.

He climbed the first two steps but stopped, catching a glimpse of white in the back seat of her car. He glanced into the house then stepped back to the car, squinting, hoping that what he saw was a magazine or newspaper. His fears were confirmed. A plastic covering with "Saks Fifth Avenue" laid on the back seat.

Damn.

He walked back inside and laid the groceries on the counter. Cheryl returned from the bedroom, her long brown hair now out of the conservative bun that she wore for work as a legal secretary. Her designer outfit was now exchanged for a baggy sweatsuit, which only exaggerated her chubby figure.

"Cheryl, I thought we decided to cut down on the expensive clothes," he said without turning to her.

"You decided that, not me." She took a plate from the cabinet.

Schmedly stood wagging his tail at the entrance to the kitchen. Danny pointed down the stairs and waved his finger for the dog to retreat, which he did.

"We can't afford it," Danny said.

"Then you'll have to work harder or get your father to give you some money."

She flipped down a small under the counter TV and switched it on.

"Cheryl, you can't keep spending money this way."

Their eyes met for the first time.

She raised her voice slightly. "Like I said, you'll just have to work harder."

Danny hung his head as he left the kitchen. He stopped before descending to the workshop and gazed with disgust at the professionally decorated living room. Ultra modern furniture was accompanied by small, strangely shaped statues. Décor such as this was more suited for a wealthy household rather than their middle class status.

He continued down, but as he passed the front door, he froze – his stomach knotted. He had almost forgotten his daily chore – the bringing of the mail. He returned with a handful of envelopes. He stopped at the bottom of the stairs.

A fluorescent bulb, one of many in a long row of fixtures spanning the lower level, flickered. Four long tables set together end to end were littered with computers in various stages of repair. Against a wall was an unfinished wooden desk covered with papers but in an orderly fashion. A Budweiser logo swept back and forth as a screen saver on the computer monitor atop the desk. Two file cabinets sat adjacent and a cork bulletin board displayed colorful pushpins holding reminders of overdue bills. This was the accounting and customer service department. In the far corner was Danny's refuge.

Schmedly greeted him with a low "woof". Danny quickly quieted him.

"C'mon over here and open the mail with me."

Danny motioned for the dog to follow him to his makeshift den. A black leather recliner sat in front of a console television – both more than a decade old. He tapped the TV remote, turning on the news. Schmedly jumped into his lap and licked his face.

"Hey you're kinda heavy for a lap dog. Thank God I have you. I don't know what I'd do without you."

He sifted through the mail, separating bills from the junk – it was two to one in favor of the bills. He sliced open envelope after envelope from credit card companies and department stores. He stared at them – at forty years old, this was not the financial position he wanted.

"She's killing us, Schmed."

Danny could hear Cheryl pull a chair out from under the kitchen table upstairs. They were both hungry but dinner would have to wait until she was finished.

"We can eat soon." He pulled the dog close but then nudged him off his lap as the business phone rang.

"Dillon's Computer Repair," he answered. "Oh, yes; that'll be delivered to you in the next couple days – we're almost finished with it... Very good, thank you."

He walked to the table where the repaired computers were boxed and ready to be sent out. He lifted a tag on one and slid it to the beginning of a line.

"He's a good customer; let's get this out to him tomorrow."

Schmedly scratched at the back door.

"You want to go out? Okay, c'mon, I'll take a walk with you," he said, throwing on a jacket. He pushed open the door.

Schmedly immediately ran to the fence and barked. Danny was right on his heels, grabbing him and holding is mouth closed.

"You want to upset the witch?"

A quiet laugh came from the other side of the fence. The yard was dark but Danny could still make out the silhouette of man and a large cylindrical object.

"Kanook?"

"Yeah Danny, I'm just searchin' the heavens. You wanna come over and take a look through the telescope?"

"Not right now. I'm hungry and so's the dog. Just waiting for her to finish."

The tall thin figure came to the fence and reached over to pet Schmedly.

"She just got home?"

"Yeah." Leaves swirled around his ankles - the brisk November breeze gave him a chill. His jaw trembled as he tried to talk. "Let me get back in and see if she's done eating."

"Hey, you never answered me on my wife's cousin, Barry Leonard. He's only in Hartford for a month, man. Then he goes back to LA. Maybe our only chance to see him do his thing for a while," Kanook said.

"I'll think about it - I'm not too keen on the whole idea... but let me think about it. Let you know in the next couple days." He gave a wave. "C'mon Schmed."

He tiptoed to the stairs and listened. The TV was on in the living room, meaning the kitchen was clear. "Let's go; I'll feed you," he whispered to the dog, who already knew the routine of sneaking quietly up the stairs.

Danny reached under the counter and took out a can of dog food. Schmedly danced around in circles - something Danny never tired of watching.

"Danny, is it possible for you to feed that dog downstairs from now on?" Cheryl called in from the living room - or as Danny liked to call it - the temple. "I had a white hair in my food tonight."

He didn't answer, confused that she had asked him to do something instead of demanding it.

"By the way, how was your day?" she asked.

Danny stood up straight and smacked himself on the side of the head to make sure that he wasn't dreaming. He bent down next to Schmedly who was nose deep in his food. "Somebody stole our Cheryl and replaced her with a robot."

He peeked into the living room. From his angle he could see her profile as she sat in her vibrating massage chair. He watched as she lifted a brandy snifter to her lips and immediately understood the reason for her congeniality. She gulped down the remainder of the liquor.

Danny bent over and whispered into the dog's ear. "She's drinking again but I must say she's much more pleasant to be around. Maybe tomorrow I'll buy her a case of booze. Hey -

maybe if I'm lucky I'll get to have sex tonight." He stood and laughed loudly.

"Danny, what are you laughing about? Did you hear me before?"

He thought a brief minute of polite conversation would be refreshing even though it was the liquor speaking.

"What did you say? I didn't hear you."

"I said 'How was your day?'"

Danny tried to find something interesting to say but there were no new contracts and no new money coming in to appease the queen.

"Nothing much happened today – same as every day."

"Oh," she replied with a yawn, and the conversation was over.

Danny sat at his desk and leaned back in his chair. His black, thick rimmed glasses, which were eons old, were now heavy on the bridge of his nose. He rubbed his eyes and held the glasses up to the light. After a quick clean, he was almost ready. He opened the top desk drawer and took out a comb. He stroked it across his slightly greasy, receding black hair as if he were about to go on a date. He hummed quietly as he moved his mouse over the pad, bringing the computer out of hibernation. He logged on to a chat room.

"Hi guys," he said as he typed in the words.

The words "Hi Danny" popped up twelve times on his screen. He looked to see which of his computer buddies were online. This was the only place where he and others could feel safe talking about their shared torment.

"Where's Sid?" he typed.

Someone came back with, "I spoke to him on the phone – she smashed his computer."

Danny shook his head. He knew that to these men this chat room was their only form of friendship – a place to console each other.

Danny had allotted a half an hour for his friends. The computers behind him required his attention and soon he was into a broken laptop. By midnight he could no longer focus. He gave Schmedly a nudge. The dog lifted his head with a yawn.

"Bedtime," he whispered.

Schmedly got up shaking himself and almost fell over. Danny got behind him and helped him up the stairs. He tiptoed to the master bedroom door and peeked in. Cheryl snored lightly. He could see her face from the glow of a small night-light. He went into the opposite bedroom where Schmedly was already stretched out on the bed.

"Hey, save some room for me, will you?"

The dog thumped his tail as Danny lifted the covers and slid in.

"Goodnight pal."

By six the next morning, Danny was back in the workshop. Cheryl would be extra ornery after her drinking the night before and he didn't want to cross paths.

They could hear her walking in the kitchen and sat quietly awaiting her departure. She hadn't said a word and he had hoped it would stay that way but luck wasn't on his side.

"Danny...Danny, where are you," she yelled.

"Down here."

"I forgot to mention last night that we're going to dinner with some people from my office on Friday. We're going to that new restaurant, Shine."

He didn't say a word. He knew that it was a pricey restaurant but rather than start an argument, he sat quietly. The front door slammed – they were free for nine hours.

Schmedly stood at the back door.

"You want out? You want to wait for him?"

Danny let him out to wait for his assistant, Tommy. Within ten minutes, Danny heard talking outside and Schmedly barking. He held open the door – the excited dog came running in search of a ball.

"Hey Tommy."

"Hi Danny," he replied, bending down to pull the ball out of Schmedly's mouth. He gave it a soft roll under the table. The dog went scampering after it.

Tommy stood tall and was of Pakistani descent but spoke perfect English. He had only been working with Danny for a month but he was already an indispensable assistant. He knew his way around the inside of a computer and had one important attribute – Schmedly liked him. That was Danny's sure-fire way of telling if a person was genuine.

"No time for play now Schmed. We have lots of work to do," Danny said.

"Okay Tommy, this is what I need you to do." He handed Tommy a small box. "I need you to deliver a couple that are done. One has to go to Hartford – it'll take you a little time. You can take the stuff later. Right now start working on that one over there," Danny said, pointing to a laptop.

Tommy seemed preoccupied and wasn't really paying attention.

"You okay, Tommy?"

"Oh yeah, sorry. It's just last night I read about a guy that I knew in high school. He was killed in an accident. It's really bothering me."

"That's too bad."

"Yeah... Nice guy too."

"Maybe I can hook you up with Kanook for some tickets to Barry Leonard. Maybe your friend will contact you – if you believe in that stuff."

"First, what's a Kanook?" Tommy asked.

Danny laughed. "I've mentioned my neighbor, Kanook, haven't I? Half Native American, half Eskimo." Danny thought for a moment. "Yes I did – you even met him once."

"Oh, the guy next door," he said, unscrewing the bottom panel of the computer.

"Well he's rather an odd duck but real good people. Really into alien stuff and astronomy. His wife's cousin is Barry Leonard – the guy who speaks to the dead. Ever hear of him?" Danny asked.

"Oh...Yeah, I saw a show on him once. He performs all over the country... I guess the best word is performs. Funny... I wouldn't figure you for someone who would believe in that kinda thing, Danny."

"I thought about trying it. Thought maybe I'd be able to hear from my mom. This guy is coming to Hartford this weekend. I don't know – then there's the problem of my wife. I'd have to sneak."

"Sneak? To go see a psychic?" Tommy asked with both sympathy and disbelief.

"I don't want to get too much into it but let's just say that my wife and I don't really get along too well."

"Okay."

"Let me know if you want to go, Tommy, and I'll see what I can do."

Early afternoon brought a light rain. Danny helped Tommy pack his truck with computers to be delivered.

"Remember, don't take any wooden nickels," Danny said.

Tommy just looked confused.

"Just go."

Danny turned the corner toward the back door. "Have you been a good dog today?" he called to Schmedly who waited inside. Schmedly knew this signal – it meant let's go to Grampa's. The dog was so excited he could barely bark. Danny opened the back door for the out of control mutt.

"Easy now, easy. You want to go see Grampa?"

As Schmedly calmed a bit, his bark returned. Danny watched and laughed, for with every woof that he let out, his one half flopped ear would stand for a second, and then fall again.

Danny harnessed Schmedly into the van's passenger seat and off they went. Schmedly's window was cracked just enough to get his nose out for the passing scents. Within fifteen minutes, they were on a country road just outside their residential community. Even with the rain, the freedom of being out of the house – the jail – was exhilarating. How nice it would be if it were just the two of them. Danny glanced over at his dog as he held back tears.

Danny stopped at the guard booth of his father's gated community. The security guard waved him through. Stately homes on acre plots lined both sides of the Belgian block curbed street. As he passed the community center, Schmedly let out a long bark, sounding almost like a howl, knowing they were near.

"Grampa's house, Grampa's house," Danny yelled, egging him on.

He pulled into the driveway. Danny's father, George was already at the front door. He was rather a non-descript gentleman of average height and grayish white hair.

Schmedly was now in a frenzy. Danny unhooked him and leaned over to open the door. The dog, his nails losing grip on the driveway, ran towards George. They disappeared into the house before Danny was out of the van.

Once inside Danny knew exactly where to find them – the kitchen, where the dog biscuits were.

"Not so many, Dad. Last time he didn't eat dinner when we got home."

George was down on one knee as Danny came in the kitchen.

"Did you hear me?"

"I heard you, I heard you. This is only the first one," he said, having a tug of war with the dog.

Danny opened the refrigerator and took out a container of orange juice. He poured while watching his father act like a child, sliding around on the floor. Schmedly let out a playful growl as they both tugged on the large biscuit. Danny knew it couldn't last long and after a minute George was reaching for a helping hand to lift him.

"Oh, my back," he said, as he rubbed his lower lumbar. "How are you, Son?"

They embraced and then settled in the expansive living room.

"So, how's things going over there?" George asked.

"Nothing different, Dad."

"Danny, you gotta get out. You gotta leave. Come here and live with me." He looked down at Schmedly, who was lying at his feet. "Tell your father that you want to come live here with me."

Schmedly stood up and barked.

"Dad, every time I come here the conversation starts out the same. Just once I'd like to talk about something else before you start in. You don't get it... it's not that easy. I'll lose my house."

"So what? This'll be your house when I die. Start living here now."

George got up and searched around. "Now where is that thing? Here it is."

He held up a remote control. "Look what I had put in." He hit the button and the fireplace flame lit automatically.

"Look, dad, all this stuff is nice but I worked hard for my house."

George cut him short.

"But you're in a prison with that bitch. Now I told you, when I die, my will states that you get nothing 'til you divorce her – so just leave now and get it started."

Danny looked ashamed. "I can't, I just can't."

George nodded his head. "You're afraid. I understand but you don't have to tell her. Just move out in the middle of the day. I'll hire a crew."

Danny kneeled on a couch under the picture window and looked out over the front yard.

"Dad, she's got something on me, all right? I never told you because I figured you'd be pissed."

"On you? What could she possibly have on you?"

He let out a deep sigh. "I wasn't exactly honest with my taxes for past seven years."

"Oh, Danny, how could you let her find out about that?"

"When we first got married, she had these visions of me making millions fixing computers. Things were different then – we got along great... I told her everything. Now... well you know."

"If you go to the IRS and tell them what you did, you'd get by with just having to pay the back taxes and penalties."

"We're talking lots of money, Dad."

"I've got lots of money – let's fix it."

"Can't let you do that, Dad. Could we talk about something else? I feel like shit now... now that you know I've got this hanging over my head."

George walked back to the kitchen. Schmedly's ears perked up hearing the rattling of the biscuit box again. He returned with a glass of juice and biscuit, gently dropping it between the front paws of the lying dog. He sat the glass down and ran for the phone.

"Hello? Hello?" he placed the phone back down. "Every day I'm getting these hang ups. Really annoying. C'mon, I'll beat you at a few hands of gin."

It was already dark when Danny backed out his father's driveway. He had to hurry if he wanted to beat her home. It was better that way – no questions about where he was.

Across the street from his father's, a dark colored van had just turned off its lights. Danny pulled away, and then slowed as he saw the silhouette of a man outside the van. He thought about going back to get the plate number but knew that all vehicles entering the development had to sign in and were expected by a homeowner, unless the guard recognized the driver. He drove on.

Friday night came too soon. Danny reluctantly took his only suit from the guest bedroom closet. He once had space in the master bedroom walk-in but now it held so many designer outfits that there was little room for anything of his. Cheryl had laid a tie on the bed for him. He examined it front and back.

"Cheryl, don't you think this tie is a little bold?"

"No, it's fine. Just wear it," she called back. "And put your contacts in."

"But they kill my eyes."

"You can't go to a high class restaurant with these people wearing those silly looking glasses. Now put the contacts in."

He sat on the bed with his head in his hands. Schmedly, who had been lying on the floor, came up from behind and licked Danny's ear.

"I know Buddy, I know."

Danny dressed slowly. When it came time to put on the tie, he turned to Schmedly. "What knot should I go with? I'm thinking a hangman's noose."

"Let's go, I'm waiting for you," Cheryl yelled from the living room.

"Coming, my little piranha fish," he murmured under his breath. After putting in his contacts, he walked out.

"Let me see," she said, spinning him around and brushing lint off his shoulders. "Doesn't look bad. Let's go."

Danny approached the driver's door. Cheryl came up behind him.

"Get on the other side, I'm driving. Your driving sucks."

Danny glanced around at the neighbors' houses, praying that no one was watching. He walked to the passenger side.

The valet opened the door for Cheryl and handed her a numbered ticket. Once inside they were greeted by the maitre d'.

"We're a bit late for the Carlson party. Seven o'clock - party of eight," Cheryl said to the man.

"Right this way, Madam."

The only thing on Danny's mind was a strong drink but he'd need a second to forget the price of the first.

"Cheryl," an older gentleman called out. "We started to think you weren't coming."

"Blame my husband. He took his time getting ready."

They made the rounds of shaking hands and kissing hello. The men at the table stood and waited as the maitre d' slid Cheryl's chair in.

"That's a beautiful dress," one of the wives noted.

"Gucci," she announced proudly.

"I guess your computer company is doing very well, Danny."

He gave a little nod and smile and then glanced at Cheryl. Trying to avoid conversation, he picked up a menu and prayed that it wasn't one of those menus that didn't include prices. This was going to cost him. He searched for what he thought would be the least expensive item but it seemed that everything was stuffed with lobster, covered with lobster or drizzled with lobster sauce.

The waiter hovered over Cheryl, his pad in hand, as she perused the menu.

"I think I'll have the surf-n-turf," she said, handing the waiter back the menu. "But make sure there's nothing in any of my food with nuts - very important."

"I understand, ma'am," the waiter said, making a note. He looked toward the men for their orders. Danny had decided on stuffed pork chops although he would have been much happier with a bowl of warm broth to save money.

He sipped from his glass of water, trying to hide his uneasiness. These weren't his kind of people. He would have been much more comfortable chatting with the waiters.

Cheryl had just finished her salad when Danny noticed her face turn a fiery red.

"Is it real hot in here all of a sudden?" she asked.

Danny, who was about to put a forkful of food into his mouth, stopped and dropped it onto the plate. He knew what that question meant although Cheryl herself hadn't figured it out yet.

"How's your breathing?" he asked.

She gave him a panicked look, quickly realizing what he was asking. She stood up, as did Danny.

"Sit back down and don't panic. Give me your bag," he said.

"What's going on," one of the women asked.

"She may have eaten something with nuts - she's allergic," Danny replied. "Someone call 911."

Cheryl started to wheeze and became light headed. She slumped in the chair. Danny fumbled with her bag as he searched for the kit. He pulled out a small plastic box and withdrew a hypodermic needle.

The entire restaurant was silent, watching Danny as he laid her down on the floor. The waiters and maitre d' huddled around him. He injected a dose of Epinephrine into her upper arm.

"Now what?" the waiter asked.

"Now we wait for the Epinephrine to take effect and get her to the hospital."

Danny's heart pounded as he watched Cheryl's body slipping into anaphylactic shock. None the less, he couldn't seem to escape the thought that he no longer had to pay for the meal and there would be no doggie bag for Schmedly.

"You still breathing okay?" he asked her.

She nodded. He draped his jacket over her and used another man's jacket as a pillow.

"The paramedics should be here soon," he said.

Within fifteen minutes, paramedics rolled a stretcher into the restaurant and put an oxygen mask over her face. By then she was almost unconscious.

"We need to intubate her – she's not getting any air here," one of the paramedics said.

He had the tube down her throat on the first try. Her chest now raised and lowered but not at a normal rate. The paramedic squeezed air into her lungs with a plastic bottle. Her face was still red and now began to swell. She was still starving for oxygen.

"You wanna ride with us to the hospital?" the second paramedic asked Danny.

"No, I'll follow you. I need a way to get back home."

The paramedic who had inserted the tube held a stethoscope to her chest and listened.

"Her heart rate is way out of whack here. We need to get her there fast." He ripped open a package and jabbed a needle with another dose of Epinephrine into her arm.

Danny held an IV bottle the paramedic had handed him. "Just hold it for a minute 'til my partner gets a free hand. Hold it higher," he said, grabbing his wrist and raising it up.

As they wheeled her out, Danny stood in shock. Tears rolled down his cheeks, "Cheryl, oh God, Cheryl," he cried.

Her friends offered Danny a ride to the hospital but he didn't hear them. He finally came around after one man gave him a gentle shake, "No, no, I can get there okay."

He picked up Cheryl's purse and walked toward the door. He felt true sorrow but in the back of his mind he felt what he hadn't in many years – possible freedom.

Chapter Two

Danny sat in the emergency waiting room. It had been an hour since hearing from anyone on the medical staff. He had only been called to fill out paperwork.

Two couples from the restaurant sat across from him. Directly to his left, an old woman slept across three seats. It was obvious that she hadn't bathed in some time. The TV above them featured the local news, which they all feigned interest in to avoid small talk. Without being rude, Danny had subtly let it be known that he would rather be without questions. He hadn't any knowledge of how Cheryl had portrayed their relationship to these people.

A doctor carrying a chart came from the treatment area. "Dillon? Mr. Dillon?"

"Right here." Danny walked over and shook his hand.

"I'm Doctor Weller. Your wife is stable but she's in for a rough ride. We can't seem to get her heart rhythm quite right. I don't think it's life threatening but... I can't guarantee it. She's going to be in for a couple days at least." He looked down at the chart. "I see she's been in before for this."

Cheryl's friends gathered behind Danny and listened.

"Yeah, she's been here twice for the same thing."

"Maybe it's time she stopped eating out. The next time might kill her."

"You tell her that. It'll save me a fortune," Danny joked.

The doctor laughed. "You can go in and see her. She's in A3." The doctor addressed her friends. "Immediate family only."

"Danny, you'll come tell us how she is, right?" Cheryl's girlfriend asked.

"I'll come right back as soon as I see her – no reason for you to wait around here after that. Write down your numbers and I'll call you later," he said, pleasantly. He turned back to the doctor.

"She's going to be okay though?" he asked, not knowing which answer he wanted.

"She should be but like I said, it's going to take a little time. This is a tough thing to predict."

Danny walked through the automatic doors and looked above the closed curtains for the stall number. The suffering in this expansive ward was obvious from the loud moaning, crying and deep coughing. He spun around, unable to find the number.

"What number are you looking for?" a nurse asked him.

"A3."

She pointed him to the far corner of the ward. A nurse was just coming out from behind the curtain.

"Are you her husband?"

"Yes."

"She's breathing on her own. We were able to remove the tube but she'll be on oxygen for a good while. I'll be back a little later to see how things are."

Danny put on a bright face and pushed past the curtain. She turned her head to look at him.

"How you feeling?" he asked.

She tried to speak but with her tongue still swollen, the words could not be formed. She just nodded and looked up at the ceiling.

"Doctor says you're going to be in for a couple days. They'll move you out of here and upstairs like last time I guess," he said, moving a cart away from the side of the bed to get closer. "Anything you want from home?"

She shook her head.

"Want me to call any of your friends?"

She shook her head quickly this time. Danny forgot that her vanity would never allow anyone to see her like this.

"What about your family? Want me to call them? Maybe they'll come up from Georgia quick if they know you're in the hospital."

She opened her eyes wide and made a face as if Danny were being a wise ass. He knew that she would never want to worry them over her condition. He always thought it peculiar how she could care for and treat them like human beings but him...

"Some of your friends from the restaurant are outside. They weren't allowed in. I promised I'd let them know how you were doing. I'll run out and tell them how you are."

Cheryl's friends rushed toward him as he passed through the doors.

"She can't talk because of the swelling but she feels okay. Time will tell."

One of the women handed Danny a piece of paper. "Here are my numbers. You can just call me and I'll let everyone else know what's happening."

"Okay and... really thanks for coming."

Danny waved goodbye as he pushed the button for the automatic door. He took his time walking back to the bed. What would they or rather he talk about? She couldn't converse and even if she could they'd have nothing to say. At least when she was situated in a room there would be a TV.

"I told your friends you're okay. I have their numbers and I'll call them with any news."

Cheryl didn't acknowledge his words.

"Do you want me to stay?"

She just gave him a look of "Are you kidding?"

"Fine but how 'bout I go to the store and bring some magazines?"

For an instant Danny thought he saw a glimmer of appreciation and walked off to the gift shop.

Danny walked through the parking lot, cell phone in hand. He was afraid to make the call but it was inevitable. He dialed.

"Hello?"

"Dad, it's me. I'm at the hospital. Cheryl had another allergic reaction at the restaurant."

George paused for a moment. "How is she?"

"You don't have to pretend, Dad. I know your feelings. She's going to be in for a couple days."

"This is it. This is your chance to move out clean. Be gone by the time she gets home, Danny," George said, excitedly.

"Dad, c'mon. I can't just move out like that. She needs someone to take care of her for at least a week."

"I'll hire a freakin' nurse. Listen; stop over here on the way home. We'll talk."

"I gotta get home for Schmed. I'll... I'll stop by tomorrow."

"Call me. Let me know what time."

Danny was more than a half mile from home when Schmedly sat up from a sound sleep on the kitchen floor. As Danny drew closer, the dog became more excited, running up and down the stairs. By the time Danny pulled into the driveway, the dog was dancing in circles.

"How's my doggie?" he called as he opened the door. "I know I promised leftovers but we had a little problem." He followed the dog down the stairs to the back door and then outside.

"Kanook? You over there?"

"You betcha'. Stars are twinklin' tonight. You just comin' back from dinner?" he asked, walking toward the fence.

"Cheryl had a bad reaction to something she ate. She's in the hospital."

Kanook glanced back at his house to see if his wife was in earshot. "Perfect time to pack up and move out, man."

"That's what my dad said."

"Well then do it – I'll help you."

"Nah, I can't. She's going to need my help when she gets home."

Danny recalled the past two occasions when Cheryl had come home from the hospital. She was almost nice – she appreciated him – and that felt good. Maybe she would change this time.

"At least come with me to see Barry Leonard talk to the dead."

Danny thought for a moment and for the first time in many years he was excited about doing something. He didn't have to get her permission. He could just go. But his high ended abruptly.

"What am I thinking? I have to go to the hospital." He took a ball from Schmedly's mouth and threw it toward the back of the yard.

"Make something up. We can go like Sunday in the afternoon. It'll be a trip."

A smile came to Danny's face.

"Yeah... yeah, okay, let's do it. I can go see her in the morning and make something up. We'll talk more about it tomorrow – I'm freezing here. Not to mention the fact that I can't wait to sleep in the big bed. I'm sick of that little bed me and Schmed have to squeeze on to."

Danny blew into his hands to warm them as he held the door for Schmedly.

"Let's have hot chocolate and cake and cookies and what else?"

He looked down at Schmedly, who hadn't seen his master this happy in ages.

"And let's really piss her off – let's eat it all in the living room."

Schmedly let out a bark of agreement as Danny boiled hot water. He filled two plates, one with cookies for himself and the other with dog treats. He carried them into the living room. Schmedly hopped on his hind legs as he followed, sniffing the air. Danny stopped short as he approached the massage chair.

"Maybe we should just eat this stuff in the kitchen, then come in here."

He did an about face. They dined on junk food and dog treats until they were both sated. Crumbs littered the floor.

"Know what? Let's forget the living room and go straight to bed – the big bed."

Schmedly scampered down the hall and turned right into the guestroom. Danny followed but turned left into the master bedroom. He wondered how long it would take for the dog to come looking for him and soon after, a confused pup poked his head into the off limits.

"You found me? C'mon up here. We're sleeping like kings tonight."

Danny thought about what he had just said. Other people – normal people – slept like this every night. Schmedly jumped up on the bed while Danny played with the remote. Within minutes both were snoring.

By midmorning, George and Danny had already begun their ritual of playing gin.

"So how is she?" George asked, not looking very concerned.

"I called the hospital this morning and they said she was the same. Stable."

"You've got the chance to get out now and not have to rush. We'll fix the IRS thing. She won't have nothin' on you."

Danny got up and paced around the table. "You don't understand. She needs me now. When she needs me, she's nice... kind. I'm hoping she'll change when she gets out. Maybe coming so close to death she'll change."

"Did she change the last two times?" George asked, pointing to a card he had thrown down.

"She did for a while. Maybe this time it'll be for good. It was really good... when we first...you had to see her face when I brought her some magazines from the gift shop." Danny spoke softly, "It almost looked like she loved me again."

George was far from convinced. "Okay, Danny, give her this one last chance. Then promise me you'll get out if she goes back to the same way she was." He waited for an answer.

"All right Dad. If she doesn't come around this time, I'll make the move."

George jumped to his feet and howled, setting Schmedly off on a barking tantrum. Danny immediately regretted making the promise, knowing his father would be on him constantly to comply.

Danny left Schmedly with George for later retrieval on his way back from the hospital.

He rolled in reverse down the driveway. Snow flurries filled the air, even though the sun was peeking in and out. Once in the street, he looked back. Schmedly stood on the couch watching him out the front window.

The hospital parking lot was full, as was the emergency waiting room. Lines formed in all directions. He waded through the people searching for the door. Even though he had high hopes for Cheryl's new found love for him, he wasn't in a real rush to see her. He approached the nurses' desk.

"Is my wife still here or did they move her?" he asked, looking back in the direction of the spot she had filled. "Last name Dillon."

"No, she's still back there. We don't have any beds available yet, so she's staying here," the nurse said.

"How is she?"

"Oh, I wouldn't know. You'll have to ask her nurse or find the doctor... if you can. It's been crazy."

"Thank you."

He slid past the curtain where Cheryl lay. She was dozing. He reached out his hand to rub her cheek but pulled away.

"Cheryl? You awake?"

She looked up at him and nodded.

"How do you feel?" he asked.

She shrugged her shoulders but still wasn't able to talk.

"Let me go find your doctor."

After a quick consultation with the doctor, Danny returned. "He says your heart still isn't quite right and that you'll be here 'til at least Monday."

She rolled her eyes in disgust.

"They'll hopefully have a room for you in a couple hours. At least there'll be a TV. I'm guessing you're kinda bored."

She tried to talk but couldn't. She made a motion of writing. He opened a drawer next to the bed where he found a pen and paper. She scribbled "more magazines – better yet book."

"Okay, I'll run down to the gift shop and see what they got."

He took his time weaving through the corridors. Time in the hospital was time served whether or not he was actually with her. He bought two magazines and a paperback and delivered them back to her. Now he needed to muster up the courage to set the big lie in motion.

"Listen Cheryl, I've got this big customer that needs his stuff delivered early next week. I figured, though, with you coming home around then it'd be better if I went tomorrow and got it over with. It's up near Hartford. What do you think?"

She mouthed, "Okay".

He spent two hours sitting next to her while she thumbed through a magazine. There was no conversation. The nurse finally broke their silence.

"A bed just became available. We're going to move you now. Mr. Dillon, there's no reason for you to stay – you can't come up with her."

Two orderlies waited behind the nurse while Danny said goodbye. He watched as they wheeled past, an IV bottle still swinging overhead.

He stepped lively in the parking lot, thinking about Sunday's big plans. The anticipation wasn't as much for the venue as it was for the freedom. He never gave much thought of the afterlife and the thought of someone speaking to the dead seemed more like a carnival sideshow trick. He gave a quick call to his father that he was on his way back and to order food.

* * * * *

They sat at the dining room table, eating pizza and watching college football. Danny leaned back in the chair and patted his small potbelly. Schmedly chomped on a pizza crust.

"I didn't tell you but I'm going with Kanook tomorrow... up to Hartford," Danny said with his mouth full. "His cousin is that guy who speaks to the dead."

George stopped chewing for a moment and smiled, "If you speak to your mother, find out where my putter is."

"Dad!" Danny said, looking toward the mantle where his mother's ashes sat.

"Just a little joke. I don't believe in that crap, do you?"

"Not really but it's a day out."

"Have a great time," George said, carrying a plate into the kitchen.

Danny waved as he pulled away from the house. About half way down the block, headlights approached. A dark van, similar to the one he had seen in front of his father's house, crept past. The silhouette of the driver's face looked familiar but it was too dark to identify him. Danny slowed, deciding this time maybe he should get the plate number. Two cars followed behind the van and by time he was able to spin his car around, the van had disappeared down one of the many side streets in the development. There was also a large construction area where new homes were being built. He dare not take the Mercedes onto any dirt roads on a wild goose chase.

That's strange - he was going so slow. How could I lose him?

Danny stopped at the front gate.

"Excuse me," he called to the guard. "A dark van passed me down the road a ways. Any idea who it was?"

"I'm sorry, I can't give out any information. I can tell you that we check out everyone that comes through - if that helps."

"It's okay. I just thought I recognized the guy, that's all."

* * * * *

Early Sunday morning, Danny sprang from the bed and danced his way to the bathroom. Schmedly was so comfortable in the big bed, he barely moved. After showering, Danny checked the time and guessing that Kanook was already up at eight, dialed his number.

"Hello," the sleepy voice said.

"Hey, it's Danny – you still asleep?"

"I was. Time is it?"

"It's eight. Sorry to wake you but I figured if we're going into the city, we might as well make a day of it. You know, walk around, have lunch. I mean c'mon – she can't talk so she can't call me."

"Give me an hour," Kanook said groggily.

Danny let Schmedly roam a distance on his retractable leash in Kanook's driveway. The dog knew there was something up as he sniffed around nervously. Kanook came to the front door and waved them in.

"Okay, Schmed, you're going to stay with Sandy today while we're out."

At first the dog didn't want to climb the stairs, knowing he was going to have a baby sitter while his master was at play. But after hearing Sandy's voice, a light bulb lit up. He had stayed there before and was treated with table scraps and even a small steak once. His tail wagged as he pulled Danny inside.

"Hi, Sandy. Thanks for taking him."

"Oh no problem. Happy to have him. How's Cheryl doing?"

"She's still stable – at least that's what they call it. Still can't talk but the doc said she can come home tomorrow night."

Danny bent down in front of Schmedly right inside the house. "Now you be good. I don't want a bad report when I get back."

Schmedly licked his face in acknowledgement, and then followed Sandy to the kitchen. Danny looked Kanook up and down.

"Problem?"

"Thought maybe you'd dress a little more... well dressy."

Kanook looked down at his garb - jeans and army boots with a fatigue jacket. A green bandana with a white peace sign circled his forehead - he was the quintessential throw back to the sixties.

"I told him he needed to wear something a little nicer," Sandy called from the kitchen. "See what Danny's wearing?"

"I was going to take off the bandana when we got there," Kanook said.

Danny tried not to laugh but his smirk could only hold back so much. Kanook sighed, feeling like a young boy being sent to change his clothes by his mother. He disappeared around the corner and down the hall.

He returned minutes later in brown corduroys and a denim jacket - his hair pulled back in a small ponytail. Danny had anticipated Kanook's change of clothes to be less than a vast improvement and had no comment other than, "Let's go," when he returned.

Kanook did eighty along the empty highway in his rickety old station wagon. Danny hummed along to a 70's tune playing on an old eight-track tape deck Kanook had mounted under the dash as a joke.

"All right, tell me more about this guy and speaking to the dead," Danny said, lowering the volume.

"You've seen him on TV, you said, right?"

"It's going to be the same type thing? He just picks people that he thinks... how do I word this. When a spirit comes through, he matches it up with the person in the audience?"

"Basically. And today is invitation only so there's going to be a smaller group. This way hopefully everybody gets connected to a loved one. I'm hoping to speak to my son," Kanook said, choking up. "Haven't spoken to him in five years."

"But he's been dead for ten."

"I've spoken to him through Barry before."

Danny looked surprised. "You never mentioned that before."

"Yeah, I know... didn't think you'd take me serious, man," he said, cracking the window and lighting a cigarette. "But now you're going to see what it's like to be there and... and... well, you'll have to experience it yourself – you'll see."

Danny's stomach got a quick tickle of butterflies at the thought of his mother contacting him through this medium.

"I just don't see why people need to talk to the dead – if that's really what's happening."

"Don't you want to know if there's an afterlife?" Kanook asked.

"What for? If there is I'll see all my friends and family when I go. If there isn't, I'll never know because when I die... that'll just be the end. Like when you fall asleep at night, you don't know that you went to sleep until you wake up. You have no memory of falling asleep, right?"

Kanook smiled and shook his head. "You're a strange dude, Danny."

"I'm just saying, when you die, it might be like falling asleep and never waking up. You'll never know that you went to sleep and you just never wake up."

"It ain't like that. I'll bet that after you see this guy, your whole outlook on life will change."

Danny glanced at the speedometer. "We're not really in a rush, Kanook. Try and keep it under a hundred, will you?"

He lifted his hand off the wheel to see his speed. "What, I'm doin' seventy-eight."

"And another thing," Danny started to say, making Kanook roll his eyes. "Why does everyone want to live 'til they're a hundred? Why do people go to such extraordinary lengths to prolong their life?"

Kanook glanced at him like he was nuts. "Danny, you gotta get out more. And do me a favor – don't ask Barry any of these questions. He gets lunatics asking him crazy stuff like this all the time."

"Sorry, I'll just observe."

"No, I want you to interact. Just don't flip out on me."

He breathed a sigh of relief when Danny stopped talking, then reached down and turned the volume back up to give him the hint.

Kanook took the exit ramp and within a mile they were inside the Hartford city limits. Like two boys out on their own for their first time without chaperones, they spent hours exploring the city. By the time they reached the hotel both had runny noses from the cold.

Kanook approached the concierge. "Where is Barry Leonard doing his thing today?"

"Down that hall," the woman said, pointing his way.

"We'll just go into the audience seats right now," Kanook said. "After we'll go back and see Barry backstage."

"Whatever you say."

Kanook gave the man at the door his name and they were let right in. The room was set up like a typical daytime talk show. Rows of chairs and a small stage. The lighting was low to give an air of mystique while classical music played lightly.

"Sit in the front. This way you can turn around and see the people's faces as he tells them things he could never know," Kanook said.

Danny plopped into the chair, grateful to get off his aching feet. People streamed in and by the time the room had filled, his interest was piqued. People exchanged pictures and belongings of their deceased loved ones that they had brought with them.

A young woman in a business suit climbed the five steps to the stage. "Welcome, everyone, to Bringing Peace From Beyond with Dr. Barry Leonard. We ask that you refrain from any picture taking. Being a small invited group today, Barry hopes to have time to accommodate everyone here. And now your host and noted psychiatrist, Dr. Barry Leonard."

The group applauded as he took the stage. His appearance was how Kanook had described - a fiftyish man of medium height, a bit chubby, balding with gray sideburns. Just an average everyday looking man with no telltale signs that he could communicate with the dead.

"Thank you all for coming today. Like Kelly said, we're a small group and I hope to help you all in contacting someone you've lost. Can everyone hear me okay? I don't think I need a mic here today."

Everyone murmured yes; he continued. His voice was loud and his speech crisp.

"Unfortunately I cannot guarantee the loved ones you seek will come forth. Many times people that you haven't thought about in many years may pay a visit. So let's get started and hopefully you will understand why I say 'death is but the beginning'."

Barry put one hand over his eyes and waved the other as if chasing spirits away. Danny frowned and leaned to Kanook. "Looks kinda silly."

"Shhhh, just watch. You'll change your mind," Kanook whispered.

They watched as Barry went from person to person, telling each about lost loved ones. There were few people with dry eyes. Even Danny as skeptical as he was, found himself reaching for a tissue now and then. Barry was able to tell many what keepsakes they had brought with them. That was the only time Danny was suspicious. Could there have been a watchful eye – a hidden camera that had given Barry the heads up on what people were carrying?

Barry made his way across the room, finally stopping in front of Kanook.

"Kanook, my old friend, it's good to see you."

Kanook stood up and they embraced.

"This is my cousin-in-law everyone. I haven't seen him in awhile. It is very difficult for me to contact the person he so wants to communicate with because I knew the young man as part of my family as well."

Tears already poured from Kanook's eyes as he sat down. Barry stood with his eyes closed and waited for a message.

"My friend... your son is here. He's communicating that he hears your prayers everyday but... I think he's showing me that you're not in the usual praying spot? I don't know what that means, Kanook."

"I do," he said as a huge smile spread across his face.

"He's trying to show me a new life in yours – a baby maybe."

Kanook jumped up. "A baby – oh God no!"

The audience burst into laughter.

"No, now I'm not sure it's a baby – doesn't feel like a baby. You know what... just keep that in mind for the future, okay?"

"Danny, remind me on the way home to hit the drug store, man. I better be real careful," he said, sitting down again.

"Let me move on here. I'll see you afterwards and we'll dig deeper. Who's your friend?"

Danny reached out his hand.

"That's my neighbor, Danny. I'm hoping he'll be more of a believer than he was when he came in."

Barry stared at Danny. "Funny, I don't get much on you. We'll talk afterwards as well."

Barry turned and took a few steps but then stopped short. He spun back around to Danny. "Do you know a Jo or Josey? I believe maybe a cat? Do you know he's watching over you?"

Danny fell hard to the back of his seat. His mouth dropped open. Barry just smiled and went on to the next person.

"You okay, man? You're turning pale. Looks like you just seen a ghost. Who's this Josey?"

Danny couldn't speak. He just stared at Barry who had his back towards him, speaking with another person.

Kanook laughed. "Told you. Kinda freaky ain't it?"

It took Danny a few seconds before he was able to get words to flow. "It's Jonesy not Josey – that was my cat when I was a kid. How could he... I mean you couldn't have told him about Jonesy – I never told you," Danny said in amazement.

"He's the real deal, man."

After Barry had finished dazzling the audience with his unbelievable ability, the three met for dinner at the hotel restaurant. Danny's mind had been on overdrive since Barry had mentioned Jonesy and his list of questions grew by the second.

Once seated, Danny let loose. "How could you possibly know about my cat? I mean he died like thirty years ago."

"Sorry Barry," Kanook said, "he's a little overwhelmed by the cat thing."

Barry waved his hand. "It's okay, it's okay. You don't think I've had people question me to death about what I've told them?

I've had people accuse me of spying on them to get information before they came to see me."

"So that's how you knew," Danny said, with a laugh.

"Danny, I'll answer all your questions but first things first." He held up his hand for the waiter. "Bring me a scotch and soda." He pointed to Danny and Kanook. "Boys, what'll you have?"

Kanook said, "Same".

"And you sir?" the waiter asked Danny.

"Any light beer's good."

Danny looked at Barry to see if he was ready to handle the bombardment of questions that awaited him.

"So Kanook, how's Sandy? I haven't seen her in a while. Why didn't you bring her?" Barry asked.

"She's doin' okay." He turned to Danny. "Yeah, why didn't we bring her?"

"You're asking me?"

"No, it's because she wanted me and Danny to have a day – you know just the boys," Kanook said.

As the light conversation went on, Danny realized Barry was just a regular guy. He wasn't a circus attraction and the need to pin him down as an imposter faded. Instead he waited for Barry to initiate any explanations which he did soon after.

"So, Danny, you have questions." Barry took his drink from the waiter's hand. "Let's first see if I can contact anyone around you."

Danny looked around. "Right here? You're going to do it here?"

"It's not like I'm going to start chanting or anything."

Barry closed his eyes. Unlike their initial meeting in the staged room Danny waited with anticipation for Barry's visions.

"I'm getting an older woman, Danny. She appears sad but not for herself. She's very unhappy for you. Does this make sense to you?"

Danny dropped his head. "Yes, unfortunately it does. I think you're speaking with my mom."

"This is strange. She... she sends a warn..." Barry's eyes opened wide. Danny quickly picked up a deceptive look. "I'm sorry but I've lost her, Danny."

Danny wasn't buying it. "Wait – you were about to say something. You were going to say that she sends a warning?"

Barry couldn't hide the truth. "Danny, she was sending some kind of warning but I don't know what."

"Do you have any idea at all?"

Barry shook his head. "That's why I didn't want to say anything. I didn't want you to worry about something I can't give specifics on."

The thought of a warning from beyond the grave sent a shiver down Kanook's spine. He downed the remainder of his drink and held his glass up in the air to summon the waiter.

Danny watched Barry for a moment, carefully analyzing his face. Noticing that Barry didn't want to make eye contact, Danny knew there was more. "Barry, there's something you're not telling me."

"Danny, c'mon, man," Kanook said. "Give the guy a break."

"No, Kanook, it's okay. He's right."

Kanook sat up straight. Danny braced himself.

"If you must know... what I got was the warning of impending doom."

Danny's mouth hung open slightly but no words would form. Kanook was also silent.

"I'm sorry to tell you this but I have no idea what it means. I've never experienced that feeling from beyond before – never."

"Great, just great," Danny said. "Is this doom thing just for me or the whole planet?"

"I think it was just for you – I'm sorry I can't tell you more. When I felt what she was trying to communicate, I lost the mental ability to continue." He sat back in his chair. "Losing contact with a spirit because I was startled has only happened a couple times."

"What was it before that made you lose the connection if it wasn't a warning?" Danny asked.

"It was the way the spirit had died both times. So violently it made me nauseous." He lifted his glass. "Now Danny, you can't let this vision control your life. Maybe by me telling this it will... say make you drive a bit slower and thus avoid a major accident. Only means the warning worked."

Danny wasn't totally convinced.

"I wish I could spend more time with the two of you but I'm booked for the rest of the night. I have meetings with TV people and also two interviews. Just have time to eat and run. You can always come back."

"Not so easy – my wife is in the hospital and when she's out I'm going to have to be there constantly to help her."

"I'll be in the area for some time. Kanook can track me down." Barry raised his glass in a toast. "To our dearly departed."

Barely a word was spoken for the first fifteen minutes of the ride home. Danny sat behind the wheel – Kanook was near unconsciousness after the four scotch and sodas.

"You know, Danny, I've heard of games being called on account of rain but never a dinner called because of impending doom," Kanook said, slurring his words.

"I couldn't eat after hearing that. Maybe it would be different if he told you to expect a disaster. Remember how you felt when he told you Sandy was going to get pregnant."

"Oh shit, I forgot about that, man."

"It was you who told me this guy is for real, remember?" Danny snapped.

"He's been wrong before."

"Has he?" Danny asked, sounding uplifted.

"No never – I'm just getting you back for reminding me that Sandy might get pregnant."

"Ah you prick!"

"Look, just relax. Deal with whatever it is when it comes. Worrying won't help you."

Danny drifted off contemplating his *impending doom.* "Guess you're right."

* * * * *

Danny jumped out of the car and walked quickly toward the front door. Sandy opened it, letting Schmedly tear out of the house, almost knocking him over.

"He let me know when you were about two minutes away," Sandy said. "He jumped up and ran to the door. How does he do that? How does he know you're... like a mile away?"

"I don't know. It's eerie though." Danny shook Kanook's hand. "Thanks for the day out. I enjoyed the freedom. I really have a lot of thinking to do after seeing Barry in action. It was pretty cool."

"I told you. And he's here for a while yet. We can go again," Kanook said, his words tailing off when he realized that Cheryl would be home soon.

"I'll cherish the memory... and of course in the back of my mind I'll have the thought that I'm probably going to die a hideous death soon. Thanks for that."

"Aw, man. Barry said you may have already changed your fate by him mentioning it." Kanook held tight to the handrail, trying to pull himself into the house.

"Uh-oh," Sandy muttered, as she saw the condition of her husband.

"I wouldn't take advantage of him – I mean in the bedroom tonight, Sandy," Danny said, laughing.

She gave a confused look. "What?"

"I'll tell you later," Kanook said.

Danny led the dog across the front yard and glanced back. He stopped, seeing Sandy was having trouble dragging Kanook inside.

"You need some help?" he called over.

Kanook waved him off.

Danny flopped into the living room chair. His body was unaccustomed to long outings where any type of physical activity was involved. He reached for the phone. The nurse at the floor station gave him the same report as earlier – stable with a probable release Monday. He dialed George.

"Hi, Dad, I'm back from a great day."

"How was the ghost guy? Did you hear from your mother?" George said, laughing.

"Yes... I did and... and the guy told me Jonesy was watching over me."

George was silent for a moment. "How could he know Jonesy and what did your mother say? You sure he didn't ask you a lot of questions to fish things out of you?"

"He didn't ask me anything at all. The guy just knew. He was amazing."

"Huh, that's interesting."

"He said Mom was well and sends her love."

George choked up, thinking about his lost wife. He coughed trying to cover his emotion.

"Yeah, and the promise I made to you about Cheryl – I'm keeping it. I had such a feeling of freedom today that I decided if she goes back to the way she was, I'm leaving her."

Chapter Three

Danny stood outside Cheryl's room holding a small bouquet of flowers. He smiled and tried to hide his uneasiness as a nurse walked past. Was she the new Cheryl or the old? The way he looked at it, he was a winner either way.

"Hi, Cheryl, you awake?"

She stretched and yawned. "Yeah, I'm just dozing. Not much more to do. There's only so much TV a person can watch." She pointed at the flowers. "For me?" she asked, her voice still a bit strained.

"Oh, yeah, for you."

She stuck her nose into the bouquet and inhaled. "They smell nice. You really appreciate things more after near death."

Danny wasn't sure if she meant appreciating him more or just the flowers? He wanted to look directly into her eyes but was afraid. Cheryl let the flowers drop onto her stomach. "Danny, I don't want to fight with you anymore." She started to cry.

Danny sat on the edge of the bed not knowing how to comfort her - it had been so long since he had even touched her. She reached out her hand and ran the back of her fingers down his cheek, startling him.

"I want it to be like it was when we first married," she said.

Danny didn't know how to react. Even though she was his wife, she was a stranger. He would have to get to know her all over again.

"Okay," he said nodding. "I'm willing to try if you are."

She smiled; something Danny hadn't seen in years. The doctor came into the room followed by an orderly pushing a wheelchair.

"You're all set. Now just take it easy for a couple more days and you should be as good as new," he said, flipping through her chart. "Do you have any questions?"

Danny looked at Cheryl and shrugged his shoulders. "I don't," he said. "Oh wait – what kind of medication is she on?" he asked.

"No medication. She was just on Benadryl. Okay? The orderly will wheel you out."

Cheryl dozed for most of the drive home. Danny was grateful, not really knowing what sort of conversation to strike up. He ran through all the changes that would have to take place in order for them to have the relationship that once was. Did she really mean it this time? They would have to share the same bed again. Eat together. She would have to stop her compulsive shopping and most important – what about Schmedly?

They pulled into the driveway. Cheryl looked around with sleepy eyes.

"We're here already. I'm still so tired. All I want to do is sleep."

Danny unlocked the front door and opened it for her. Schmedly, expecting Danny, retreated up the stairs upon seeing Cheryl in the doorway. Cheryl climbed the stairs. Schmedly wanted to get to Danny but she blocked his way and bent down at the top step.

"Hi Schmedly."

He backed up.

"That may take him a little while to get used to – you being nice to him." He was walking on eggshells and regretted saying it, fearing it would anger her.

"Baby steps," she said.

Dinner was awkward. For the first time in years, they sat at their kitchen table and ate together. Conversation was scarce so Danny turned on the TV. Schmedly was so confused that he went downstairs, sending up an occasional moan.

"Listen, Cheryl, can we talk?"

"Okay, let's talk."

"Are you serious about us, you know, getting along again?"

She sipped a glass of water. "Yes, I am."

"I mean, for us to really get back to the way we were, you'd have to cut the spending down to nothing 'til we get rid of the debt," he said meekly.

She nodded but Danny was still suspicious of her new demeanor. Near death or not, no one does an about face like she was showing now. There had to be something else – but what?

That evening they watched TV together in the living room. Schmedly was even allowed to sleep on a sheet in the forbidden zone. Danny's stomach churned as bedtime approached. If they slept in the same bed, would there be sex?

His answer wasn't far away. At ten o'clock, she stood and reached out her hand. Danny looked back at his perplexed canine as she led him down the hall. Danny could swear he saw Schmedly shake his head before he followed them.

Danny slid under the covers while he waited for Cheryl to come from the bathroom. Schmedly put his snout on the bed, looking for his spot.

"Not tonight, Schmed. Let her get used to you, then you can sleep up here," Danny whispered.

The dejected dog circled a small mat Danny had placed next to his side of the bed, and flopped with a thud. Danny felt bad but this was sex and sex took precedent over the dog's hurt feelings – besides, how long could it take to be over? Five minutes...maybe? He flipped on the TV. He grew impatient.

Cheryl walked back into the room. She dropped her satin robe as she crossed the room and joined him. The first kiss was awkward but quickly turned passionate. He slid his hand down her body.

Hey, this isn't half-bad.

He was about to make his move when Schmedly jumped on the bed and flopped down against Danny's back. He turned and gave the dog a shove but that only made him roll on his back. He gave Danny a cute look hoping he would get the okay to stay but...

"Danny, I'm losing the mood with that dog on the bed."

"All right, dog, off you go," he said, giving a good heave.

Schmedly jumped to the floor, put his nose in the air and went to sleep in the other room.

"Now where were we," he asked.

She reached over and turned out the light. She returned with a teasing smile.

A week had passed. Danny was growing accustomed to being treated like a human being again. Simple things that most took for granted - watching TV in a comfortable chair, eating at the kitchen table and of course sex, were all treats for him. But still, in the back of his mind, there was the fear of Dr. Jekyll turning again into Mrs. Hyde.

It was Tuesday evening. Danny had finished his deliveries. He squeezed the van into the garage, which he rarely did, to repair a broken headlight.

He sat tinkering in the workshop when Cheryl opened the front door. She paraded into the bedroom, carrying the spoils of a shopping spree.

Danny crept up the stairs and down the hall. While Cheryl undressed in the bathroom, he tiptoed into the bedroom and leaned over the bed where three dresses still on hangers and in their plastic wraps, were laid.

"What's this?" he asked loudly.

He could hear her take a quick, deep breath in the bathroom.

"What are you doing here? Where's the van?"

"In the garage. I thought we said the shopping would stop for a while," he said in a non-threatening voice.

She came into the room wearing only her underwear.

"I just bought a few things, that's all."

She tried to get between Danny and the bed but he had already lifted the plastic and found the price tag of one on the dresses. His eyes opened wide. He was only able to mouth the price, which was two hundred dollars. She pulled the garment away.

"I didn't buy anything all last week," she complained.

"Two hundred dollars for one dress? How much were the others?"

"None of your business," she yelled. "Get out now while I try these on." She gave him a shove.

"Cheryl, these have to go back," he said, hoping she would give him a guilty look and agree.

"I work hard. I want nice clothes," she said, raising her voice slightly.

"I understand you work hard but not to buy six hundred dollars worth of dresses at a clip."

"I'm keeping them," she said, now more defiantly.

Danny took a couple of steps back and realized – the bitch was back. He walked down the hall with Schmedly close behind. He motioned for the dog to continue down the stairs. He stopped and waited, hoping to hear Cheryl's voice call him to apologize. The call didn't come. He slunk down the stairs.

Back in his tattered chair, Danny wondered where he was sleeping that night. Things had been so good that he decided to try and reconcile the short spat – he couldn't go back to the way it was – and then there was the promise to his father and more importantly, to himself. He felt queasy.

"Schmed, you stay here."

He met Cheryl in the kitchen.

"Can we talk about this?" he asked.

"What's to talk about?" she said, curtly.

"Things going so well..."

She cut in, "And now they aren't."

He stood between her and the refrigerator. "I can't believe you would..."

"Move out of the way." She tried pushing him to the side.

"No, we're going to talk about this," he said, trying to sound unafraid.

She grabbed his tee shirt by the shoulders and tried to pull him away from the refrigerator door but could not. She reached back and slammed her hand palm first into his mouth and then again to the side of his head. With his arms up high to fend off the blows, he backed away and stopped at the head of the stairs only to see her taking out a container of milk as if nothing had happened. He stood in astonishment – it was like her rage had built up inside all week and was unleashed in one violent barrage. This was not the first time that she had hit him but he wanted it to be the last.

He ran back downstairs. As he picked up the phone, he felt his lip, which was slightly swollen from the punch. He took his hand away – a small amount of diluted blood covered the tip of his index finger.

He dialed, knowing his father would give him the "I told you she'd be back to the bitch again," but Danny just wanted out. His father's phone rang ten times without an answer before Danny hung up. He turned to see the wall clock.

Seven o'clock. He should be home. Maybe at the neighbors?

Schmedly sat facing Danny.

"We're back to the way we were, Schmed."

The dog lay down and let out a sigh. Danny flipped on the TV.

Hours later, Schmedly touched Danny's ear with his wet nose. Danny, his head limp against his shoulder, awoke with a start.

"Oh, shit, I fell asleep. What time is it?" he turned to see that it was ten o'clock. "Oh Schmed, I'm sorry. C'mon, we'll eat."

He stood up, and then froze. After so many years of falling asleep in that chair, he had forgotten how in the past week so little time was spent in it. Somehow he knew his days in the dungeon would return.

He climbed the stairs but stopped half way up and stood on tiptoes to see if Cheryl was in the living room. Seeing it was clear, he motioned for Schmedly to continue. He feared Schmedly would enter the living room but to his surprise the dog stopped on the boundary line as if the past week had never happened.

While Schmedly ate, Danny dialed his father's number again. He couldn't get into a conversation about the situation with Cheryl right down the hall but he needed to know that he was there. The phone rang many times before Danny hung up.

I wish he would get a cell phone - or least an answering machine. Where could he be?

Danny slept downstairs all night but he didn't sleep well. Recurring dreams of his father kept him on edge and at 6:30 he dialed the number again. There was still no answer. Danny wiped his eyes.

"C'mon, Schmed, we're going to Grampa's."

He was so absorbed in the thought that maybe his father had suffered a heart attack that he gave no mind to Cheryl sitting at the kitchen table. He filled a travel mug with coffee and snapped the lid on.

"Where are you going?" Cheryl demanded.

He didn't answer. She sat with her elbows on the table, reading the newspaper and sipping coffee. Danny thought he heard her laugh. As he glanced at her, a smile quickly faded. He grabbed his keys and ran down the stairs. Schmedly followed.

Danny sped towards his father's house. His stomach churned as he pictured his father lying on the floor. He dialed George's house from his cell phone but still there was no answer. He was now in a panic. Schmedly, sensing Danny's fear, growled and barked as they approached the front gate of his father's development. He stopped at the gate. The guard waved him through but Danny motioned for him to open the window to the booth.

"Do you know George Dillon?"

"Sure," the guard replied.

"Have you seen him leave yesterday or today?"

"No." The guard could see that Danny was uneasy. "Something wrong?"

"I don't know yet."

Danny chirped the tires of the van as he raced down the road. In the rearview he could see the guard standing in middle of the street, watching him speed away.

As they approached the house, Schmedly startled Danny with a loud growl – nothing like Danny had ever heard. He stopped the van. Schmedly was now trying to bite his way out of the harness.

"Calm down," he yelled, as he released the catch and opened the door.

Schmedly ran straight for the front door as Danny jumped out and fumbled with the keys, looking for the right one. But as he neared, he realized he didn't need it. The storm door was closed but the inside door was open a crack.

"Dad! Dad!" Danny yelled, entering the house as Schmedly pushed past him barking. He ran from room to room and into the garage.

The car was still there but there was no sign of George. Danny searched all the rooms; nothing looked ransacked but his wallet was not in sight. His keys remained on the kitchen counter.

Schmedly had stopped barking but now whimpered as he lay only feet from the front door. Danny knelt next to the now trembling dog.

"What is it, Schmed?"

Danny had only to look a few inches from the dog's front paw. One small spot of what appeared to be dried blood. Danny reached his index finger to touch it but pulled back, realizing he might be compromising evidence of a crime. He dialed 9-1-1 on his cell phone.

"This is 9-1-1. What's your emergency?"

"I think somebody..." Danny choked up. "I think someone may have hurt my father."

"What's your location?"

Danny gave the dispatcher the information needed.

"I'm sending police to the address right now. Do you need paramedics?"

"No, he's not here."

"Someone's on their way. What's your name?"

Danny was no longer listening. He stood up, snapped the phone shut, and threw it onto the couch. It immediately started ringing, the 9-1-1 dispatcher trying to reestablish an open line. He ignored it.

He took Schmedly by the collar into the kitchen while he got a plastic bowl. He returned and placed it on top of the blood spot to preserve it. The phone continued to ring.

Danny yelled at the dog, "Find Grampa, find him." He hoped the dog could dig up more blood splatter or at least some clue to his whereabouts. He was careful not to upset anything as he followed the dog around the house. Schmedly sniffed the air and growled on occasion but was unable to uncover any other evidence.

Police cars, their lights flashing, screeched to a halt in front of the house. Police with hands on their guns, ran up the driveway. Danny held his hands in the air as the officers looked in the front door.

"This is my father's house and he's gone."

The officers cautiously stepped inside.

"You say he's gone. Do you think he's hurt, what?" the officer asked.

"The door was open and he hasn't answered the phone since yesterday."

One officer walked around the house as the other asked more questions.

"Your name, sir?"

"Danny Dillon."

"Could he be at a neighbor's or maybe went on a trip...?"

Danny pointed at the upside down plastic bowl on the floor. The officer bent down without taking his eyes off Danny.

"I think it's blood," Danny said.

As the officer bent down, Schmedly, who was lying quietly curled up on the couch, caught his eye.

"That your father's dog?"

"No; he's mine. I know something's really wrong when he just lies there like that. He's kind of a special dog – special senses. He knows, he knows," Danny said almost in tears.

More officers came through the door.

"What've we got?" one asked.

"Missing person." He pointed to Danny. "His father. Might be a blood stain here."

"Mr. Dillon, is there any way your father could be somewhere else? A friend's, a relative's?"

Danny was shaking his head through the officer's questions.

"See, right now all we got here is a man that's not home and maybe a spot of blood. There's no sign of a struggle or forced entry." Danny's look of distress swayed the officer. "Look, we'll canvas the neighbors and see if anyone saw or heard anything."

"Okay," Danny replied.

By now all the neighbors were outside, huddled in groups, many still in pajamas with overcoats on. The officers began questioning them. Within a minute, one of the officers returned with an elderly woman. Danny met them in the driveway.

"Mr. Dillon, this lady says she saw your father leave with two men in a dark van last night."

"Hi, Mrs. Wright."

"Hi, Danny. I saw him get into a van but I didn't think anything of it," she said. "Is he all right?"

"I don't know. I don't know where he is but that must've been the van I saw hanging around lately." Danny smacked himself in the head. "I didn't take down the plate number. Wait," he yelled. "The guard booth – they should have it."

"We'll check it out soon as our boss gets here," an officer said and with that a fourth police car pulled up. A tall thin officer got out. "It's the sarge – he's the one that makes the call here."

Danny watched as the sergeant and the other officers huddled in the street. He could see one officer doing most of the briefing. He pointed at Danny and at the house, then at Mrs. Wright. After a few minutes the sergeant took Danny inside.

"I'm Sergeant Hicks." He shook Danny's hand. "We had a call about a man with a gun in his belt from a convenience store owner last night." They walked up the driveway. "They drove a dark van. I don't know if it's the same van or not but we caught a glimpse of an older gentleman in the back of the van on the security tape. I'm inclined to treat this as a possible abduction. Where's the blood stain?"

Danny pointed to the bowl as they entered the house. Another officer came in behind them, carrying a small orange identifier cone, which he put in place of the plastic bowl.

"Okay, Mr. Dillon, I'll call the detectives. Let's all stay outside here until we know what's up." He ushered Danny out. "We'll need you to check out that security tape to see if you can identify the man as your father – only problem is the picture quality ain't that great."

"Let me just get my dog from inside."

The sergeant motioned for an officer to accompany him in. "Just get the dog and come right back out," he said to the officer.

"Hope Grampa's all right."

They sat in the back of a patrol car; Schmedly was curled up with his nose on his tail. The dog rolled his eyes up and looked at Danny without lifting his head. From Schmedly's expression, Danny knew that there was something seriously wrong. The dog was special that way.

Police circled the house with crime scene tape. Danny trembled as he watched an unmarked car ease up to the house. Two men in suits got out and were met by the sergeant. After a brief conversation, they walked towards Danny, who had already gotten out.

"Mr. Dillon? I'm Detective Marone. This is Detective Caloway. Before we touch anything inside, we want to talk to you. We'll run you down to the station."

"What about my dog?" Danny asked, pointing in the window of the van.

The detective looked in. "Does he bite?"

"No, he's very well behaved – almost human."

The detectives looked at each other. "Almost human, huh?" Caloway said. "You can bring him with you. I doubt anyone will mind. We'll just tell the boss that the dog's a witness."

Danny opened the door and clipped on the leash. He led him back to the detectives' car.

"Hop in the back. We're going to take a quick look inside," Marone said.

Danny sat with Schmedly's head on his lap. The neighbors still mulled around in groups. They shook from the cold but a kidnapping in the quiet neighborhood took precedent over chilly air.

Danny waited for fifteen minutes before the detectives exited the house. Marone got behind the wheel. Caloway turned to Danny from the passenger seat.

"Do you know anyone with a dark colored van that he might've left with?"

"No... no way. Check with the booth – they should have a record."

"We'll have someone check that out. What I want you to do on the way to the station is try and think of any enemies he might have – anyone who would want to hurt him."

Danny laughed. "Just one and she's probably on her way to work right now."

"Who would that be?" Marone asked.

"My wife."

Chapter Four

Danny sat on a metal folding chair; Schmedly sat on the chair next to him. This was an interrogation room – he wondered why he was here and not at a detective's desk. The room was cold and dimly lit – bars on the window kept out most of the outside light. The décor and atmosphere were intentionally dreary to keep a criminal in discomfort. A strong odor of stale cigarette smoke permeated the air. Danny envisioned detectives enticing a perp with a Marlboro to make him talk.

The two detectives entered; both stopped short upon seeing Schmedly sitting like a person on the chair.

"So he is almost human." Marone said. "What's with the floppy ear?"

"That's just a fashion statement."

Both detectives dropped a pad on the table and sat across from them at the long wooden table.

"We had a guy check with the guard booth. Seems they don't pay them very much and if there are no problems, they get a bit lax. The guard on duty didn't take a plate – was probably watchin' TV. Just waved him in. They're so many workers

coming in and out with the new construction, you know?"
Marone said.

"Mr. Dillon, we have to look at all the possibilities here.
Please don't be insulted by our questions, okay?" Caloway said.

Danny shrugged his shoulders, not really understanding
what he was being told.

Caloway, who sported a goatee but still looked to be the
unthreatening type, started the questioning.

"Your father has a nice house there. What's he worth?" he
asked.

"Oh, I don't know – probably three million, give or take,"
Danny said.

Marone whistled. "Wow, that's a bunch. Where were you
last night?"

"Me?" Danny asked loudly, startling Schmedly. "You think
I had something to do with this?"

"It's just standard procedure. We gotta ask this stuff. We
don't know you. You wanna be ruled out, right?" Marone asked.

"You're right, you're right. I understand. I was home all
night. My wife... she can confirm it. Actually she's the one you
ought to be questioning but don't tell her I said that."

"Explain," Marone said, interlocking his fingers in front of
his face and leaning forward on his elbows. He easily made up
for Caloway's lack of intimidation. His deep-seated eyes and
tobacco stained teeth almost gave him the appearance of a
corpse. He resembled the detectives from the comics of the
1950's.

"My wife and I don't exactly get along. She spends every
penny we have and then some. When I tell her we're broke,
she yells for me to go to my father for the money. He
understands the problems I have with her so he does give me
money sometimes but I never tell her."

"So how do you think she's involved?" Caloway asked.

Schmedly was getting uneasy sitting so he jumped down off
the chair and lay down.

"How do I think she's involved? I don't know but she's evil
– pure evil. Guarantee she's got a hand in this," Danny said,
looking past the officers and out through the metal bars.

"You said she was home with you last night?" Marone asked.

"Oh, yeah, but if someone took my father for money – she's involved. She would never kill him though; she knows he took me out of his will 'til I leave her. If he dies, I get nothing 'til she's gone. She knows that."

"How does she know that?" Marone asked, jotting down notes.

"My father told her to her face. Wasn't a pretty scene."

Danny had seen a water cooler when he first walked in. He pointed to it. "May I?"

"Sure, go ahead." Caloway said.

The glub glub glub sound of the water bottle brought Schmedly over for a look.

"You want some?"

The dog licked his lips as Danny bent down and put the paper cup under his nose. He slurped and slobbered water onto the floor while the detectives waited patiently.

"Is this your dog or your son? Man, the way you treat him. I should get treated so good," Caloway said.

"He's my buddy – my best friend in the world. We'd give our lives for each other if we had to."

"Okay, let's get back. Now the van – you told the sarge that you had seen it before?" Marone asked.

"Yeah, I saw it in the neighborhood twice," Danny said.

"Remember anything about it? Blue or black? Anything?"

"No, I can't think of anything. There was nothing out of the ordinary about it." Danny scratched his head. "Hey, shouldn't I be home in case someone calls?"

"Yeah, we're getting the electronics ready," Marone said.

"Electronics?"

"Don't you ever watch detective shows? We're treating this like a kidnapping rather than just an abduction because of his wealth. We're going to forward all the calls from your father's house to yours. We don't know where they're going to call. This way we only have to tap your home phone," Caloway said.

Marone stood up. "About your wife... we'll need to question her. The way you've spoken about her, she don't sound so pleasant."

"That would be putting it mildly but she'll put up a good front."

"The problem you have is, she's not gonna be too happy about us askin' about arguments that she had with your father... and that she dislikes him etcetera. She's gonna know that you told us about things," Marone said, raising his eyebrows.

The detectives waited while that idea sunk into Danny's head.

"I understand she's going to be upset with you asking questions... but you know what – I don't care. I'm already resigned to the fact that I have to move out. I'll start moving into my father's place temporarily."

"Not yet. Not 'til we find out if someone's lookin' for money. You have to be by the phone at your house. Besides, wouldn't look too good... you moving into your father's right after he disappeared," Caloway said.

There was a knock at the door before a head poked in "We're ready," the officer said.

"That's our electronics guy. Let's go."

Within an hour of reaching Danny's house, the phone wires had been plugged into the machine. It was ready to record and trace any incoming calls. Danny had cleared a desk in the workshop where an officer would man the phones.

Tommy sat on the far side of the room, attempting to repair a computer but the excitement made it difficult to concentrate. "Hey, Danny, you want me to go home or something?" he asked.

"No, we don't really know what's going on, Tommy. We might not get a call at all and besides, these guys aren't going to be here all the time – just one guy on the machine."

Danny walked over to Tommy and put his hands on his shoulders. "Look, I may not be a lot of help around here for awhile and we really need to get some of this stuff out. Peoples' businesses are counting on getting these PC's back. So if you can put in overtime..."

"Sure, no problem."

The two detectives and two communications specialists were hovered around their recording device. One of the officers raised his hand. "Before you go up, just want to tell you how this works. We have your father's number forwarded to your home number. It will give us a distinct ring – here' I'll show you." He pushed a button. Two short rings instead of the usual one were emitted. "We're not recording your business lines. We really don't think they'll come in on them but with a quick signal to the officer it can be switched over so all bases are covered. Any questions?"

Danny shook his head.

"You guys mind if I let the dog down? I got him locked upstairs."

"No, send him down. He won't bother us," Marone said.

"Put his bed by me. He can sleep over here," Tommy said, pointing down to the floor next to him.

Danny started up the stairs when Detective Caloway called to him. "Mr. Dillon, we're about ready here. You wanna call your wife and have her come home."

Danny cringed. "I'll call her now."

He continued upstairs, and opened the door for Schmedly. Being unaccustomed to strangers in the house, Schmedly avoided the officers as he ran down the stairs. Tommy lured him over with a biscuit but the dog was too nervous. He approached each officer and after sniffing each individually, ran back upstairs.

Danny sat in the living room with the portable phone in his hand. Schmedly put his snout on Danny's arm and gave a couple of tail wags as if to say everything would turn out all right. After a couple pats on the head, Danny motioned the dog to lie down. He dialed the phone.

"Cheryl, it's me. I think you need to come home," he said, his voice a bit shaky.

"What's wrong?"

Danny hesitated. He was so sure she knew something about his father's disappearance that he just wanted to say, "You know damn well what it's about," but he kept his head.

"My father is missing."

"Missing?"

"Kidnapped - well, we think kidnapped. There are detectives here and... well you should come home right away."

"I'll be right there."

Danny looked at the keypad of the phone as pushed the button to disconnect the line. Did she seem concerned or was there the "I know something you don't know" sound to her voice?

Danny yelled down the stairs. "She's on her way."

The two detectives joined him upstairs.

"When she gets here, why don't you take the dog out back? But don't go far in case the phone rings. And by the way, if we do get a call, just stay calm. The machine will start recording immediately and without any noise on the line. The caller won't know that anyone's listening. Keep him on as long as possible," Marone said. "Gotta tell ya though, in all probability, there most likely won't be a call."

Danny looked surprised. "I thought that's what we were waiting for."

"If the people who took him have half a brain, they'll know we're here and can trace them in an instant."

"Then why the machine downstairs and the twenty four hour guy down there?"

"That's just in case whoever kidnapped your father is stupid. We gotta cover all the bases."

Danny stared at his watch for forty minutes. A car door slammed. He jumped off the bed in the guestroom and waited at the head of the stairs. Schmedly, on Danny's command, fled downstairs and lay on his bed next to Tommy.

The front door opened and Cheryl came in.

"What's going on?" she asked, removing her long coat.

Danny looked into her eyes as he walked toward her down the stairs.

"We think my father's been kidnapped."

"By who?"

Danny watched her closely.

"Danny, answer me. What's going on?"

"One of his neighbors..."

The detective cut him off, coming up the stairs.

"Hi, Mrs. Dillon. I'm Detective Marone. This is Detective Caloway," he said as he ushered them up to the kitchen. "Mr. Dillon, why don't..."

Danny took the hint quickly and continued down the stairs but stopped to try and hear the questioning.

"Danny, where are you going? Wait a minute – you don't think I had something to do with this, do you?"

"We just need to ask you some questions just like we did with your husband."

"What did he tell you?" she asked loudly. "Did he say I had something to do with this?"

"Ma'am, it's just routine. We need to check everyone."

Cheryl had the look of a wild woman as she sat at the kitchen table.

"Go ahead, ask me."

"We know you didn't get along with his father. Is there anyone else that you know that would want to hurt him? Anyone else in your family?"

"Anyone *else* that would want to hurt him? So you're saying I want him hurt."

Marone slumped, sighed and looked up at the ceiling. "Mrs. Dillon, we have to eliminate everyone."

The officer who monitored the tape machine downstairs caught Danny attempting to listen in and ushered him out the back door.

Danny sat in the backyard while Schmedly sniffed around. Suddenly the dog sprinted toward Kanook's house. Danny heard the sound of crunching leaves.

"Danny, is everything all right?" Sandy called from the fence.

He got up and walked in her direction. "Hi, Sandy. My father was kidnapped last night."

"Oh, my God," she gasped, covering her mouth. "Do they know who did it?"

"No, well, we think he was kidnapped. We don't know where he is and there's no other explanation – no reason for anyone to want to hurt him other than for money. We're waiting to get a call or something. The police are checking his ATM and credit cards to see if any money was withdrawn."

"Oh, my God. I can't believe this. I'll call Kanook."

"No, don't. He'll come rushing home and there's nothing he can do to help. I'm going to have my hands full with Cheryl in a bit anyway. The detectives are questioning her."

"Is there anything we can do to help?"

"Just say a prayer, I guess."

Danny looked at his watch: twenty minutes had passed. What could they be asking her – and more important – what was she telling them? But then he realized she was a natural liar and they wouldn't crack her with days of questioning.

The back door opened. "Mr. Dillon, c'mon back in. We're done with her." Caloway called.

Danny looked up at the kitchen window. He pulled the detective to where Cheryl couldn't see if she looked out.

"Did you find out anything?"

"Nope, if she knows anything, she's keeping it to herself. We asked her if she'd take a polygraph... let's say she was less than enthusiastic about it."

Caloway held the door open. Marone was just coming down the stairs. He waved a videotape in the air for all to see. "Just dropped off a copy of the tape from the convenience store."

Danny pointed to the TV and rushed the tape into the VCR. The three men huddled close to the picture. Tommy leaned back in his chair for a glimpse but his eyes met Caloway's. He quickly turned back to his work. Caloway kept looking in Tommy's direction. He tapped Danny on the shoulder and whispered "What's his story?"

Danny looked at Tommy. "Who, Tommy?" he asked before he realized what Caloway was asking. "Oh no, definitely not – he has no knowledge of my father... or his money."

Caloway didn't look convinced but focused on the TV. Marone, already having viewed the tape, watched for Danny's reaction to it.

Danny set the tape in slow motion. He trembled a bit, fearing he was about to see his father held captive.

"No, run it at full speed first," Marone said.

Danny hit the button. The first shot was from a camera positioned behind the clerk. They watched as a man reached for an item higher up on a rack next to the register.

"There's the weapon," Caloway said as the man's jacket lifted just high enough to sport the revolver.

"Mr. Dillon, you recognize that guy at all?" Marone asked.

Danny shook his head. "Not at all."

"We'll be showing this tape to the guard who let them in. I'm sure he no longer has a job," Caloway said.

The tape, which had already been edited by police forensics, lost focus for a moment as it rolled into the next camera shot. This angle was from the side of the man, pointing out the front door and directly into the windshield of the dark colored van. Danny sat forward close to the screen as the two detectives got down on one knee to get a better view. The driver seat was empty but there was a man in the passenger side and another behind him in the center of a bench seat. Danny fixed on him but the picture was grainy through the distortion of the front door and windshield glass.

"This is a waste," Danny said. "There's no way I can tell if that's him or not. Can't even tell how old the guy is... looks like an older guy but..."

"Yeah, I agree this ain't helpin' at all. Let's just use the shot of the guy at the counter. We can broadcast his face in the media and see what we get. It's better than nothing I guess," Caloway said.

"We're going to leave now and canvass your father's neighbors again. We'll take the tape to the media and make a stop at the convenience store – see if the clerk who worked that night can tell us anything. Hopefully somebody saw something and they'll call us." Marone reached into an inside pocket of his overcoat. "Here's my card with my cell number. If you need

me, call me. We'll leave the officer here. If you get a call, he'll
let us know."

"Mr. Dillon, we'll let you know if anything comes up,"
Caloway said.

"Thanks for all your help, Detectives."

Danny closed the door but didn't let go of the knob right
away. He dreaded this moment. He turned. He could see Cheryl
at the kitchen counter. He walked up the stairs not noticing
that Schmedly was close behind him. Cheryl was pouring a cup
of coffee as he entered the kitchen. Without turning around
she yelled, "What the fuck did you tell those guys?"

"I just told them you didn't get along with my dad, that's
all."

"Bullshit. They knew a lot more than that." Her voice was
getting louder. Schmedly hid under the table. "You think I had
something to do with this, don't you?" Her voice was now at a
fevered pitch.

Danny backed away, speechless.

"See, you can't answer."

"I only answered their questions," he said, slowly.

Cheryl approached him, pointing her finger at him. "Let
me tell you what you're going to do. You're going to call those
detectives back and tell them I had nothing to do with this."

Danny turned away as she came closer, trapping him in the
corner behind the kitchen table.

"You hear me? You call them back!" She was now
screaming so loud that her voice was cracking. She finally lost
control. With all her strength she slapped him in the middle of
his back. The hollow sound echoed throughout the house. She
smacked him again in the back of the head. Danny cowered,
raising his arm to fend off the blows. She grabbed his arm with
her left hand and with her right rained down punches to his
head and neck.

Schmedly came from under the table. The once docile and
friendly dog was now snarling and snapping like a ferocious
wolf. He approached her, now only a foot away. She trembled
as he pressed her against the wall.

"Danny, tell him to stop," she screamed.

He continued to snap, his feet coming off the ground higher with each lunge yet he hadn't touched her. Danny watched in amazement. Drool sprayed into the air with every compression of the dog's jaws.

"Call him off!" she yelled again.

Danny tried to speak the words, "Schmedly no, stop!" but the words wouldn't come.

Schmedly allowed Cheryl to move to the left as he turned, keeping himself between her and Danny. He steered her away from the wall, finally giving her the chance to escape the kitchen. The dog gave two final snaps as he chased her into the hallway. He stopped and gave a look of "that's what it feels like, bitch".

Schmedly turned back to Danny, sneezed twice and walked to him, wagging his tail as if nothing had happened. Danny knelt down and held his best friend.

"I promise we'll be out of here real soon. You are the best."

Danny could hear Cheryl talking loudly on the phone. She opened the bedroom door a crack and yelled, "I want that dog out of this house." She slammed the door.

"Hey guess what, Schmed? I think we're sleeping downstairs tonight."

Danny had forgotten for a moment about Tommy and the police officer who were now on the landing next to the front door. The officer had his hand on his gun and they both looked as if they had seen a ghost.

"Everything okay up here?" the officer asked.

Danny nodded.

"Thought you were being killed up here," Tommy said. "And what was that werewolf sound?"

They waited eagerly for an explanation.

"My wife is a bit upset that the detectives questioned her about my father's disappearance. She thinks I told them she had something to do with it. The snarling was Schmedly. He got a little pissed when she was..." he looked embarrassed and dropped his head. "When she was hitting me."

Schmedly stood with his usual sweet little dog expression. The officer looked at Danny, then at Schmedly and then back at Danny. "That little dog made all that noise? What, is he possessed?"

Danny kept his voice low. "I didn't know he had that in him... but I would do the same for him."

"You know, Mr. Dillon, there are laws to protect you," the officer said.

"Yeah, that'd look great in the papers – that my wife got arrested for beating me. Right now my concern is my father. I'll deal with her later."

Danny sat in his chair. He channel surfed until he found a local news station and did the only thing that he could – he waited. The detective hadn't said when they would release the missing person report to the media. He flipped through a magazine trying to erase any pictures from his mind of his father tied, chained or maybe tortured. He wept quietly while hanging his arm over the side of the chair, stroking Schmedly's head.

"Mr. Dillon, what time does the mail usually come?" the officer asked. "Most likely too early for a ransom note but just in case."

Danny looked at his watch. "Might be here now. I'll go check."

He ran up the stairs. Cheryl had the TV turned up in the bedroom. Danny smiled as he realized she was too afraid to leave the room. He came right back inside, flipping through mail as he walked down the stairs.

"No, nothing out of the ordinary here. Just a pile of bills."

"Tomorrow we'll have someone pick up the mail at the post office in the morning so we don't have to wait," the officer said.

That evening, Kanook sat on a folding metal chair next to Danny. Each had a beer and Schmedly had a rawhide bone.

"So what's the next step?" Kanook asked.

"Any minute, according to the detectives, the story should hit the news. Maybe someone will know something. If that doesn't work, we can only wait and pray that they want money and it wasn't a murder."

"Police check his credit cards?"

"Yup. Nothing – no withdrawals from any ATMs or banks."

"Did they..."

"Wait, here it is."

Danny turned up the volume. The replacement officer on the night shift stood behind Danny's chair as the broadcast began. A picture of Danny's father took up the entire screen as the newscaster asked for help in finding him or for any information about the abduction. They cut away from George's photo to a reporter live at his house. The yellow police tape fluttered in the wind behind him as he gave the details of the disappearance.

"I wonder if they'll find anything at the house. They're doing a DNA test on the blood stain on the floor," Danny said quietly.

"They already know it's his blood type."

"Look, they're most likely after money. Just get it and give 'em what they want, man. It'll have a happy ending," Kanook said.

"Let's hope."

Schmedly snored lightly in his bed next to the recliner. Danny opened his eyes; the TV was still on. He glanced at his watch and sat up quickly – there was still time to get some supplies from the kitchen before Cheryl was ready to leave. He assumed she would go to work after the previous day's ordeal. The officer still waited at his post for a call but the only calls that had come through were friends and relatives asking questions and lending support.

He pointed to the officer. "You said milk and sugar, right?"

"Yup. Thanks, Mr. Dillon."

"Let me ask you..."

The officer raised his hand. "You're going to ask how these things usually turn out, right?"

"Yeah, how'd you know?"

"I could see by your expression – I see it a lot. Every case is different. There is no one answer for every kidnapping."

The front door opened a crack and the doorbell rang simultaneously. "Mr. Dillon?" Marone called.

"C'mon in," Danny yelled, running halfway up the stairs.

Marone held up a manila envelope for Danny to see.

"They want money?" he asked, breathing quickly.

"Yup, and lots of it. Four hundred thousand," he replied.

Detective Caloway followed Marone inside. Cheryl came from the kitchen to the top of the stairs. "Did you tell them I had nothing to do with this whole thing? Did you?"

"Not now, Cheryl. We just got a demand letter for four hundred thousand dollars," Danny said without looking at her.

"Now this isn't the original. We made a copy. Forensics is going over the original for prints or any evidence they can find but I have to tell you, the letter and envelope looked very clean. They were very careful."

Danny felt relieved. A ransom note meant his father was still alive. He took the envelope and walked to his desk. Out of the corner of his eye, he could see Caloway whispering to Marone.

"What... what is it?" Danny asked.

Marone was hesitant – Caloway nudged him.

"They sent a picture too."

Danny turned over the envelope and shook it. A single page typed letter fell out. He began to read.

If you want to see your father alive again follow these instructions. Don't bring the police. If we see them he's dead. We want four hundred thousand dollars in unmarked unsequenced 100-dollar bills. You have 2 days to get the money. We will contact you with more instructions.

He turned the envelope over again and looked for the picture. Marone reached into his jacket pocket, taking out a small envelope.

"Here." He handed it to Danny.

His heart sunk. He took a deep breath and pulled out a snapshot of his father sitting on an old wooden chair. Masking tape covered his mouth and his hands were bound behind him. His eyes looked dark and a small cut stood out on his cheek. The blood hadn't been cleaned off and it had caked over the wound. Tears streamed down Danny's face; the feeling of helplessness was too much.

"Four hundred thousand?" Danny said. "This would have to be someone that knew he had that much cash, no?"

"Nowadays Mr. Dillon, with technology they can find out everything about anyone," Marone said.

"She would have an idea of how much money he had," Danny said in an angry voice, pointing toward the ceiling.

"We've got nothing on her now. Best bet is to get the money, pay them and then we catch them. They usually do something stupid. It's easier than trying to find them first," Caloway said.

"Something stupid like killing the victim?" Danny asked.

"Look, I'm not going to lie to you. They already know if they're going to kill him or not. We can only give 'em the money and pray. We'll do everything in our power to get him back safely."

Danny looked startled at the officer's candidness.

"I'm assuming you can get that kind of money?" Caloway asked.

"As long as you guys come to the bank or brokerage house with me and explain. They're not just going to give me his money and I certainly don't have four hundred thousand bucks myself."

"Right, we'll head out in a little bit. Do you know which bank?"

"Yeah, I have everything in my safe," Danny said, pointing toward a far corner at a two foot high tarnished brass plated safe.

"Start going through it so we know where we're going," Caloway said.

Cheryl leaned over the railing at the top of the stairs. She stood in bare feet so not to be detected. She had heard much of the conversation. As the men readied to leave, she tiptoed back to the bedroom.

Chapter Five

Danny accompanied the two detectives into the branch office of The First New England Bank. He put a brown leather suitcase on the floor in front of the manager's desk and waited for the man to finish his phone call. Seeing the three men with such serious faces seemed to alarm the manager. He hung up the phone and stood up. Danny reached out his hand.

"I'm Danny Dillon. These are Detectives Marone and Caloway."

They stepped forward and produced their badges.

"We really need your cooperation in this matter," Caloway bent down to see the manager's nameplate. "Mr. Tully."

"Yes, of course. How can I help?" He waited to see who would explain the situation.

"My father has been kidnapped. They want four hundred thousand dollars. My father has an account here with one hundred thousand dollars. I need to withdraw that in unsequenced hundred dollar bills."

The manager looked surprised.

"We don't keep that kind of money on hand here. I'll need to get approval from my superiors. Then we'll have to make a request for a delivery of the money."

"How long will that take?" Caloway asked.

The man looked confused for a moment. "I don't know. I was never in a position like this before. I'll start making calls. There are certain procedures that need to be followed." He pointed to the chairs. "Have a seat and I'll get right on it." He looked around, seeing one of the tellers standing idly, he phoned her. "Janice, please come out here and get these gentlemen some coffee."

The bank manager made his call, taking notes as he was given instructions. Within minutes, he was finished.

"Gentlemen, apparently this was on TV last night and I missed it. My superiors didn't. We can accommodate you with that money by this afternoon. We'll have a special armored car bring the money from other branches. But first I need your badges and your precinct along with your boss's name."

Both detectives put their badges on the desk. Caloway scribbled the head of detectives name and number and handed it to Tully.

"Very good then. All I have to do is verify that you are who you say you are... oh and Mr. Dillon, can I have some ID?"

"Sure," Danny replied, handing him his driver's license.

The manager held up the identification of each man and compared the pictures to the actual person. Appearing satisfied, he said, "I'll need to call your boss and we can get this show on the road."

He picked up the phone and made the call.

"Mr. Dillon, how many places do we have to go to for the rest?" Marone asked.

"First, could you guys start calling me Danny?"

Both officers nodded and smiled.

"It's got to be banks only. The stock brokerages won't have access to cash like the banks will. So we need to go to two more places."

"Hey Detectives, what's goin' on?" a voice came from behind them.

Two uniformed officers shook hands with the detectives. "We got a call to check out if you guys were really detectives or not."

Marone and Caloway turned back to the manager. "I'm sorry gentlemen but ID cards are easy to forge. My higher ups called 9-1-1 to send them just to make sure you weren't phonies."

"No, you're okay Mr. Tully. I know these guys – I wouldn't leave a donut around them but they're real good guys." The officer turned to Marone. "I got my account here. Tully's okay."

"Thank you and I'm sorry that I had to do that, Detectives, but..."

"Don't sweat it. Just get the man his money," Caloway said. "I'll do my best."

The two other banks were as accommodating as the first and a plan was set to have one armored car pick up the money and deliver it to the First New England Bank branch. From there a police escort under the cover of night would deliver the money to Danny's house.

That evening Danny sat downstairs with Kanook, waiting for the big delivery. An unmarked car sat in front of the house and would stay there for the duration. The officer who manned the phone-tapping machine was now armed with a semi automatic weapon. The officer's cell phone rang. He answered it and gave Danny a nod.

"This is it," Danny said to Kanook.

Danny went to the garage and opened the door. Four officers armed with semi-automatic rifles were already in the driveway. The armored truck backed in and the back door swung open. Marone and Caloway stepped out; Caloway carried a dark suitcase.

"Okay, inside," he said.

Danny watched the truck speed out of his driveway as the garage door lowered. It all happened in twenty seconds.

With the suitcase sitting on top of the center worktable, the two detectives, the officer, Danny and Kanook, all gathered in front of it. Caloway did the honors popping it open. There was a loud gasp and then dead silence for a few seconds.

"Wow, never seen that much green before," Kanook said.

"Sure is pretty," Marone remarked.

"Would be a lot nicer if it wasn't going to pay the ransom for my kidnapped father."

The other men were silent once again, having forgotten for a moment that delivery of this money meant life or death for George.

"All we can do now is wait," Danny said.

"We're going to head out, Danny," Marone said. "If you get the call, you have our cell numbers. Also keep in mind we're keeping four men outside just in case."

"Right. Thanks for all your help, guys."

The weekend went without any contact from the kidnappers. The detectives had no new leads. Danny looked haggard from lack of sleep and food. He had only eaten two small meals over the two-day period. Kanook did his best to care for his friend but there wasn't much he could do to comfort him. The one thing Danny did enjoy was freedom to move about the house as he pleased. He had grown accustomed to waiting for Cheryl to finish eating or for her to leave the house before going upstairs but she now had such a fear of Schmedly, that the dog now ruled the house.

It was Monday, mid-morning. Even though Danny's heart wasn't in his work, he rejoined Tommy in fixing the backlogged computers. The phone had already rung so many times that the anticipation of a call had lessened.

Marone stopped in to check on Danny. The detective sat for a moment in the recliner, watching the news.

A few minutes before noon the phone rang.

"Is this Danny Dillon?" the caller asked in a low voice.

Danny snapped his fingers. Marone jumped up and looked over at the officer manning the taping machine. He gave Marone a nod and thumbs up.

"Yes, I'm Danny," he replied. A burst of hot blood shot through his body.

"Did you get the money?"

"Yes, I have it. Let me speak to my father," he demanded.

"He's fine. As long as you follow my directions, he'll be okay."

"Let me speak to him!"

Danny could hear muffled sounds while the kidnapper covered the mouthpiece and spoke to someone in the background.

"Danny," George's voice sounded strained.

Danny froze for a second. "Dad, are you okay?"

"I'm okay Danny. Just do what they say."

The kidnapper came back on the line. "Now be home tonight precisely at six o'clock for more instructions... and remember – don't involve the cops."

The line went dead. Danny laid the phone back on its cradle and looked at Marone, who was leaning over the machine.

"It's a cell phone, Detective. Older model, no GPS. Most likely stolen so having the number won't help but now I contact the cell phone companies. They can tell me which cell tower the call went through. We'll have an idea of where they are but won't be able to pinpoint them."

"Then what good is having this contraption here? It's useless," Danny said.

"We had to try, Danny. If they were stupid enough to call from a house, we could've grabbed 'em. Unfortunately they seem to know what they're doing," Marone said. "Now we wait 'til tonight. I'm going to head out. I'll be back around four. You still got an unmarked outside." He put on his overcoat and left through the garage.

Danny sat with his elbows on the workbench. He ran his hands up his face until his fingers locked tightly into his hair. Hearing his father's voice would only make the wait more unbearable.

Outside one reporter and a cameraman chased after Marone. "Any truth to the rumor an armored car pulled into this driveway? Did it deliver ransom money?" the man asked as Marone jumped into his car.

"No comment." He drove away.

Both detectives returned to Danny's house at four o'clock. To their surprise Cheryl answered the front door.

"He's downstairs," she said. Her expression was almost slightly apologetic.

Danny sat with Schmedly on his lap in the recliner - a cordless phone held tightly in his hand. Kanook sat across from him, drinking a beer.

"No calls yet, right?" Marone asked.

Danny shook his head.

"What's with your wife, Danny?" Caloway whispered.

"I know, she actually asked me how everything was going with my father. Maybe she feels guilty. I don't know."

"You really think she's got something to do with this?" Kanook asked.

"I've given it a lot of thought. Her brother would have to be involved. She couldn't do it on her own."

"We're still looking into her brother. Trying to locate him. Your wife told us he lived in Georgia but we can't find him. And no calls were made from this house to Georgia other than to her parents who say they haven't spoken to the son in a while," Marone said. "He's a drifter apparently."

"Maybe you should give her the benefit of the doubt," Kanook said, taking a long swig of his beer.

"She's in this. I know it," Danny said. "I've been wracking my brain to figure it out... and I will."

"We tracked the phone the call came from this morning. It was stolen. We also tracked the call to a cell tower about thirty miles from here. Unfortunately, we can't pinpoint a call and we can't go poking around. Last thing we want is to spook them," Caloway said, throwing his overcoat on the workbench. "Actually there is a way of tracking a cell phone but if the battery is removed you can't. They knew that and removed it."

Danny's hand was sweaty from holding the phone so tight. He wiped his hand along his pant leg and opened and closed it repeatedly.

"All we can do is wait, wait, wait," his voice trailed off.

At exactly six o'clock, the phone rang. Danny jumped out of his chair, as did the detectives.

"Wait," Caloway said.

He looked back at the officer on the machine. Getting the thumbs up, he pointed to Danny.

"Hello?"

"This Danny?" the voice asked.

"Yes."

"Listen carefully. Do you know where Lisbon Park is?"

"Yes."

"Go there in a car with no tinting and come alone. If we see the cops your father dies. Understand?"

"Yes."

"Take the money to the third hiking trail entrance – Dikers Way Trail. Put the money next to the trail sign and leave it. Got it?"

Danny finished scribbling the instructions down on a pad.

"I got it."

"Twenty minutes. Come alone or he dies."

"Twenty minutes? Wait, let me speak to my father first," Danny said in desperation.

"Twenty minutes – better leave now."

"Wait... wait," Danny yelled into the phone but the man had hung up.

Danny walked in a circle, confused and stressed by the immediacy of his task.

"Stay calm, we'll be close by," Marone said.

"Close by. I don't want you anywhere near me. You heard what he said."

"We'll stay right outside the park just in case something happens to you. It'll be far enough away."

Danny didn't look happy about their plan but there wasn't time to argue. Marone and Caloway both dialed their cell phones while walking to the machine.

"Another cell phone, guys. I'm sure it's stolen too," the tech officer said.

"Check it out anyway. Let me know," Caloway said.

Danny threw on his coat and picked up the suitcase. Marone, now off his phone, walked over to him.

"First, stay calm. Just do what the man said. Second, this suitcase has a transmitter in it so we can track them. Unfortunately, they've been pretty smart so I doubt the money will stay in it long but we have to try."

"What car you gonna take?" Caloway asked.

"My wife's Mercedes – it's got clear windows." He picked up his wallet and keys. "Let me go. I don't want to take a chance on getting stuck in traffic somewhere."

Schmedly followed Danny as he hauled the suitcase through the garage. He hit the button for the garage door and then the button to pop the trunk of the Mercedes. The detectives and Kanook followed. They shook his hand and wished him luck. Kanook added a hug after the handshake. Danny looked at the living room window while Kanook embraced him. He could see Cheryl's shadow against the blinds as she peered out.

Danny pointed at Schmedly to hop across the front driver seat into the passenger side as he held open the door.

"Hey wait," Marone said. "You're not taking the dog with you."

"He's coming. I wouldn't think of going without him."

By Danny's expression they saw there was no way they would change his mind. He followed Schmedly into the car and bent forward to see if Cheryl was still at the upstairs window. He smiled when he saw that she was.

"Hey Schmed, do me a favor and dig your claws deep into the leather. Mommy's watching."

Danny set his cell phone in the cradle and dialed his business number.

"Okay, Danny, we're here. Just leave the phone line open and take us through what's happening," Marone said. "Caloway will be following you most of the way there – I'll have him on another line."

"Right."

He drove to the park entrance. There were no lights but a half moon helped lead the way to the trailhead parking lot.

"I don't see anyone yet."

He pulled back on the headlight high beam switch and proceeded, coming to a crawl at the first two parking lots. Schmedly growled as they approached the third. An arrow carved into a small wooden sign with the words "Dikers Way Trail" carved under it pointed to the right. He drove in.

"I'm at the third parking lot now. I'm pulling in. I see the sign for the trail itself." A shiver went down his spine as Schmedly let out a hair-raising growl.

"What was that?" Marone asked.

"Schmedly."

"God, sounded like a bear."

He put the car in park, opened the glove compartment and hit the button to open the trunk. He also opened the passenger window.

"Schmed, you stay here unless I need you."

With the car still running, he stepped out and panned the parking lot. He bent back inside the car and leaned toward the phone.

"Still don't see anyone. I'm going to take the suitcase out now."

The wind gave him a chill as he walked back toward the trunk. He lifted the heavy suitcase out, walked it to the sign and dropped it before returning to the car.

"I did it. Now I'm driving toward the parking lot exit."

Danny knew he was supposed to leave immediately after the drop but his curiosity prevailed. A short distance from the lot, he parked the car and turned off the lights. After waiting for three minutes he decided to return to the original plan. He reached for the ignition key but off in the distance the sound of what he thought was a chain saw made him stop. In his rearview mirror he could see a flickering light off in the woods. He opened his window – the sound became identifiable. It was a motorcycle – a dirt bike. They could take the money through the back trails for thirty miles without being seen.

"They're coming by motorcycle. They're taking the money through the woods."

"Danny, you did your job. Now get out of there," Marone said.

Danny watched for a few more seconds. He could see the silhouette of a rider against the light from the headlamp as the bike turned around and roared back into the woods.

"He's gone. I'll be right home."

Danny arrived home in half the time it took him to get to the park. He flew into the house. Cheryl jumped from the chair in the living room.

"How did it go?" she asked.

He didn't answer. He raced down the stairs.

"Anything yet?" he asked the detectives.

"You have to give them a little time, Danny. The guy on the motorcycle might not even be back to where they have your father. The suitcase was dumped a thousand feet from where you dropped it. They knew we would track it," Caloway said, pointing to a GPS system screen on a laptop.

Danny sat in his chair.

"So all I can do is wait then."

"We have our guys on the scene where you dropped the money to get track prints from the bike and anything else we can find," Marone said.

"But they said if they saw cops, they'd kill him," Danny yelled.

"Relax. They're far away from that place and are probably heading for an airport. Oh, and keep in mind that your father may remain tied up for days... hate to have to tell you this but it could happen. They may wait 'til they're wherever they want to be before contacting us on his location," Caloway said.

"If we don't hear anything for twenty-four hours, we'll start a massive search for him in the area of the cell phone calls. By then we'll know they're gone and it'll be fairly safe," Marone said.

Kanook handed Danny a beer. "I'll stay with you through the night, man."

"We'll be stayin' for a little while too but outside," Marone said. "If we don't hear from him in an hour, the command truck is comin'. We'll leave the officer in here on the machine in case he calls and we need a trace."

"I'll get a sleeping bag and sleep on the floor next to Schmed," Kanook said, going to the garage.

Danny would have preferred solitude but didn't want to hurt Kanook's feelings. He did feel a bit upbeat though, now that the money had been delivered smoothly. He actually felt hungry for the first time in days. He climbed the stairs but got dizzy halfway up and had to hold onto the banister. Schmedly looked down at him from the landing and barked once to encourage him to continue.

Danny stuck a dog food can in the opener and pushed down on the switch.

"How did it go?" Cheryl asked from the kitchen entranceway. She looked at Schmedly who gave a quick return glance but was more interested in the spinning dog food can.

Danny was startled and didn't know whether to be nice or to give her the cold shoulder – being nice might net some information but he was not that good an actor.

"Why do you care, Cheryl? You hate the guy and he doesn't much care for you – the way you treat me."

Without saying a word, she left the room.

It had been three days since the ransom had been paid, yet there was no contact with Danny's father. The detectives had little to go on. A massive search had turned up nothing. The telephone-tracking machine had been packed and hauled out. Danny had lost all faith that George was still alive. He hadn't showered or shaved in three full days and he had eaten only a few bites of food.

It was noon. Danny sat by himself watching TV while he waited for Kanook to arrive. The business phone rang incessantly but he let the machine answer. Irate customers left nasty messages, wanting to know where their broken computers were. He barely even noticed. Tommy walked in, throwing a McDonald's bag on the table before diving for the phone. After receiving a few choice words from an unsatisfied customer, he carried the bag to Danny.

"Danny, you gotta eat something."

Schmedly sat up and sniffed the air. Tommy handed him a cheeseburger and Danny a bag of fries.

"Got salt?"

"Yeah, right here."

Danny ripped open a small salt packet and dumped it into the bag.

"Danny, I know you're not into hearing this but we're really getting backed up and the customers..."

"I know, Tommy. You don't have to tell me."

Kanook walked in the back door.

"Kanook, I need your help, buddy."

"Name it, man."

Tommy and Kanook glanced at each other wondering what the favor was. They kneeled next to him as if waiting for a dying man's last request. Danny rolled to his side in a fetal like position to face Kanook but was uncomfortable. He struggled to bring the recliner upright but lacked the strength. Kanook reached and pulled the chair lever.

"Kanook, you know the guy we went to see? Barry something..."

"My wife's cousin, Barry Leonard."

"Yeah, him. Can we go see him again? He still around?"

"Yeah, he's in New York and is gonna be there for a while. I'll take you tonight if you shower." He waved his hand past his face.

Danny smiled for the first time in days. "A shower it is. You go call him and make sure he can see us."

"Sure."

"You remember when we were there? He told me of impending doom."

"I didn't want to bring it up," he said, returning to his feet. "I need to know if my father is dead and I believe he can tell me. I mean he was able to name my cat, Jonesy, from when I was a kid. I spent hours thinking about how he could have known that. He couldn't have unless he really can talk to the dead."

"Told you he's good."

"I'd love to see this guy too," Tommy said.

"Not today, kid. I think we need to see Barry alone. I'll get you tickets though," Kanook added.

Danny reached into the bag that Tommy had put along side of his chair and unwrapped a hamburger. He started to eat. Kanook pulled Tommy aside. "Get him in the shower right away. We don't need him upstairs when she gets home." He opened the back door. "I'll run home and call Barry to see what's up."

Tommy unscrewed the cover to a printer.

"He in the shower?" Kanook asked, returning through the back door.

"Yes, thank God. I couldn't take any more. He stunk!"

"Yeah, I know. I finally got hold of Barry and he's going to see us before his show tonight so we gotta leave soon. I'll run up and move him along."

Schmedly ran down the stairs upon hearing Kanook's voice.

"Hiya mutt," Kanook said, scratching the dog behind the ears. "Hey, Tommy, any chance you can stay late 'til we get back? I don't want to leave Schmed home alone with her. You never know what might happen, you know?"

"I was staying anyway."

Danny came down the stairs looking like a new man, although his eyes were still sunken.

"You speak to him?" Danny asked.

"Yeah, we can meet him any time between four and six. Let's hit it now to make sure we don't run into traffic. Tommy's stayin' late so Schmed'll be okay."

"Tommy, don't leave him here alone with her," Danny said, pointing to the dog. "If you have to leave, take him with you, understand?"

Tommy nodded as he answered the phone once again.

"Let's go, man."

As they drove, Danny obsessed about Cheryl's involvement in the kidnapping. He finally let loose.

"You know she's gotta be involved. The way she's acting. She's being nice again and she's acting like she cares about my father."

"Danny, you gotta calm down with this. You have no proof. The cops got no proof. There's no phone records of her talkin' to her brother like you thought."

Danny wasn't listening to Kanook's logic.

"The only thing I can't figure is how she's going to spend the ransom money without being caught. I mean she can't put it in the bank."

Kanook rolled his eyes.

They stood at the hotel's front desk.

"Gentlemen, please have a seat and he'll be right with you," the girl behind the counter said.

They mulled around waiting until a woman called out to them.

"Are you Kanook?" she asked.

"Yeah, that's me."

"I'm Kelly, Barry's assistant. He's just getting finished meeting with someone. Please follow me and I'll take you to his room. You can wait there."

Once upstairs, she swiped her plastic card key through the electronic door lock. It played a five-note tune acknowledging that entry was permitted. They walked into a two-story suite with floor to ceiling windows. Being immediately drawn to the view, both men were silent as they gazed from the twenty-story room.

"Man, I guess Barry's doing okay," Kanook said.

"Gentlemen, there's a bar over there. Please make yourselves comfortable. Barry will be here shortly."

She left the room.

"Wow, this place is unbelievable. The kind of place that Cheryl would give her right arm to stay in whether it bankrupted me or not," Danny said.

Both men popped a beer and sat in front of the big screen TV. Kanook flipped through the channels. Danny wasn't as comfortable. He got up and paced near the windows. Could he trust the visions that Barry might bring from the other side?

The front door opened.

"Hey, guys. Glad to see you again," Barry said.

Kanook walked over and hugged him. "Thanks for seeing us on short notice."

"Kanook, any time you need help, you just call."

He turned to Danny and shook his hand. "You have some questions I understand."

"My father was kidnapped and I need to know if he's alive."

"Come sit... first I need something to drink," Barry said. "Kanook has given me some heads up on the matter and I did see the story on the news." Barry poured a glass of orange juice. "I'll do the best I can, Danny, but remember they don't always come."

"I understand... just try is all I ask."

Barry took a long drink and put the glass down. He then moved the coffee table away from the couch where the men had been sitting. "Kanook, give me a hand with this." Together they moved a large chair to face the couch and sit only two feet away from it.

"Danny, sit here in front of me," Barry said, as he sat in the chair.

Danny was already on the verge of tears. He sat and faced him.

"Now Danny, I can only tell you what I see. If I'm not sure, I will not make a guess. I will not speculate. You may come away from here with more questions than when you arrived. You understand this, yes?"

Danny nodded as he glanced at Kanook who sat on the far side of the room.

"The most important thing is if your father has passed, he needs to give you something... something so you know that it's him, understand?"

"Yes, some kind of proof only I would know," Danny said.

"Exactly. Let's begin. Give me your hand."

Danny reached out. As Barry's hand touched his, Danny felt what he though was an energy pass through him but wasn't sure if it was merely his desire to believe. Barry closed his eyes while holding tight to Danny's hand. He began to breathe heavily.

"I see an animal... I get the name Joe... Joan?"

"Jonesy, my cat from when I was young."

Barry shook his head for Danny not to speak for a moment.

"There are quite a few... spirits coming through. There is a woman... older than you... a very happy woman – bubbly. Name of Edna... Edna... something like that with the cat."

Danny sat with his eyes open wide and jaw hanging. Tears began to steam down his cheeks.

"My mother's name was Edwina," he whispered.

"She's here with us now. A very happy woman, yes?"

Danny's mind was close to a short circuit. Now his mother was happy?   "Yes... she was very happy in life but last time she was warning me."

Barry shook his head but did not open his eyes. "Wait 'til I'm finished."

"Sorry."

"Danny, understand they don't actually speak to me in full sentences like we speak but communicate symbolically and I can sense names. She is now putting her hand on her heart to show her love for you."

Danny's body quivered. Kanook looked on in awe, wanting desperately to fill a glass with scotch but he dared not move.

"Now... I have a younger male. May have died from... something with the head – looks like head trauma."

"My cousin Chris. He was hit by a car when he was twenty."

Barry's eyes opened for the first time. He looked into Danny's eyes and then to the floor. "Sometimes when someone has passed recently, they have to adapt to their new existence. They usually have another spirit to guide them. Your cousin is guiding someone to me - an older male."

Danny's heart sunk but he was not surprised. Barry again closed his eyes. Thirty seconds passed in silence.

"The man has passed recently. He is very sad, not for himself but for you."

Danny's body now trembled violently. Barry held Danny's forearm tightly with one hand and with the other pushed down on his knee, in an attempt to keep it still.

"He... he shows me that you are suffering. He is opening his arms wide... this shows he is happy where he is and not to mourn for him."

"Is it..." Danny swallowed hard. "Is it my father?"

"I don't know, Danny. Wait - another woman comes to me - older also. Now... the older gentleman is pushy. He really wants to come through. And I really feel that he is new to his surroundings."

Barry started to breathe heavily. For an instant Danny thought Barry was having a seizure. Kanook started to stand but Barry resumed the reading.

"He puts his hand on his heart for you. He is fading... but ... he's showing me... I'm seeing the... this is strange. I've never seen this deep a color before - it's beautiful and not of this Earth. He's showing me a - I think it's a bicycle - a deep green bicycle? Does that make any sense to you?"

Danny jumped off the couch. "Oh, my God, he is dead," he screamed, locking his fingers together behind his head and squeezing his head between his arms. He fell to the floor and sat with his back against the couch with his elbows on his knees. Barry and Kanook rushed around to that side.

"You all right?" Kanook asked.

"When I was twelve... my father got me this green bike that I had wanted so bad," Danny said in a low, even voice, his body rocking back and forth.

Kanook looked at Barry. "So he is dead then."

"I only tell what I see, Kanook."

Barry kneeled next to Danny.

"Before he faded the one thing I did notice was his aura was very bright – one of the brightest I've ever seen. That means he was a good person in life. I'm sorry to bring this news to you Danny."

Barry patted Danny's hand and stood up. Danny calmed for a moment. Questions now swirled through his mind.

"How come my mother didn't bring him to you?"

"I don't have all the answers, Danny. It's just the way it happens. I can't even tell you that it was your father that I saw."

Kanook stood behind the bar. Finding the scotch, he poured two shots.

"Barry, you want one too?"

"No, I have a show soon. It keeps me from concentrating."

Kanook downed the shot and carried the second to Danny, who was just standing up. His hand still shook but was able to hold the tiny glass. He threw the liquor to the back of his throat and swallowed.

"The bitch killed him. I can't believe she knows he's dead and she's laughing behind my back. Barry, could you tell the way he died?"

Barry had his back to Danny but Kanook could see his face as he answered. It looked as if Barry was about to tell a lie.

"No, Danny. I did not see how he died. I'm sorry."

"Was there anything else? Anything about a vicious woman involved with his death?"

Barry stood behind the bar. "No, Danny, I didn't see anything like that."

The ride home was quiet for the most part. Danny obsessed to himself over what he believed was his wife's knowledge of George's disappearance and now his murder.

Kanook walked with Danny through the back door. Tommy was still working at the same bench. Schmedly ran and jumped at Danny who had squatted down to meet him.

"I know, I missed you too, buddy."

"What happened?" Tommy asked.

Kanook looked at Danny. "Do we tell him?"

"Yeah, I have no problem telling him." Danny sat in the chair next to Tommy. "The guy told me that my father is dead."

"Wow... but how do you know he's right?"

"He told me things that he could never have known unless my father was the one he was communicating with."

"Wow, that's weird."

"Sure is. Now I have to put away whoever did it," Danny said, looking upstairs.

"Oh, boy," Kanook said. "Danny, promise you won't do anything crazy."

"I am going to confront her. Even if she denies it, I'll be able to see her eyes and get an idea."

"That's it for me. I'm getting out of here while the gettins good," Tommy said. "I don't want to be around for this."

Tommy grabbed his keys, patted Schmedly on the head and quickly left.

"When you doing this?"

"Right now. You want to come watch?"

Kanook put his hands up and backed towards the door. "Not me, man. I'll call 9-1-1 if I hear shots though. Be careful what you do. Call me if you need me." He laughed. "But not if you need help loadin' a body."

"All right, get out," Danny laughed but his face quickly turned solemn the instant Kanook was out the door.

He could hear Cheryl upstairs in the kitchen. He walked toward the stairs, Schmedly followed.

"You better wait here." He put up a retractable gate Cheryl had left at the bottom of the stairs. It came with a note stating the upstairs was now off limits to the dog. Cheryl washed a dish as Danny walked up from behind. He opened the refrigerator and took out a beer.

"Where were you?" she asked.

"I was with Kanook." He popped open the beer. "We went to see his cousin, Barry Leonard. The guy who speaks to the dead."

Cheryl froze for an instant. "And what did he say?"

"He said my father was dead." Danny hesitated, nervous that his plan could backfire. "And he said someone close to me was responsible."

She dropped the dish, breaking it in the sink. "Do you still think I had something to do with this? You idiot – how could I have done it?" she yelled.

Danny summoned all his courage. "I don't think you did it but I think you know who did."

She took a deep breath. "I've been trying to be nice to you 'cause of your father but now you can go fuck yourself. I had nothing to do with it and I don't give a shit if you believe me or not." She stormed out. "And be careful, your bodyguard isn't here to save you," she said, disappearing down the hall.

He followed her and stood in the bedroom doorway. "I'm moving out."

She came out from the bathroom, laughing. "You're leaving? Where will you go? You have no money and can't make a living without your workshop. If you move into your father's house, you'll be thrown out soon as you can't pay the taxes. And speaking of taxes, don't forget the IRS. Think I forgot about that?"

Danny could tell that she was just getting started and maybe he hadn't thought out the whole scenario well enough.

"You can't get any of his money because your name isn't on any of the accounts. And his will doesn't help you because they can't find him – no body, no death certificate for seven years."

"What are you talking about?"

"Guess you didn't know," she said triumphantly, "but if someone disappears, they can't be listed as dead for like seven years. You won't get a nickel 'til then. And I'm pretty sure the medical examiner won't issue a death certificate on the say so of a guy who talks to the dead. Face it – you're stuck here to do what I tell you." She laughed. "Now go down and make some money so I can spend it."

Danny retreated. She was right – he was a prisoner. If he left, she could turn him into the IRS. He didn't have his father's money to pay off that debt anymore.

There was only one way to regain his freedom.

Cheryl, you're not leaving me any choice.

Chapter Six

Five days had passed. Danny had given Cheryl a week in his mind to call a truce but the spending sprees increased and the bills mounted. His pleas to cut back on her shopping went unheard. His explanations of how they could lose the house also fell on a deaf ear. She would rather be out on the street than give in to his requests – unless of course she had fallback money – ransom money. He was convinced now more than ever that she had a hand in his father's kidnapping and death.

Kanook tapped on the back door as he opened it. He took a step in and froze. Danny hadn't wanted any company so Kanook hadn't been in the workshop in three days. It had the makings of a computer graveyard with parts scattered everywhere.

"Where's Tommy?"

"He only comes in now when I call him. I told him he might have to find a new job. I can't pay him."

He sat back in the recliner.

"Danny, you look like shit, man. When was the last time you showered or shaved?"

Danny turned to him. "She's got me. She's got me right where she wants me. I figured it out. It's a slow death. She'll wait 'til the money is totally gone and leave. I'll have no place to go. The creditors will be hunting me. I'll lose my business."

"Whoa, Danny, take it easy."

Danny attempted to hide his crying under a baseball cap. Mucus ran from his nose but he made no attempt to wipe it. Kanook handed him a paper towel.

"Look, Danny, you gotta snap out of this."

"Why? I got nothing left. She's just gonna leave and spend my father's money. Probably turn me in to the IRS. I'm as good as dead."

Kanook came closer to inspect a small collapsible table, which sat next to the recliner. A pad of paper with small stick figures and arrows formed a circle around the outer edge of the top page. Kanook turned his head to make heads or tails of it but Danny, catching him spying his work, grabbed the pad and buried it under his robe. Kanook only caught a two-second glimpse of the primitive drawings but was able to decipher their meaning.

"Danny, I think it's time we got you out of here. You and Schmed can stay with us for awhile."

Danny looked at him. His darkened eyes weren't giving away any emotion. Kanook couldn't read him – was it fear that he saw? Or was it grief... maybe anger. Danny's words, spoken very slowly, did give some hint.

"I'll be fine. I appreciate the offer but I'm going to take care of this." He clenched his teeth. "Me... I'm taking care of it."

Danny was no longer the man he once was. Instead of being his mild mannered, easygoing friend, he was now an unstable man on the edge with only one objective. Kanook took a step back.

"Danny, I think you may be on the verge of a nervous breakdown. Please let me help."

"I don't need any help but thanks." Danny yawned. "All I need is some sleep. I do feel better seeing you though, Kanook... my friend."

He closed his eyes. Kanook feared Danny's plans but there was nothing that he could do to stop them, short of going to the police.

* * * * *

Danny had shut off the phone ringers and the answering
machine so as not to be disturbed by his customers. He looked
toward the back door. It was still light out. He opened and
closed his mouth a couple of times, moving his tongue around,
trying to lubricate his cotton mouth. He ran his hand over his
face, rubbing the lengthening facial hair.

"Hey dog – you feel like getting up?"

Schmedly slept upside down on his bed. He let his feet fall
to the floor upon hearing Danny's voice.

Danny pulled out the pad, which was still under his robe.
He followed the crude drawings around with his finger. He
flipped the page and went over a checklist. Penned check marks
dug deep in the left margin, having been written over a thousand
times. He was sure that nothing was left out.

He eased himself out of the chair. His body was stiff from
inactivity. He turned his head and held his breath as he closed
his robe, causing his body odor to be forced upward toward his
nose.

He was ready to rehearse his plan once again. He opened
a bottom desk drawer and lifted out a bottle of clear yellowish
liquid – peanut oil. He raised it to the light and stared through
it. He swished it around as he went over his situation looking
for another way out. He couldn't leave – he had no money. If
he did leave, she would turn him into the IRS. There was no
money to pay them – it meant jail time. If he stayed, he toiled
in the basement for life. If George's body were discovered, she
could fight a divorce for years, preventing him from collecting
his inheritance. George's will clearly stated, "No divorce, no
money."

He put the bottle on the desk and took out a single paper
towel. After making believe he had dipped it in the bottle, he
walked up the stairs.

The next evening, Danny sat in his recliner. He was shaved
and showered. He sipped straight scotch from a glass. He

needed to have just enough to remove his inhibitions but not so much as to dull his senses. This was the night – Wednesday night. She always brought home Chinese food.

The front door opened – he listened. The sound of a paper bag crunching against the door jam as she pushed her way in, gave it away. Schmedly let out a couple of mild barks. Danny grabbed his snout and whispered "quiet" into the dogs ear. He then raised the volume on the TV.

He jumped out of his seat and tethered Schmedly to the center workbench leg. Opening his desk drawer, he took out a sealed zip-lock bag containing a paper towel wet on one corner. He listened for her movements. The TV went on in the kitchen. He could hear opening the closet door to hang up her coat. He could hear her footsteps walking down the hall and then the sound of the bedroom door closing. That was his cue – he dashed up the stairs with only socks on his feet and latex gloves on his hands.

Just like I rehearsed it now.

He threw a pad and pen on the counter while adjusting the volume down a touch on the TV. He opened the bag of Chinese food, looking for the soup. He knew she would eat that first. He removed the containers of food until he came to the soup on the bottom. Without taking it out of the bag, he lifted the lid off, being careful not to spill it. He reached into his pocket and took out the plastic bag. Removing the paper towel, he dipped the peanut oil soaked corner into the soup and swirled it around. He raised the towel an inch above the soup and with two fingers squeezed the liquid back into the container. Holding one hand under the towel, he carefully placed it back in the bag. He could not spill a drop. The cover was snapped back into place and the paper bag repacked.

Danny's heart sped but not to the extent that he had expected. He took a step backward and listened for a second – there was no noise – he still had time.

The next step was to search her purse, which she always left on the kitchen chair. He dug through it, pulling her Epinephrine kit out and sliding it into his back pocket. He dug some more until he found her alarm. She carried a device, the size of a cigarette pack which had a pin that when pulled, sent out a loud, ear piercing alarm to summon help if she were having an allergic attack. He put it back neatly inside her purse so she would have easy access to it. He turned the chair so her bag was easier to reach.

He scanned the room, checking to make sure he hadn't forgotten anything. He completed his checklist by taking the portable phone from the kitchen table. Once back downstairs, he stepped into the small bathroom, dropping the bag with the peanut oil tainted paper towel into the bowl and flushing it.

Schmedly moaned from across the room. He had his leash on and to him that meant going for a walk, and not being tied up.

"Shhhh, not now," Danny said.

Schmedly lay back down.

Danny grabbed the glass, which was still half-full with scotch, and downed it. He had second thoughts for only an instant until he saw the pile of unpaid bills on his desk. His eyes shot back to the stairway when he heard Cheryl humming a tune as she headed for the kitchen. It wouldn't be long now. To hear better, he stood near the bottom of the stairs and waited. There was no turning back. He could hear her digging into the bag. Then the utensil drawer opened. There was no sound of a chair being pulled out; as he had hoped, she was eating at the counter.

Danny's body got a shot of adrenaline. The thought of what he was doing began to sink in. He had made arrangements for such an episode of emotion such as remorse or guilt. He took a step back. An eight by ten picture of his father holding him as a child sat only a few feet away.

I'm sorry Dad. I know you wouldn't approve but there's no other way.

Hearing a thud from upstairs turned him back toward the stairway. He put his foot on the first step. Had she fallen? Seconds later, he could hear her fumbling around and items hitting the floor. Then the final confirmation that she had ingested his poison – the alarm.

Schmedly started barking as Danny walked calmly up the short set of stairs. He continued past the front door. As he turned up the second flight, he could see her lying there holding the alarm, which echoed throughout the house. She raised her head and waved for him to hurry.

He was hesitant; afraid that he would give in and save her. But as planned, he pictured his father tied up in a dark, dingy basement – left to die. He bent over her. "What's the problem?" he asked, taking the alarm away and resetting it.

Mouthing the words "Epi Pen", she pointed to her bag, its contents spilled on the floor next to her.

"Oh, you mean this thing," he said, pulling the kit from his back pocket.

Her eyes opened wide.

"Here," Danny said, handing her the pad and pen that he had planted on the counter earlier. "Write down where my father is and who's involved."

She shook her head but he wasn't buying it.

"Write it down or you don't get this." He held up the case, which he opened, withdrawing the needle.

"Write it down," he yelled.

It was a no win situation. She took the pad and pen. Her face grew pale and her breathing became labored. Danny got nervous that she wanted to confess but wouldn't get the chance unless he injected her. Would she give in?

Lying flat on her back, she held the pad over her head so he couldn't see her face. She didn't write but just held the pen at her side. He moved the pad away and was about to cave in and inject her but the sight of her eyes changed his mind. Instead of a panic-stricken person about to die, she looked more like a person enraged and wanting revenge. Danny did a double-take. She could see his amazement and managed a small smile as she made a feeble attempt to throw the pad at him. She gasped one last time. Her final gesture was to raise her hand back up and produce her middle finger.

Her arm fell to her side and her body went limp. He wanted to reach down to feel for a pulse, but even comatose she still frightened him. He reached out with his foot and kicked the pen away, fearing she might awaken and jab him in the neck as he bent over. He kneeled with one knee on her arm and felt er wrist. The pulse was still there but faint through his latex gloves. He dropped her hand to the floor.

Rehearsing the murder in his mind was much different than the actual killing. He had gone over a thousand times the things that he needed to deal with after she was dead. First, he picked up the alarm, wiped it off, and along with everything else that had spilled out, he stuffed it deep into her purse. He replaced the Epi-Pen in its side compartment. Then he picked up the pad and pen, laying them on the kitchen table, and sat her purse back on the chair. Just like that he was finished. He took one last look at her near lifeless body and returned downstairs.

Schmedly, who had barked through the entire ordeal, had pulled so hard on his leash that he had bent the table leg out.

"Okay, okay," Danny shouted to the moaning dog.

He unhooked the leash. Schmedly walked to the stairs and sniffed the air but didn't make an attempt to go up. Danny fell back into his chair and poured another shot, gulping it down. He motioned for the dog to come to him.

"I had to do it, Schmed. We couldn't live this way." He cried quietly. "Oh, God, forgive me – please forgive me."

Schmedly laid his snout in Danny's lap.

"I did the right thing, right?" he asked, trembling.

A chill ran down his spine as he pictured her lying on the floor. Had she died yet or was there still a spark of life left? Should he go up and try to save her? He reached out and held his father's picture. Any thoughts of pity were quickly replaced with thoughts of how fast he could access Cheryl's 401k to keep the mortgage current.

He looked at his watch almost every minute. The urge to go back up was strong – he just wanted to see her but he didn't know why. Going back up wasn't part of the plan but maybe he would take just another quick look.

"Okay, Schmed, you stay here," he said, clipping the leash back on again.

Danny crept up the first set of stairs. He held the banister tight as he leaned around to look into the kitchen. He knew it couldn't be possible but still he worried that her body would be gone as in a horror movie. Or maybe she would be sitting at the table waiting for him.

He backed away for a moment – he was petrified. After a couple of deep breaths he got on all fours and crawled up the second flight of stairs. He popped his head above the last step – she was still there. He crawled on but was afraid to get too close. From about four feet away he leveled his head with her chest to see if she was breathing. There was no movement. From the floor he inspected the kitchen once more, making sure there were no mistakes. Once satisfied, he crawled backwards without taking his eyes off her.

Back in his chair downstairs, Danny's foremost thoughts were that of the murder that he had just committed but the thoughts of freedom from the tyrannical bitch soothed him. He sunk deep into the chair. He would wait another hour and make the call to 9-1-1.

Schmedly gave a low growl – Danny perked up – he knew that sound. It meant someone was coming. Then the unexpected – the doorbell rang. He jumped up. His first thoughts were that the police had come, but how could they know? The bell rang again. Schmedly barked twice.

"Shhh, quiet," Danny whispered as loudly as he could. He grabbed the dog. "No," he said into the dog's ear.

"Danny? You all right?"

Oh shit...Kanook.

Kanook now had the storm door open and was banging on the inside door. He was now only inches away from discovering Cheryl's body. This was not part of the plan.

"Okay, okay... I don't answer the door," he said to himself while pacing around his chair. "He'll worry and call the police. I'll make believe I was out cold from drinking. They break down the door and discover her body – I'm okay here. This'll work."

But Kanook threw another wrench into the plan. Danny's eyes opened wider when Kanook's voice was no longer coming from beyond the door. He had a key to Danny's house and was now one step inside.

"Danny? You okay?" he called.

Danny thought quickly and sat back in the chair, holding the dog by the collar. He could still pull this off. He released the dog and acted unconscious.

Before Schmedly made it to the stairs, Kanook yelled, "Cheryl, Cheryl," as he ran up to her body.

Danny could hear Kanook above him in the kitchen as he yelled to the 9-1-1 operator, "My neighbor's wife on the floor here. I think she's dead."

Danny had a decision to make – when was the right time to make his entrance? Feeling like he had overcome the problems that Kanook had introduced, he decided to wait. The phone conversation upstairs went on. He listened.

"CPR? Yeah I know how but I never really did it... I mean on a real person."

Kanook dragged Cheryl's body away from the counter. "I'll try mouth-to-mouth first," he said.

He blew into her mouth but her chest raised only slightly.

"I can't blow any air in – wait, she's allergic to nuts, I think. I bet she's having a reaction. She carries a needle with her."

Danny was again up out of the chair in a flash. He looked at his watch. Cheryl had only been out for a short time. If Kanook found the needle and injected her, he might save her. He walked to the stairs and listened.

"Found it," Kanook said.

There was silence for a moment.

You found what? You found what? Danny thought frantically.

"I've injected her but I don't know how much air I can get into her."

Danny held his head tightly in his hands. He wanted to run up and stop Kanook from going any further. Kanook would understand but the 9-1-1 operator would not.

"Danny, where are you?" Kanook yelled.

Danny grabbed the bottle of scotch and drank as much as he could – he needed to be totally inebriated to explain away his failure to respond to Kanook's repeated calls.

"Yeah, I'm down here. What... what you doing up there?" he called in his best drunken voice.

"You all right?"

"Yeah."

"Get up here. Cheryl's on the floor, man. Don't you hear me callin' you?"

Danny thumped his feet heavily on the stairs as he went up. "What's the problem, Kanook?"

"Cheryl must've ate something," Kanook said.

Danny stopped short at the kitchen doorway trying his best to look surprised. "Oh, my God, what happened?" He fell to his knees but didn't know how to act. He couldn't fall over her body crying. "Is she dead?"

"Not yet."

Kanook continued CPR with the help of the 9-1-1 operator until sirens blared in the distance. Danny's heart pounded with the sound. The paramedics would surely intubate her. If she lived, it was over for him.

"I hear the sirens, thank you," Kanook said to the 9-1-1 operator and hung up.

"God, I hope she makes it," Danny said.

He looked at Kanook for the first time and then quickly turned away. The smell of scotch was strong.

Kanook put his hand on Danny's shoulder and with a serious face said, "You better sound more convincing when the cops get here."

Red and blue lights shot through the front windows. Doors slammed. A police officer and two paramedics burst through the front door.

"Up here," Kanook yelled.

Danny covered his mouth and leaned back against the wall. "What we got?"

"His wife," Kanook said, pointing to Danny. "Allergic reaction we think."

One paramedic took a pulse as the other attempted to blow air into her mouth.

"No airway, gotta intubate. Pulse?" the paramedic asked.

"Very weak," the other answered.

Danny listened in horror. They were going to save the bitch.

"Who injected her?" the paramedic asked, spotting the Epi Pen on the floor.

"I did," Kanook said.

"How long ago?"

" 'Bout... twelve minutes I guess."

The last massive gulps of scotch that Danny had taken were kicking in and he could barely stand. The officer, getting a good whiff of Danny's breath, helped him to the living room.

"You been doing some drinking tonight, Mr....."

"Dillon, Danny Dillon and yeah I had a few drinks."

Kanook kneeled in front of Danny as the officer talked on his radio.

"Mr. Dillon, are you somehow related to the Dillon that was kidnapped recently?" the officer asked.

"My father."

The officer took out a cell phone and dialed. The paramedics were just coming out of the kitchen with Cheryl on a stretcher.

"You want to ride with us?" the paramedic asked.

"I'll bring him over. I want to get some coffee in him first," Kanook said.

Danny watched as Cheryl's limp body rolled past on the gurney. He glanced up at the wall where some of their wedding photos still hung and wondered how a marriage could go from "I do" to a husband killing his wife. Tears streamed down his face, not as much for sorrow as for the fear of being caught if she lived.

Kanook took a step into the kitchen. The officer was just coming out. He put his hand up.

"Sorry, I need to ask that you don't enter the kitchen."

"I just wanted to make some coffee."

"No can do. I just spoke to the detective involved with the kidnapping and I have orders to seal this house as a crime scene."

Danny cringed but was confident they couldn't indict him on any evidence in the house. He need only concern himself about Cheryl pulling through.

C'mon you bitch die.

"You heard the officer?" Kanook asked Danny.

"Yup."

"Let's go. I'll take you next door and get some coffee in you. Then we'll go."

"And take that barking dog with you," the officer said.

With all the commotion, Schmedly's barking hadn't penetrated Danny's mind.

"All right, I'll get him."

"Whoa, wait a second. Is he friendly?" the officer asked.

"Yes."

"Let's go," the officer said, escorting them out the front door. "I'll bring the dog up. We want everyone out."

Two more police cars pulled up outside as they waited for Schmedly on the front steps. Danny could hear the officer inside talking. He opened the door. Danny turned, reaching for Schmedly's leash, but instead was ushered back inside.

"Change of plans. Go sit in the living room. I'll bring the dog up for you," the officer said.

"What's going on? I have to get to the hospital."

"The detective told me to keep you here 'til he comes. Just doin' what I'm told."

"Am I under arrest?" he asked, severely slurring his words.

Kanook gave him a shove. Danny tripped up the first step.

"Just have a seat in the living room. I'll get your dog – you're sure he won't bite me, right?"

"No, he'll be okay," Kanook said.

The officer waited for them to sit. "Don't leave those chairs," he ordered.

Kanook waited for him to disappear down the stairs to talk to Danny in private but another officer came in the front door.

"Danny, listen to me," Kanook whispered, "they're going to question you. Don't say a word. You're too drunk."

"No, no, I'm okay."

"You're not okay and you might... you might slip."

Danny looked Kanook in the eyes but only for an instant. "Slip with what?"

"Danny, I don't know if you had anything to do..."

He was cut off when the two officers came up, one being pulled by Schmedly.

"Here's your dog, Mr. Dillon."

Danny wrapped his arms around Schmedly's neck and swayed back and forth. Kanook looked concerned, fearing the detective would take advantage of such an opportunity.

"Danny, I'm sorry, but I gotta tell you that you better look more like a grieving husband than you do now. You look like a worried drunken mess and if I were a cop..."

Danny looked up without letting go of the dog. Tears rolled down his face.

"You know how she was. How upset could I be?"

"If it's now a crime scene, you better look a little upset."

Danny heard voices outside and immediately recognized Detective Caloway. He was a bit relieved that it wasn't Marone who was the more aggressive of the duo.

"Hi, Danny... Kanook," Caloway said, coming up the stairs. He bent down to pet Schmedly. "What happened?" Danny thought he detected a tone of disbelief.

"I was passed out downstairs. Next thing I know, Kanook is screaming that she's on the floor."

Caloway sniffed the air. "You been drinkin'?"

"Yeah, that's why I was out cold."

"So she was at work, right? Then she comes home... then what?" Caloway asked.

"I never heard her come in."

"You didn't say a word to her... no hello... nothin'?"

"Even if I had heard her... you know the situation here, Detective. We didn't go up to eat or anything 'til she was done and out of the room."

"Who's we?"

"Me and Schmed."

"Oh yeah – you and the dog."

Caloway pulled out a pad. "Now Danny, we gotta seal the place off 'til we investigate what you're tellin' us. I'm sorry but because of your rocky relationship with your wife... you know, we gotta check it out."

"I understand."

"Marone will be here soon. We were both at home when the call came in." Caloway sat on an ottoman. "Now Danny...

wait you know, Mr. Kanook, is it? Could you do me a favor and head on home?"

"You mean, I'm not allowed to go to the hospital?" Danny asked.

"We'd feel better if you stayed for just a little while. Just 'til Marone gets here."

"Mr. Kanook... could you..."

"Oh, yeah sure," Kanook said as he stood up. He took a step and then stopped. Danny gave him a nod of reassurance.

"But stay close," Caloway said, "We're going to want to talk to you, too."

Danny stopped breathing for a moment but then realized that Kanook had nothing to give them. They could torture him and get nothing.

"I'll be right next door. I'm gonna call in sick for tomorrow, Danny."

"Thanks."

Caloway excused himself and made a call on his cell phone. Danny was nervous but confident that he could explain away anything thrown at him. He went into a deep daydream, playing over every precaution that he had taken. The alcohol made it hard to concentrate but it all still added up - there were no loose ends.

"Hey, Caloway," someone yelled up.

"Yeah, who's that?"

"Forensics," the man called back.

"I'll be right there. Get some pictures of the kitchen, will you?"

Danny started to replay all the TV shows that he had watched about how sophisticated the forensics of the police could be. The one thing that stuck in his mind was that in every case, the bad guy always got caught.

"Okay Danny, let's have it from the top. When did she get home? Were you here the whole time? Give me the whole story minute by minute."

Caloway sat back down on the ottoman.

"I told you I was passed out downstairs. Kanook let himself in and found her. I heard him screaming and came up. He had injected her and then the paramedics showed up."

Caloway jotted down some notes.

"Why did Kanook come in?"

"Guess he was worried when I didn't answer the phone for a while."

"All right, just sit tight here for now," Caloway said.

Men carrying black cases stepped into the kitchen. Flashes from a camera went off every few seconds. Danny reached for the fancy French phone, one of Cheryl's prize living room pieces, but then pulled his hand back – was he allowed to make a call?

"Hey, Detective?" Danny called.

"Yeah, Danny."

"Can I make a call?"

"Yeah, go ahead." Caloway came in from the kitchen. "Danny, you're not under arrest or anything. Everything we're doing is routine."

The front door opened. Detective Marone walked in.

"What's the story?" He saw Danny through the wrought iron bars as he came up the stairs.

"I'll be right with you, Danny," Marone said as he pulled Caloway into the kitchen.

"Okay."

Danny sensed what they were doing wasn't routine. Routine is letting the husband of the dying wife accompany her to the hospital. He dialed Kanook.

Marone popped his head back in. "Wait, who are calling?"

He gestured to next door. "Kanook, my neighbor."

"No, hold off on that," Marone said.

"But Caloway just said I could."

"Just hold off. Let's get this all squared away."

The detectives came back into the living room, both looking very serious.

"Danny, we need you to come with us to the station," Marone said. "We have questions."

"Like what?" Danny's heart began to pump hard.

"Not here. C'mon grab your things."

Danny realized that he must have missed something that they picked up on.

"Let me call Kanook and have him take the dog over there, okay?"

Marone took the phone from Danny's hand. "What's his number? I'll call him."

Kanook was at the front door in seconds. Danny handed him the dogs leash and he guided Schmedly back to his house. Danny waited by the front door. Was he to be handcuffed? Did they know something? Even if Cheryl had been saved, there's no way she could have spoken yet. Or could she?

Once again, Danny sat at a table in an interrogation room. Unlike his previous visit when questioned about his father, this room had a two-way mirror.

Marone and Caloway joined him. Caloway handed him a cup of coffee.

"Danny, we're not going to lie to you. We have our suspicions on what you're telling us. You said she was allergic to nuts, right?" Marone asked.

"Yeah, that's right."

"We took the menu from the bag where she got the food and sent an officer to the restaurant. We sent Officer Chin who speaks Chinese so there'd be no mistakes. According to him, they knew your wife well there and cooked in clean pots when she ordered to avoid what happened tonight." Marone said.

"I don't know what to tell you."

Caloway took over the questioning. "Danny, if the food wasn't prepared with nuts, they got in between the time she left the restaurant and the time she ate it. Any idea how that could've happened?"

"No, I never saw the food. I never heard her come in. Kanook found her."

"You told me you always waited for her to finish and leave the room before you would go up. That right?" Caloway asked.

"Yeah, but I didn't know she was home."

Danny sipped from a cup of straight black coffee. He was now a stimulated drunk but was able to think clearly enough to be careful. He gained confidence as he went on. He sipped his coffee whenever he needed to stall.

"When she came home, did she leave the food alone at all?"

"I told you I was out cold."

"The clothes that she had on when you saw her leave on the stretcher tonight, were they what she would have worn to work?" Marone asked.

"I didn't really notice what she was wearing."

"She had on sweats. Would she have worn that to work?"

"No, you know she wouldn't. Why would you be asking me that?"

"The paramedic said that someone injected her with the Epi Pen – who was that?" Caloway asked.

"My neighbor, Kanook."

Caloway held his hands palms up at shoulder height. "Any reason why we should be looking at your neighbor for this?" He then clapped them together in front of him.

Danny thought about this answer very carefully and came up with the perfect response. "No."

"Well, he was the last person to be with her alone before you got there."

"Yeah, so?"

"We'll be bringing him in for questioning later."

Danny didn't protest the threat of questioning Kanook – they were only trying to get his reaction. He knew that.

"I'm sure he'll be cooperative."

"Danny, if we find nuts in that soup, we are going to have a problem if we can't find out how they got there. We've both spent a good deal of time with you and we understand what she was putting you through. If the torment finally got to you, let us help. Maybe we can work a deal."

Danny knew that working a deal was just another way of getting twenty years instead of twenty-five. Better to get none and live a good life.

"I had nothing to do with her death," he stated forcefully.

"Okay, Danny, we'll have someone take you to the hospital," Caloway said.

Marone put his hand on Danny's shoulder as he passed him. "I can only imagine what you must be going through right now."

"Anything new on my father's case?"

"We woulda told you, Danny." Marone stopped before getting to the door. "I'm not going to lie to you. We've exhausted our leads and may have to put the case in the dead file 'til something new comes up."

"Already?" Danny said in utter disbelief. "It hasn't been that long."

"We have nothing to go on. I'm sorry but we've gone over every lead a thousand times." Marone could see the disappointment in Danny's face. "Look, what I can do is maybe give the case to another detective. We do that sometimes if we hit a wall. Sometimes new blood finds something we missed."

"Oh and Danny," Caloway said, holding the doorknob. "We're going right now to pick up your neighbor – don't call him. Wait here and I'll send someone in to get you."

The detectives sat together in an empty office. Both looked at sparsely written on pads.

"What's your guess?" Caloway asked.

"One of em did it. Hard to tell if Danny is lying because he's still drunk. I know we're going to find nuts in that soup." Marone said.

Caloway tapped a pen on his head. "But why didn't whoever did it throw the soup away?"

"Too hard to hide the container. I gotta believe this was planned to make it look like the restaurant was at fault."

"Let's go get Mr. Kanook and see what he has to say," Caloway said.

"Agreed, let's bring him in. I'll send a car from the area. You wanna give him a call and let him know we need him. I have to let the boss know what we got," Marone said.

"Right."

* * * * *

Kanook watched and waited for his ride. A police van still sat behind Cheryl's Mercedes. An officer stood guard outside.

"How long are they going to keep you?" Sandy asked.

"Have no idea but I know what they want to ask me."

"If Danny did it, you mean?"

"Yup."

Sandy got up the courage to ask. "Do you think he had something to do with it?"

"Absolutely."

Sandy's jaw dropped.

"What are you going to tell them?"

"Nothin'. Absolutely nothin'. I didn't see nothin', hear nothin'. She got what she deserved."

Not agreeing with murder but knowing what Danny's life was like, Sandy didn't respond.

"Here's my ride," he said. "If you go to bed before I get home, try to keep Schmedly off my side so I can get in."

"Bed? I can't sleep now. I'll be up," she said.

He hopped into the back of the patrol car.

Caloway greeted Kanook at the front desk.

"Thank you for coming, Kanook."

"Where's Danny?"

"We just took him to the hospital to see his wife," Caloway said, escorting him to the back rooms. "Have a seat in here."

Kanook did what most people did when left alone in an interrogation room – he walked up to the two-way glass and put his hand across his forehead trying to see through. He got a whiff of alcohol and wondered if Danny had been in the same room.

"Hello, Kanook," Marone said. "Have a seat. Hopefully this won't take long."

Kanook knew whenever a cop said that, it meant you're here for a long while. He wondered if he was to be held under a spotlight 'til he cracked.

"How's Cheryl?" Kanook asked.

"We called a few minutes ago," Marone said. "She's doing pretty well. They think she's going to come out of it." Both detectives watched for his reaction but there was no flinch, no uneasiness.

"That's good news for her I guess," Kanook said.

"That means... what?" Caloway asked.

"She put Danny through hell. You know what I'm talkin about – you spoke to her."

"That still doesn't give anyone the right to attempt to murder her," Caloway said.

"Murder? How do you know there was an attempt..."

Marone cut in. "Okay, let's start from the beginning. Tell us what happened."

Caloway took notes.

"I called Danny a bunch of times but there was no answer. The state that he was in... I was afraid something happened to him, so I went over."

"And then what?"

"I knocked. No answer. I had a key so I opened the door. I saw Cheryl on the floor and ran up."

"Did you see Danny?"

"No but I called his name."

"Did he respond?"

"No."

"Okay... continue."

"I called 9-1-1, injected her and that's it."

Marone stared for a moment. "You know we saw some signs of a struggle. You sure she was passed out when you got there?"

"Absolutely."

"Did you see Cheryl come home?" Caloway asked.

"No."

"How long were you in the house before you called 9-1-1?"

"Oh jeez, maybe twenty seconds."

"And had you been in the house earlier before coming and seeing her on the floor?"

Kanook suddenly had a revelation that the detectives were questioning him about his possible involvement. He stood up. "Wait, you're questioning me? You think I was involved? I thought you were askin' if Danny had something to do with it... but me?"

Caloway stood up. "Now just relax - it's just routine."

"Routine my ass." Kanook put his hands on the table and leaned toward Marone. "Lawyer... now!"

"We have all we need. You're free to go... for now." Caloway added.

Kanook stormed out but did an immediate about face. "You know you guys got some balls. You don't even know if there's been foul play and you bring Danny here instead of the hospital. Ya drag me here instead of lettin' me go with him. Now get me a ride to the hospital."

The two detectives sat in the room - both quiet, trying to piece together what had happened.

"Well, what do you think? Danny or his buddy... or did they both pull it off together," Marone asked.

"I don't know. Let's wait for the results of the tests on the soup. I have some ideas how we might catch the killer in a lie."

Chapter Seven

Kanook stepped off the elevator and turned the corner to the ICU waiting lounge. A huddle of people cried in the hallway. He bowed his head and walked past.

Danny sat in a far corner, his head back on the chair and his mouth open wide. He snored lightly. Kanook gave him a light shake. Danny looked around, unaware of his surroundings for a moment.

"Oh, hi, Kanook." He rubbed his eyes.

"Any word on how she is?"

"I spoke to a doctor... what time is it?" Danny asked, trying to focus on his watch.

"Nine o'clock," Kanook said.

"I guess I spoke to him half hour ago maybe. Said she's in bad shape and he couldn't tell me if she'd make it or not."

Kanook looked shocked and then angry. "That's not what our detective buddies told me. They said she looked like she was going to make it."

Danny sat up straight too quickly and got dizzy.

"They said she was going to pull through? When was that?"

"Like forty minutes ago."

"I better find the doctor again then."

"You stay here and I'll see what I can find out. Those fuckin' detectives must've told me she was okay just to see my reaction." He paused for a minute. Danny waited while Kanook's wheels turned. "They wanted to see if I was there before she went unconscious – like if I shoved a peanut down her throat. They wanted my reaction to her surviving."

Danny, even in his drunken state, was able to see what the detectives were doing. By attempting to implicate Kanook, they were hoping that Danny would confess to relieve his friend of the accusations. Or if Kanook thought he would be implicated, he might turn on Danny.

"Mr. Dillon?" a voice called.

"Over here," Kanook called back as the doctor walked over. "I'm Kanook, his neighbor."

They shook hands and stood looking down at Danny.

"You can see her for a few minutes, that's all. And I have orders to be with you the entire time that you're there – I'm sorry."

"Danny tells me she's in bad shape. Any reason why the police would think she's going to pull through?" Kanook asked.

The doctor shook his head. "I give her a fifty-fifty chance of making it. The next twenty-four hours will tell all."

Danny tried to hide his uneasiness. Fifty-fifty wasn't good as far as he was concerned. He would have felt more confident with seventy-thirty – against.

"The last few times she's had these reactions she's pulled through," Danny mumbled.

"All depends on how fast she got the epinephrine. She gets it immediately and she's got a fighting chance. The longer she goes without getting oxygen, well..." the doctor said.

"All right, let's go in."

He reached out his hand for Kanook to pull. He stood up but his legs buckled underneath him. Kanook held him steady.

He took a couple of steps. "Feel like shit."

A nurse stood on the far side of Cheryl's bed while the doctor stayed at the foot. IV tubes invaded both arms while an intubation tube ran into her mouth. A machine on the nurse's side hissed as a collapsible bladder opened and closed like an accordion.

"That machine is breathing for her," the doctor said.

Danny leaned over the rail of the bed. He hadn't rehearsed which terms of endearment to use, not realizing that a nurse would be so close by. He certainly couldn't speak his mind and say, "Die bitch die". He knew his words wouldn't sound genuine so he turned and buried his head into Kanook's chest. Kanook, startled at the embrace, instantly caught on and held his friend tight.

"C'mon buddy," he said to Danny while turning to the doctor. "He's in shock. Maybe we can come back in a little while?"

"Maybe in an hour or so we can let you back. This is a busy floor."

"Thank you."

With his arm around Danny's shoulder, he walked him out.

"We'll catch a cab home and get some..."

"Coffee, I need coffee," Danny said.

"Okay and maybe get a shower and then we'll come back."

A police car remained in front of the house. An officer sat, filling out papers. The evidence team was gone and Danny had the okay to reenter.

He opened the front door hesitantly. Having Schmedly would have given him more courage. He climbed the stairs. There was no evidence that Cheryl had lain dying on the kitchen floor. The Chinese food was gone, as was her purse. He wondered what the police had taken from downstairs.

He filled the coffee maker. Back in the living room, he fell hard into a chair. His mind wandered in the dead silence.

"Fifty-fifty chance she'll make it," he said out loud.

"All right, all right, you'll see him," Danny heard Kanook yell as Schmedly dragged him across the lawn.

Kanook breathed heavily from the short run as he opened the front door. Schmedly scampered up the stairs, meeting Danny who was now back in the kitchen.

"There's my doggy," Danny said, kneeling and hugging the mutt.

He pulled out a large biscuit from a container under the sink and handed it to the dog.

Kanook poured two cups of coffee and led Danny into the living room.

"Too eerie for me to stay in the kitchen," Kanook said.

Danny sipped from the cup. "Ah, man that's good."

Kanook opened his mouth to ask one of the many questions he had but instead just went with, "What next?"

"I have to call her parents. Funny thing is, they don't know about Cheryl... what she's been like toward me. To them she's an angel. They're going to come here and I have to sound concerned - like I really care."

"Do you care at all?" Kanook asked, watching Danny closely.

Danny thought for a second. "Would you think me a bad person if I said no?"

"I wouldn't think you a bad person if you told me you killed her. I know what you were goin' through."

Kanook waited for a confession but didn't get it. He still didn't know for sure that Danny had done it. He just knew that his friend wouldn't really mind if his wife died from the allergic reaction.

"I better go down and make the call. It'll probably take me a few minutes to figure what to say. Why don't you head home for a little while... you know you don't have go back with me."

"It's okay, I already called work and told 'em I'd be out."

"Thanks," Danny said. "Hey, take Schmed back to your house now, will you? He can keep Sandy company."

Kanook finished the last swallow of coffee.

"Oh, I almost forgot – when we head back you gotta tell me about what the detectives asked you at the station." Danny said.

Danny played it down as if it was only a passing interest but in reality his insides squirmed to know what the detectives had asked. Maybe he could get a glimpse of what they had up their sleeves.

Danny sat at his desk downstairs, staring at the phone. Calling his in-laws would be an easy task compared to what lay ahead. Maybe a hint now that the police were questioning his involvement would lessen the shock when they arrived. And what would he say to them if she awoke? Would they ever believe the torture he had endured that forced him to attempt her murder? He looked up toward the ceiling.

God, please forgive me for the lies that I'm about to tell.

He dialed.

"Hello?" the sleepy voice said.

"Hello Alice? It's Danny," he said in a low voice.

"Danny? What's wrong?" she asked instinctively in her heavy southern accent.

"Alice, it's Cheryl. She's had another reaction. She's in the hospital."

"My God, how bad is she?"

Danny began to cry - not for Cheryl but for her mother and father. Only for an instant he regretted his actions - for taking a child from her parents.

"She's bad Alice - you better come."

Danny could hear her sobs as she spoke to her husband. He grabbed the phone.

"Danny, what happened?"

"Apparently she ate some Chinese food that had nuts in it."

There was silence for a moment. "How bad is she?"

Danny sighed. "Doctor said fifty-fifty."

"We'll be there soon as we can, Son."

"Oh and Walter..."

"Yeah?"

"Never mind, call me with the flight info and I'll come get you."

"No, no, you stay with her and we'll come straight to the hospital."

Kanook tapped the horn outside. Danny climbed into the car carrying a mug of coffee.

"You ready, man?"

"As ready as I'm gonna be."

"You call the hospital?"

"Yeah, but nothing new."

"You call her parents?"

"Yeah, they'll be here in the morning. I felt so..."

Danny caught himself before admitting to feeling bad about lying to her parents. Kanook sensed a near miss. They both knew that a confession was not too far off.

"You felt so... what?"

"I just feel bad for them. They don't know what Cheryl's really like."

"Oh."

"So tell me what the cops asked you," Danny asked.

"Oh, bunch of stuff. They pissed me off. They asked me questions like I was involved. Asked me if I was there earlier in the day. Asked how long before I called 9-1-1. Stuff like that."

"They asked me all kinds of questions too, but I just told them what happened," Danny said. "I'm sure I'll be questioned again. Maybe you, too."

They drove on in silence. Danny was fidgety – partly from the large amounts of coffee and more from a question that he needed to ask his best friend. A question that would all but quench Kanook's desire for the truth.

"Have to ask you a question."

"Sounds serious."

Danny choked up. "If something were to happen to me... like I died or something... would you take care of Schmedly?"

Kanook turned and rested his chin on his right shoulder; his right wrist lay on the steering wheel. "If something were to happen to you? Like going to jail?"

Danny didn't face him. "Yeah... like going to jail."

"Already spoke to Sandy about it. It's cool – we'll take good care of him."

"Remember when Barry said you might have a new addition to the family? I think he meant Schmedly not a baby."

"Wow, never thought of that."

Danny sniffled and tried to hold back his tears but the thought of never being able to hold his dog again overpowered him. He broke down.

"I couldn't take any more," he whimpered. "I did it. I put the shit in her soup and tried to get a confession on my father in exchange for the needle."

Kanook was stunned even though he had suspected what had happened. "Wish you hadn't told me in a way. If they put me on a polygraph, they'll see I'm lyin'."

Danny waved it off. "Can't use it in court – I'm sure they need physical evidence."

Kanook thought for a moment. "You fought with her? That's why there were signs of a struggle?"

Danny stared at the floor. "There was no struggle," he said, barely audible. "Feel like a coward."

"So you watched her go out, man?"

"Yeah."

"Wow... remind me never to piss you off."

Danny waited for more questions.

"Then why'd the cops say there was a struggle?"

"Maybe they thought one of us or both of us held her down and poured the soup down her throat."

Kanook pulled into the hospital lot and parked. He put his hand on Danny's shoulder.

"Mums the word, man. I'm with you all the way - even if it means hoping she dies."

They stepped off the elevator. Danny still had puffy eyes from his crying jag in the car. He went alone through the automatic doors into the ICU, stopping at the nurses' station. "Anything new on my wife, Cheryl Dillon?"

He held his breath. The doctor walked up behind him, startling him. "I'm sorry there's no change and I'm afraid I have some bad news." The doctor looked around and ushered Danny to an empty office. "We're going to do a brain scan to see if there's brain damage."

Danny tried to look concerned, then just stared down at the ground. There was a party happening in his head that he needed to conceal.

Brain damage would be good.

"Mr. Dillon?"

"Oh I'm sorry. I was just thinking about what that meant."

"I'm sorry to say I'm losing faith that this will have a good ending. I'm not sure help got to her in time. I'm sorry."

"I understand," Danny said.

"Why don't you wait outside and I'll call you when you can see her, all right?"

* * * * *

Kanook sat in the midst of sleeping, unshaven and unkempt people, all awaiting news of their loved ones in the ICU. He caught a glimpse of Danny approaching in the hallway. Their eyes met – Danny motioned with his head for Kanook to follow to a more secluded area.

"The doc says that she may have brain damage and he doesn't think she's going to make it."

Kanook nodded while in deep thought. He looked around before speaking. "What do I say at time like this... congratulations?"

"I'm glad to see you smiling, Danny," a voice called from down the hall.

He spun around. "Detective..."

"I was just in to see your wife. She's not doing well," Marone said.

Danny was caught by surprise.

Kanook jumped in. "C'mon, man, his wife's inside on a respirator and you're here harassing him?"

Marone got close to Danny's face. "We got the test results back on the soup. Peanut oil in the soup. Now how did that get there?"

"No idea," Danny said.

Marone turned to Kanook. "You got any idea?"

"Nope."

"I think one of you does know – or both of you. Have a nice night, gentlemen. I'll be in touch."

They watched him walk down the hall.

"Don't sweat it, man. If he had something, you'd be in cuffs."

Both men fell into the soft chairs of the ICU waiting room. Danny's head pounded as the alcohol left his system. Within minutes Kanook was snoring. Danny watched TV until his eyes grew heavy.

* * * * *

Danny awoke to someone shaking his arm. His eyes would only open a sliver. He sat up straight and tried to identify the two people standing in front of him.

"Danny, it's us..."

Danny's eyes slowly brought into focus his grossly overweight in-laws – both wearing baggy clothes in an apparent attempt to hide the years of southern fried cooking.

"Oh, Alice, Walter, I'm sorry. What time is it? How'd you get here so fast?" He tried to stand but he got dizzy. "Where's Richard?"

"Our son comes and goes. We left word at a friend's for him...how is she?" Alice asked.

"I don't know. The doctor was supposed to come get me. Guess I fell asleep." He looked around. "Where's Kanook?"

"Let's go see the doctor," Alice said, dragging Danny by the arm.

They approached the nurses' station. "We'd like to see our daughter, Cheryl Dillon," Alice said.

"Give me a minute to find the doctor," the nurse said.

The same doctor was still on duty. Danny introduced Cheryl's parents.

"I'm sorry to say your daughter is not doing well. It appears that her organs may be shutting down."

Danny knew that this would be hard to endure but they weren't going through the hell – and they would never be told if possible of their daughter's treatment of him. He watched as they embraced and cried.

"Soon as we get someone from security up here, we can go see her," the doctor said.

"Security? I don't understand," Alice said, wiping her eyes.

The doctor looked at Danny. "You didn't tell them?"

"Didn't have a chance. They just got in."

"Tell us what, Son?" Walter asked.

Danny sighed to make it sound less credible. "The detectives who are investigating my father's disappearance have to follow protocol and have security by her side while I'm there. Apparently I'm a suspect in Cheryl's allergic reaction."

Her parents stood with a confused stare.

Danny clarified. "They think I poisoned her."

Alice's mouth dropped open. "Oh, my God, how could they?"

"I was the only one home when it happened, other than my friend coming in and finding her, so they suspect something. Don't be surprised if they ask you questions about me."

A uniformed guard came up from behind. The doctor pulled him aside, giving him instructions.

"Before we go in I must warn you that she's connected to a ventilator and a lot of tubes connected." He got very serious. "There's nothing really that I can say to describe the shock this will cause. Do you understand?"

Cheryl's mother swallowed hard. "We're ready."

Cheryl was lifeless. Alice covered her mouth. Walter wept. They touched her face and hands and called to her but there was no response. The guard remained on the opposite side of the bed keeping Danny at the foot.

Danny watched her parents, checked out the machines, looked up at the ceiling but couldn't look at Cheryl. A nurse brushed by and startled him as she handed the doctor test results.

"I stand corrected," the doctor said, holding up a piece of paper. "These tests show her actually improving a bit. I am amazed."

Danny held his breath. This was becoming a roller coaster ride that he didn't want to be on. The decision was made – he would stay day and night and if she awoke he would go on the run.

Danny followed Cheryl's parents' back to the waiting room. Marone and Caloway had Kanook pinned in a corner. The detectives followed his eyes as he saw Danny come out. They made a beeline for Cheryl's parents.

"Hello Mr...."

Walter looked down at the badges that both men held out.

"Chambers, Walter Chambers."

"Mr. Chambers, Mrs. Chambers, this is Detective Caloway. I'm Marone. We need to speak with you about your daughter. We've secured a room where we won't be disturbed." Marone gave Danny a look of disgust as he ushered them away.

"What'd they say?" Danny asked Kanook.

"They just got here a few minutes ago. I told 'em that I answer nothing without a lawyer." Kanook bit off the end of a chocolate bar. "How is she?"

"Let's get some breakfast downstairs and I'll tell you."

Both carried trays as they sat at a corner table of the cafeteria. Danny threw back a couple of aspirins. His head pounded worse than ever with the news that Cheryl was attempting a miraculous recovery. Kanook stared at Danny and waited for the update.

"C'mon man, what's up?"

"She's getting better."

"No way," he whispered loudly.

"Her vitals are getting stronger. I should've known she wouldn't give me the satisfaction of dying."

"Damn, what now. You gotta Plan B?"

"Yeah, I go home and pack. I found a credit card at my father's house with a twenty thousand dollar limit. I pack and take out that cash. Then I run to Mexico."

"Mexico... what's there?" Kanook asked, taking a sip of coffee.

"I don't know but that's where people run to when they're in trouble."

"No man, that's where Mexicans run when they're in trouble. You're a white guy in a white van with a black and white dog with one floppy ear. They'll pick you out and send you back in a heartbeat."

Danny thought hard for a second. "Really?"

"Yeah, really."

"Got any ideas?"

"I guess you have to run but wait... do you know for sure she'll turn you in? Would it be better for her to hold it over your head?"

"Thought of that. No good. If she knows where my father's body is, it'll turn up. Then she'll sue me for the entire inheritance while I'm in jail. This is the best thing that I ever could've done for her."

"She ain't talkin' yet, Danny. She still might not make it but... better pack anyway." Kanook shook his head. "If you told me two weeks ago that my best friend would do... well, what you did and then had to go on the run... I never in a million years would've guessed it."

Danny glanced at his watch. "Eat faster, I need to get back up and give her parents my side of the story."

"Which is?"

"You know... just eat."

After a brief search for Cheryl's parents in the waiting area, Danny passed through the automatic doors to the nurses' station. Before he could speak, Caloway walked into view.

"Are her parents back there?" Danny asked.

"They're back there and you have some explaining to do. Wait for them outside."

Danny walked ahead of Caloway through the doors. In the hallway, he turned to him. "You know, Detective, you were very sympathetic in my father's case and I thank you for that. I just don't get the about face. You don't have any evidence against me, yet you've just turned my wife's very sweet parents against me and I may have to explain to them that their daughter isn't the sweet, dear person that they know and love. I hope you're happy with that."

"Danny, if I wasn't sure there was foul play in this case, I wouldn't even be here."

Caloway stepped quickly toward the closing elevator door. "Hold it," he yelled. A hand from inside the car stuck out and the doors reopened. He gave Danny a sly smirk and got on.

"Is it true, Danny?" a voice asked from behind.

Danny, who was normally not a good liar, was becoming better with the recent practice. This would be the biggest test of his deceitfulness. He turned to the saddened faces of his in-laws.

"Is it true Danny? Please tell me you didn't do this," Alice said.

Walter waited for an answer in silence.

"I didn't do it," he said, keeping it simple – no explanations.

"That's good enough for us," she said, hugging him. "We didn't think so."

"Danny, could your friend have done...?" Walter started to say.

"No, Walter. It was a mix up at the Chinese place. My friend is the one who tried to save her."

"We're going to have some lawsuit against that place when she's better," Walter said.

Better? He had forgotten to ask how she was.

"Wonder if I can go in and see her? How was she just now?" Danny asked.

Alice took Danny's arm. "She's actually moving around a little. "Isn't it great? She's not ready to leave us just yet – I know it. Doctor said it would be a slow process – days before she'd come out of it but I can feel it – she's going to be just fine."

"I don't think they'll let you in right now, though. Said maybe not for a few hours," Walter said. "We'll stay – you go home and get a rest."

"Yeah, that's a good idea."

"Take our bag back to the house. We only had time to pack one for both of us," Alice said. "We're going to go down for something to eat. We'll see you later. Oh, I'm sorry, Danny... with all the excitement I forgot to ask if there was any news on your father."

"No, nothing yet."

"We'll say a few more prayers for him." She kissed his cheek.

Danny felt ill on the ride home. The stress and the hangover combined to cause some slight chest pain and heartburn.

"You all right?" Kanook asked. "You look a little pale."

"I didn't think it through enough. Didn't think of the consequences... actually, I did, but I didn't figure you coming to save the day."

"I knew it! I knew I'd get the blame for this. I was just waitin' for it."

"No, no, not your fault."

"If you had just told me what you were up to..."

"Yeah, what was I supposed to do? Call you and say I'm about to kill my wife; please don't come over."

"You could have said something."

"I'm just starting to realize how many lives I've affected. They're going to keep questioning you. I had to lie to her parents - how's that gonna look if she wakes up and blabs the truth. Oh, and by the way, Cheryl's moving around now. Idiot doctors - one second her organs are shutting down and the next thing she's moving."

Kanook let him rant on.

"And on top of it all, if she doesn't come out of it, her father is ready to sue the Chinese restaurant. To get them off the hook, I'd have to confess anyway."

"They got insurance for that stuff," Kanook said.

"Yeah, but I bet they don't have enough to cover a death... well, whatever. Do me a favor and keep Schmed at your place until I'm done showering. I'll come see him before we go back."

"No problem. How long you gonna be?" Kanook asked.

Danny daydreamed for a moment, running through the chores that he needed to complete.

"I have to call her office too," he mumbled. "Call her office?" he laughed to himself. "I need to get packed."

"Danny, you all right?"

"Huh, oh yeah. Was just thinking I need to pack my stuff and get ready to go... but where? Where do I hide? I mean I don't have any relatives in the back woods or anything."

Kanook could only shrug his shoulders.

Danny walked through his front door. Like before, the silence was unnerving. He jogged downstairs and turned the TV up loud. His answering machine blinked rapidly but there were more pressing issues at hand. He pulled drawers open on his desk and then slammed them shut.

What does one pack to go on the lamb?

He ran upstairs, pulled out a large duffel bag and started filling it with clothes. He stopped abruptly, remembering that Schmedly's bowls would need to come. He ran to the kitchen, getting on his knees and opening the cabinet door. He pulled out a bowl and reached into the back, grabbing dog food cans and tossing them backward across the floor. The home phone rang – that one he could answer.

"Hello?"

"Danny, it's Alice. The doctor just spoke with us." Danny tensed up. "He said it might help her to come out of it if we played some of her favorite music. Could you be a dear and bring her CDs?"

"Sure."

"Oh and Danny, don't fill the fridge. I'll go shopping in the next couple days. I'm sure we're going to be here awhile."

Danny was dumbfounded and could only manage a weak, "Okay" before hanging up. He sat at the kitchen table, breathing heavily.

"They're staying here? They are staying here? I don't believe it." He banged his fist on the table. "How much more complicated could this possibly get?"

He filled a glass with water. He took a sip while walking but spilt it as he kicked one of the dog food cans. That simple miscue gave him the idea of leaving Schmedly with Kanook. He didn't dwell on it - he had no time for a breakdown but traveling alone would make more sense and there would be less danger if there were a police scene.

He gave another dog food can a quick kick to the side and went downstairs to contemplate his next move. He dialed Tommy's number and arranged a short meeting. The computers still in his care needed to be returned. Tommy showed up quickly.

"Hey Tommy, c'mon in."

Tommy hadn't yet been told about Cheryl's mishap but upon seeing Danny's raggedy appearance, sensed a problem.

"Danny... you all right?"

"No, not really. I need you to do me a favor."

"Name it."

"I can't explain too much now."

Tommy had a bad feeling about what Danny might need as a favor.

"Does this card have anything to do with it?" Tommy produced a business card from Detective Marone. "I found this in my door but haven't called him yet."

Danny flipped the card over. The words, "Call me ASAP," were scribbled on the back.

"Cheryl's in the hospital. She had an allergic reaction and the police think I had something to do with it."

"Wow, is she okay?"

"We don't know yet, Tommy. The cops want to question you to see if I mentioned anything about killing her."

Tommy took a step back as Danny turned away. The stench of alcohol and body odor was overpowering.

"Tommy, I want you to fix all the computers whenever you have time. But first check all the messages from our happy customers and return their calls. Deliver them when you can and charge them like half price, you know?"

"Okay," Tommy answered slowly.

"Keep whatever money you get as pay."

"We going out of business?" Tommy asked.

"Something like that. Listen, call the detective and get that over with. You can tell him you're here. I'm sure he'll want you to meet him at the station."

Tommy made the call and left immediately to meet Marone.

Danny had one knee on the front seat of Cheryl's car as he dug through a leather CD holder searching for her favorite music. It dawned on him that her parents didn't know what she liked - and his objective wasn't to snap her out of the coma but to deepen it. He threw her CDs on the floor and went to his van where he opened a vinyl case.

"Let's see... she hates this group and... where is it? Aha, the Beatles - she hates the Beatles. Let's play some of that for her."

He stuffed the CDs into a plastic bag and put them on the passenger seat of her car.

Danny found Cheryl's parents in the same seats he and Kanook had occupied earlier. Alice dropped a pair of knitting needles and smacked her husband on the leg as Danny approached. They stood up with optimistic expressions.

"Good news, Danny," Alice announced. "They're talking about taking the breathing tube out today."

"That's great," he said with a forced smile. "When's that happening?"

"Don't know, Son," Walter said.

"I brought her CDs like you asked," he said, holding up the bag.

"Take them to the nurses' desk, Danny," she said, sitting back down and continuing her knitting. "Where's your friend?"

"We took separate cars - he'll be here soon."

Danny approached the nurses' station and lifted the bag over the counter. "These are CDs. The doctor wanted to play them by her bed or something."

He could feel the nurses' animosity. Now that word had spread of a possible attempted murder, he supposed he was now persona non grata. Down a short corridor, Cheryl's doctor opened a cabinet. He looked through the glass of the cabinet door and their eyes met.

"I was just coming to get you," he said, motioning Danny to join him. "We took the tube out and she's breathing on her own."

"Great, let me get her parents."

The doctor took his arm. "Tell you what - I'll give you a minute to see her first. Everyone's so fast to convict you, but I believe in innocent 'til proven otherwise - but I will stay with you."

Cheryl's breathing was labored. She breathed through her mouth because of a remaining tube running into her nose. Deep black and blue marks encircled the areas where the IV needles entered her arms.

"Talk to her," the doctor said, as he motioned for Danny to move closer.

Danny was nervous - even in her condition he still feared her. To most, her expression was pitiful and harmless - to him it was still pure evil. He knew it was silly but as he leaned over her he felt any second that she would jump up and grab him by the throat.

"Cheryl... Cheryl," he called out softly.

He flinched as she repositioned herself and let out a deep exhale.

A nurse walked by, noticing Danny's unsupervised visit. She tapped the doctor, "You do know that..."

"Yes, I know. We were just about to get her parents and the guard." The doctor motioned that it was time to leave.

Danny rounded the corner toward Cheryl's parents sporting the best phony smile that he could muster. "They took the tube out – she's breathing on her own," he announced.

They jumped up in glee and all three hugged each other. Danny hadn't noticed that Kanook was now sitting next to them. He stood and joined in the charade.

"Go ahead in. I'll be right there. I have to wait for the escort."

"Danny, we'll see you inside," Alice said.

Danny and Kanook wandered to a secluded spot. Neither said a word. Danny squatted down with his back against the tiled wall.

"Oh well, this is it for me." He looked up at his friend. "You will take good care of Schmedly, right?"

"Told you we would," he replied in a somber tone.

"Only a matter of time before her parents know the truth... and the detectives. Tomorrow morning I hit the bank and get that cash advance off that credit card. Then I'm gone."

"Where to, man?"

"I thought of hopping a plane somewhere – it'd have to be in the US – I don't have a passport." He stood up again. "Then I figured if I was in the air when she spilled the beans, they'd be waiting for me when I got off. I want to have a little fun before I'm nabbed."

"I guess go south where it's warm at least."

"No... Vegas. Never been there... you know us nerdy guys – we fantasize about winning big and having the women hanging all over us." He started to walk away. He waved his arm for Kanook to follow. "I gotta go back in. I'm sure they're expecting me."

Danny's guard stood waiting at the nurses' station. One of the nurses pointed as he came through the automatic doors. He stopped short as he spied the firearm on the man's hip.

"An armed guard now?"

"Yes, sir, and I have to check you for weapons."

It was a humiliating experience as Danny placed his hands on the counter facing both nurses. As the guard frisked him, he almost burst out laughing thinking about how much more insulted he would have been had he not actually tried to kill his wife.

"This way," the guard said.

Alice was stroking Cheryl's forehead from one side as Walter leaned in close on the other.

"Danny, where have you been?" Alice asked.

"Sorry but I was being frisked by the armed guard."

"Wait 'til I see those detectives again," Alice said. "Danny come over here and talk to her. Maybe hearing your voice will help."

"Sorry folks, but you can't stay. This was only a short quick visit so you could see her breathing. We'll let you back in later – let her rest," the doctor said.

Danny and Kanook paced for hours covering at least a mile in front of the waiting lounge. They watched other families, who had been invisible before, pass the time crying and quarreling, waiting for news of their loved ones. The crying was contagious – once one family broke down, it spread to the others and then there would be silence until the pattern would start over again.

With no change in Cheryl's condition by dinnertime, the decision was made to go back to the house in shifts.

Kanook would stay with Walter while Danny took Alice home to freshen up.

Danny pushed open the front door for Alice to enter. She walked up the stairs and gasped at the living room.

"My, oh my... what a beautiful room. I guess you must be doing all right in your business to afford this," she marveled. "Cheryl mentioned that she had brought in a decorator but I never dreamed..."

Danny wasn't a gossip but keeping the secrets that Cheryl had kept from her parents for so long wasn't easy.

"Oh, I forgot this is your first time seeing it."

"Yes, Cheryl always insists on coming to visit us. Doesn't want us to have to go through all the trouble of the plane and all."

Yeah, that's the reason.

"And where's that nice dog of yours I've heard so much about?"

Danny almost stumbled over. "Cheryl told you about Schmedly, huh? He's next door – I'll get him."

Danny was back in a minute. Schmedly sniffed the air following the unfamiliar scent up the stairs.

"Well, hello there, Schmedly," Alice said.

The dog, startled by the stranger in the living room, approached cautiously. After a couple of stiff scratches behind the ear, he had made a new friend.

Danny grabbed his half-packed getaway bag from the guestroom and sneaked it behind Alice's back down the stairs. He noticed empty spaces where computers once sat – Tommy had been in.

"Danny?"

"Yeah," he called, coming back up the stairs.

Alice was still petting Schmedly. "Danny, I wanted to come home with you to ask you something."

Danny sat across from her on the couch. By the sound of her voice he knew the question.

"You and Cheryl get along good, right? I mean those detectives were tellin' us things that couldn't be true."

"Don't listen to them, Alice. They're always looking to put someone away." He stood up and walked into the kitchen ending the conversation before it got any deeper. "The bathroom's down the hall. If you need anything, just yell – I'll be catching up on some work downstairs."

He sat at his desk and stared at a blank screen on the computer. Thinking of how to word an apology for attempting to kill someone wasn't simple but it was something he felt needed to be done.

> Dear Walter and Alice,
>   I don't know how to begin, but there are many things that you didn't know about the relationship Cheryl and I had. I am not easy to get along with sometimes and that strained our marriage. Business wasn't going too well and I had a lot of stress on me. Why it came to me actually doing what I did I don't know. I am truly sorry for hurting you both. I'm sure that I'll have plenty of time to think about what I did when I'm caught.
>   It will not be easy to face you the next time I see you.
>   I can only hope that one day you will forgive me.
>   -Danny

He sealed the letter in an envelope and wrote "Walter and Alice" on the front before burying it under some papers in a drawer. He had avoided turning around in order to keep his composure until the letter was finished. Spinning his chair, he bent over and looked into Schmedly's eyes. The dog wagged his tail and rolled onto his back for a belly rub. Danny obliged.

"I'm going to miss you," he said as he started to cry.
The dog sat up and held out his paw.

"You know, don't you? You're a special friend. Don't
you give Kanook and Sandy a hard time. They'll take good
care of you."

He held Schmedly tight, wiping his teary eyes in the
dog's soft fur. He would much rather have lived with the
witch and her torment than lose his dog.

Alice sat crying. Walter did his best to comfort her
by keeping his arm around her. Danny stood impatiently
in front of them in the lounge waiting for the doctor to
make an appearance. Kanook came in and stopped short
upon seeing Alice sobbing.

"Something happen?" he whispered into Danny's ear.

"No, we're all just stressed waiting for this doctor."

Kanook held out a handful of candy bars. Danny
reached for one but changed his mind.

"Mr. Dillon?" the doctor called.

"In here."

Danny helped Alice up and they all moved toward
the open ICU doors. Danny's guard was waiting and for
the first time he was frisked outside in the hall – obviously
a ploy of the detectives to humiliate him further. People
from the waiting room whom Danny had spoken with
during the endless hours watched and wondered.

He joined them at Cheryl's bedside as the doctor gave
an update.

"Her vitals are stronger but I must warn you that she's
not out of the woods yet."

"Is she going to be okay?" Alice asked.

"Time will tell. I am cautiously optimistic – that's the
best I can say."

Danny noticed when Alice spoke, Cheryl's heart rate
monitor shot up from sixty to ninety five – not a good
sign. Alice bent down and spoke into her ear. Again the
rate climbed, this time over a hundred. No one else had

noticed. Danny was curious to see what would happen if he spoke to her. He tapped Alice on the back. The guard stepped closer as Danny bent over the rail. He watched the numbers and spoke, "Hi Cheryl, it's me, Danny."

To his surprise, the numbers went only as high as they had when Alice had spoken to her. He concluded that she was not recognizing voices but just hearing them.

"Mr. Dillon, could you please step away," the guard asked.

To Danny's surprise, Alice stepped back to allow him to return to the foot of the bed. She had no harsh words for the guard. She was obviously having some doubts.

"How is she?" a familiar voice asked.

They turned to see both Caloway and Marone.

"She's doing better," Alice said.

"Anything on my father?" Danny asked, trying to divert some attention away from the situation.

"Sorry, Danny, nothing," Caloway replied.

Both detectives just stood there waiting. Danny walked up to them. "You want to talk to me?"

"No; we're here to talk to the doctor and see how she's doing. That's all," Marone said.

Danny met Kanook in the hallway. "My two friends are back. Doing nothing about my father but they got plenty of time to snoop around here." Danny looked around – the coast was clear. "I'm leaving probably tomorrow."

A look of shock came over him. "Serious, man?"

"Unless you got something better?"

Walter walked out of the ICU with his arm around his wife. "Danny, do us a favor and get us some coffee," he said.

"Sure."

As Danny waited for the elevator with Kanook, Marone walked up from behind. "Danny, you got a passport?"

"No, why?"

"Just wonderin'."

* * * * *

By midnight the four had finished a large thermos of coffee. Alice's plan was to get one more visit with Cheryl before morning. The coffee helped gain an advantage over the other people in the waiting lounge who were asleep or close to it. The nurses wouldn't be as busy fighting off pesky relatives and may allow one more quick visit.

Alice walked through the doors meekly trying to play upon the sympathy of the nurses. "Any chance we could see her once more tonight?"

The nurse rolled back on her chair to look down the ICU ward. She waved for someone to come to the front. She remained in the center of the aisle until the doctor met her. She pointed at the trio. He waved them back.

"Mr. Dillon, I see they have an armed guard watching you now." This was the same doctor who had let Danny in without an escort before. He looked Danny up and down and smiled. "You don't look dangerous to me... but you will stay at the foot of her bed."

Danny's eyes immediately focused on the heart rate monitor. Again the rate jumped as Alice's southern accent filled the immediate area.

"Hi, sweetheart. We're all here."

Cheryl squirmed and let out a low moan. Alice stood up straight. Walter pushed in closer. The doctor leaned over her on the other side but didn't interfere. Danny's heart rate now sped faster than Cheryl's did.

"Say again, dear."

They waited, but nothing. Alice took her hand.

"Look Cheryl, Daddy's here and Danny's here."

Then it happened – Cheryl's eyes opened a crack. Alice was only inches away.

"Mom?" she said, showing no emotion on her face.

Alice let out a cry of joy that was heard throughout the ward. Cheryl closed her eyes again and attempted to roll on her side but her arm was tethered to the rail. She let out a moan – she was obviously in great discomfort.

Alice pushed past her husband and grabbed Danny, who had just died inside. The little flicker of hope that he had kept stashed deep in the back of his mind was just snuffed.

"I told you she wasn't ready to leave us yet."

Walter attempted to have Cheryl open her eyes for him but to no avail. Alice pulled Danny to the side of the bed. Danny waited for a nod of approval, which the doctor gave him. He leaned in close and whispered her name.

"Cheryl."

"Louder," Alice said.

"Cheryl, it's me, Danny."

For a second it appeared that she was about to say something but instead it turned into a yawn. He began to back away when suddenly her eyes opened again. When Danny came into focus she gasped, let out a small shriek and pulled away. Her eyes closed again. Alice and Walter were silent as they tried to decipher Cheryl's reaction to her husband's face.

Now Danny not only had to appear happy that his wife had just said her first word but he had to hide his guilty expression for the horrified face she made upon seeing him. He dug down deep.

"Alice, you were right – she's not ready to leave us."

"But why did she look afraid of you, Danny?" Walter asked suspiciously.

The doctor jumped in. "Don't take that to mean anything. Even when she said 'Mom' she probably only did it as a natural reaction to someone who was so familiar to her."

"You're sure?" Alice asked.

"I've seen these cases many times. Common factors usually are disorientation... memory loss. Many times they forget what happened days before an accident or episode like this. Sometimes they wake up violent."

Danny perked up. He wanted to ask for more details about her possible memory loss prior to the incident but quickly suppressed the urge.

Alice and Walter seemed to take comfort in the doctor's words as they stared at Cheryl, who was now still.

"C'mon folks, that's enough excitement for tonight. Let her rest."

Kanook was still sipping coffee and watching TV when they returned. He saw them coming and immediately knew that Cheryl was doing better. Her parents' faces were jubilant – Danny's was less than radiant.

"Oh, Kanook," Alice said, grabbing and hugging him. "She said 'Mom'."

Kanook watched Danny's face while Alice's was buried in his chest.

"Alice, you're squeezin' the guts out of that poor guy and barely know him," Walter said.

"It's okay, Mr. Chambers – I don't mind."

Alice sat down and fanned herself. "My God, I'm havin a hot flash."

Danny motioned for Kanook to take a walk.

"We'll be back in a bit, Alice. Going to hit the candy machines."

Kanook followed Danny into a stairwell. He checked to see that they were alone as voices carried a great distance in the shaft.

"Doctor said she might wake up and forget everything that happened for days before the whole thing."

"Means you'd be in the clear but..."

"But I can't wait around for that."

Kanook lit a cigarette. "So what happened, man? She said 'Mom'?"

Danny was too distraught to even ask why Kanook had lit up inside the hospital.

"Yeah and worse... when she saw me up close, she made a face like I was about to kill her."

"That don't sound good."

"Ya think?" He sat on the top stair. "I have to leave but how do I do it without causing suspicion? The detectives can't know so I can get a decent head start. C'mon, help me think of something."

"Well..."

"I just need a reason for having to leave for a couple hours. It'd have to be real important. I need to get to the bank but that's not a good enough excuse."

"Something to do with Schmedly would do it," Kanook said, nodding his head.

Danny jumped up. "You're on to something here. They know how much I love the dog and Alice seems to like him."

A door a few floors below opened and slammed shut. They could hear footsteps running up a flight. The person coughed. It echoed against the concrete walls. Another door slammed. They continued their brain storming.

"I think I have the beginning of the story," Danny said. "I tell them I have to go home because Schmedly's not feeling well. Listen, dial Sandy right now."

"She ain't up, man."

"Tell her it's freakin' important," Danny growled.

"Oh yeah... and what am I sayin' to her?"

"Nothing just talk for a minute... about the weather, I don't care. I just need to show that a call went to your house from your phone. This way if the cops check that story, it's backed up."

Kanook made the call and spoke to his very sleepy and very confused wife. He ended the call abruptly, curious to hear the next step of Danny's plan.

"She's awake and scratchin' her head. What's next?"

"Don't tell Sandy I'm leaving town. Don't want her to have to lie to the police."

"Right."

Danny thought for a moment. "We go back in there. You have to leave because you have to get up for work and I have to go with you because the dog's not feeling well. We go home and I try to sleep for a couple hours...

but keep the dog. I'd love to see him but I won't be able to sleep and I gotta get a couple hours in."

Walter was dozing when they got back. Alice stared at the other people sleeping in awkward positions.

"I've got to go," Kanook whispered to Alice as he reached out and held her hand. "I'm glad to hear she's doing better."

"Thank you, Kanook. Thanks for all your help."

Danny stepped in for his lines. "I'm going to go with him – Schmedly's not feeling well. I'll be back as soon as I can."

"Okay, Dear. The poor dog probably just misses his mother."

"Yeah, that must be it," Danny said, cracking a smile at Kanook.

Kanook's house was lit up as the two cars rolled up. They both knew that Sandy had her hands full with Schmedly who undoubtedly sensed Danny's approach. They pushed the car doors closed quietly.

The two men stood together in the kitchen. They looked at each other and fell into an embrace. Danny sobbed. "Thanks for being with me through this."

"Not to sound weird or nothin' but thanks for adding some excitement to my life," Kanook joked.

"Take good care of my buddy. I'm sure I'll get to see him again – I mean I will be back when the cops catch me."

Kanook started to say something but stopped. Danny gave him a questioning look.

"I was gonna say, you sure you want to leave? It's a real sign of guilt. I mean what if she don't remember?"

Danny leaned his back against the kitchen counter. "If you had seen her face when she woke for that brief second, you'd know by her look that she ain't forgettin' nothin'. You better head out. I need to get some things done and get some sleep. I'll need a good head start."

They hugged one last time.

Danny moved the computer mouse, bringing the PC out of hibernation. Logging on to his chat room, he prayed that some of his buddies would still be on. Battered husbands usually had an easier time using their computers late at night when their domineering mates slept.

"Yes... yes, thank God you guys are on," he said seeing that five of his cyber pals were conversing. He typed a quick message.

"Hello guys it's Danny. I have to leave and may never be able to speak to you again. Can't explain now but Stan I need you to do me a HUGE FAVOR."

"If you're on this late Danny, you must be in trouble," Stan typed back. "What's the favor?"

"Need you to go to a local payphone – leave no prints – and call me at home."

The members of this chat room were like brothers, even though none had ever met. They sought comfort from the daily abuse and none would ever admit to seeing this message or ask for an explanation.

"I'll be calling in ten minutes."

"Thanks."

Danny opened the partially packed duffel bag and sorted through it. There were enough clothes for a week or two – about as long as he expected to be on the run. Off his shelf he took down a picture of his mother and father and tucked it into a side pocket. He did the same with a picture of Schmedly.

He knelt in front of the safe and dialed in the combination. On the final number, he twisted the brass handle and pulled the heavy door open. He flipped through car titles and business papers until he realized they no longer mattered. If they all got stolen - it didn't matter - nothing mattered.

There was a loud knock on the door. It didn't startle him. He knew who it was. In the back of his mind he had hoped but didn't count on the visit. He ran up the stairs and yanked open the door. Kanook stood with Schmedly, who went wild.

"Okay, okay, I missed you too."

Two feet inside the front door, Danny hugged the dog and wept. A tear rolled from under Kanook's glasses as well.

"Sorry Danny but he was going nuts. Moaning and whining and jumping all over the furniture. I had to bring him."

"I'm going miss you," Danny said as the dog pulled away and ran up the stairs.

Danny looked at Kanook in surprise. They followed him up. "Here I am pouring my heart out and he's scratching at the biscuit cabinet?"

"That's weird, man."

"He has to know I'm leaving - he always senses it. Why isn't he upset?"

"Don't know. When you leaving?"

The phone rang; Danny ran back down the stairs. He stood but leaned over and rested his elbows on the desk.

"Hello?"

"Danny, it's Stan. This is the call you wanted, right?"

"Yep and thanks. How's things by you?" Danny asked.

"The same - what's going on? You getting out?"

"Something like that. Can't really explain it. Just check my local newspaper online and you'll see my name."

"Oh, boy - that doesn't sound good, buddy."

"It's definitely not."

Kanook came down and listened intently to the conversation, which lasted for five minutes.

"Okay Stan, we've talked long enough to accomplish what I needed. I can't thank you enough for leaving your house at this hour."

"Danny... you're part of our family... that chat room is all I got. Us guys... well, you know what I mean - us guys that live like we do have to stick together. Good luck and I hope I see you online again."

He sat down. "Thanks, Stan but... just thanks. Take care."

Danny laid down the phone. Schmedly carried a tennis ball to him and dropped it into his lap. Danny let it fall to the floor where the dog picked it up and with a snap of his neck, sent the ball bouncing across the floor. He slid and skidded after it.

"I don't believe this, Kanook. He's gotta sense that I'm at the end of my rope and he actually looks happy."

"Don't sweat it. Who was that on the phone?"

"I had a chat room buddy from South Carolina call me. When the detectives start looking for me they'll check my phone records - incoming too. I'm trying to throw them off to think I'm heading down south. I'm also going to leave my cell phone somewhere off I-95 right before I head west. They won't know which way I went. I'm pretty sure they can trace my phone's signal but it may take some time. I need every minute."

"You put some thought into this, huh"

"Yeah... I guess it's time. Take Schmedly with you."

"Take care of yourself." He gave a wave and they were gone.

Danny was exhausted. He would rather have left immediately but falling asleep behind the wheel would put a quick end to his one last Vegas fling - if he could actually make it there. He set two alarm clocks and lay on the bed. Within minutes he was snoring.

Danny was still groggy as he hit the button to open the garage door. With the keychain remote, he popped the trunk of the Mercedes and threw the duffel bag in. He then placed a large cooler in the back seat filled with all the food and water that it would carry.

He went back inside for one last look around. There weren't many positive memories in this house so leaving wasn't an emotional event other than the thought of losing his dog. He walked out the front door carrying a thermos of coffee and a travel mug. He took two steps down before stopping and placing the coffee on the stairs.

The letter.

Shuffling through his desk drawer, he removed the letter of apology to Cheryl's parents. He placed it on the kitchen table propped up against a small candleholder. The names "Walter and Alice" stood out in bold print. He backed away from it to make sure it was the first thing they would see when they came in. He adjusted it three times before he was satisfied with its position.

Sitting in the driveway, Danny turned on the wipers to remove the early morning dew. After one last deep sigh he rolled out into the street and headed for the highway.

Danny had been driving for three hours – his eyes felt heavy. He was running on only a couple hours sleep at best and now he would need to be more alert with the upcoming rush hour traffic. He pulled to the side of the highway and refilled his coffee mug.

He glanced at the road atlas, which was opened to the entire country map. He gulped down mouthfuls of coffee, then ran his finger along the southern route that he had chosen.

Over the next hour traffic thickened just a bit. He turned a radio talk show up loud to help him stay awake. He didn't have the luxury of even a short nap – at least not for another three to four hours.

Danny jumped as his cell phone rang and vibrated at the same time. He had forgotten to turn it off. He panicked and again pulled off the road. If the detectives were on to him even the ringing could help them pinpoint his location. He wrestled the phone out of his pocket and read the caller ID.

"Payphone," the top line read. He thought for a moment and then read the phone number. It was familiar yet he couldn't place it. Could this be a trick by the detectives to make him pick it up or was his sleepy mind just making him paranoid?

He hit the Send button. "Hello?"

An indiscernible female voice cried into the phone. Confused, he listened, believing at first that it was a wrong number.

"Danny, where are you?" the voice cried.

He sat up straight – it was Alice. He needed to think quick.

"Danny, she's..." Alice's now hysterical voice began.

Danny couldn't make out if the cries were happy or distressed. In the background he could hear male voices. The phone then dropped hitting something hard.

Walter came on the phone. "Danny?"

"Yeah Walter, what's going on?"

"Where are you, Danny?"

"I had something to take care of. What's happening?"

"She died, Danny. She died," Walter wept into the phone.

Danny froze; his eyes were wide open. The thought went through his head like a lightening bolt – he didn't have to run.

"Walter, what happened?"

"Blood clot traveled..." was all he could get out.

In the background, Danny could hear Alice screaming in agony. There were also men's voices, but one, sounding like Cheryl's doctor, stood out as he tried to calm Alice.

"Walter, you there?" Danny called but the receiver was hanging by its wire. Walter had gone to the aid of his grieving wife.

Danny put an earphone in his ear and laid the phone in its cradle so he could safely drive while still listening to the commotion. He pulled back into traffic, staying in the right lane to exit and turn around. He crossed the highway and put the gas pedal to the floor as he entered in the opposite direction. The traffic moved well in this direction but he needed to make time to beat the New York City traffic.

A woman picked up the phone. "Hello?"

"Hello, who's this?" Danny asked.

"This is Tina, I'm a nurse. Who is this?"

"This is Danny Dillon. My father in-law was just on – is everything okay with Alice... my mother in-law?"

"They're calming her. What has he told you?"

Danny had to sound concerned instead of jubilant. He took a second.

"He told me that my wife died... what happened?"

"I can't really discuss this over the phone," the nurse said.

Walter yelled toward the phone. "Ask when he's getting back here?"

"When...?"

"I heard him," Danny said. "I can't get back for three hours at least."

The nurse conveyed the message. Walter grabbed the phone. "Three hours? Where the hell are you?"

"I'll explain later, Walter. I'll get there soon as I can."

"Okay," Walter said sounding less than happy. "I'm going to take her back to your place."

"Okay, you have the key, right?"

"Yeah," was the last thing he said before slamming down the phone.

Danny sped down the highway with a feeling of euphoria. The words, "she's dead, she's dead," echoed through his mind. If he could explain away the driving out of state, he was home free – he had three full hours to come up with an excuse. Then something Walter had just said to him came back to him. *I'm going to take her back to your place.*

Danny's eyes shot open wide again. "The fucking letter. They're going to see the letter."

He grabbed his phone and called Kanook's house but there was no answer. They were both at work and Danny didn't have either number. He opened his wallet and took out a tiny phone book, lifting it to watch the road as he dialed Kanook's cell number. There was no answer but the voice mail picked up.

"Kanook, it's Danny! Call me back the second you get this message. Oh, God, I hope you get this. I'm in Jersey and headin' back - Cheryl died."

He couldn't help but to think that after all the bad that he had done - killing his wife and then lying to her parents - the one thing that might do him in was the one nice thing - the apology letter.

He racked his brain - then, "Tommy... Tommy, Tommy, Tommy." He lifted the phone book again and dialed Tommy's house. The answering machine picked up.

"Tommy, it's Danny. It's like..." he looked at his watch. "It's seven thirty. Call me as soon as you get this."

He dialed Tommy's cell phone but again got a recording where he left another desperate message. He left one more message on his basement business line just in case Tommy showed up to work.

He smacked the steering wheel and pushed the gas pedal further towards the floor running the car up to eighty-five. A police car passed on the opposite side causing him to rethink his speed and he brought it down.

"Maybe they won't see it," he said to himself. He then remembered how carefully he had placed the letter so they would see it.

"Shit, if they read that letter there's more than enough time for the detectives to be there waiting for me."

He slowed the car down to sixty now. He had another dilemma. Should he continue to run? The odds were they would see the letter. Or should he continue on with the possibility that the letter would be missed. Things were going his way so far on this beautiful sunny morning – why not press his luck, he thought. He drove on.

Danny, preoccupied with dialing Tommy's and Kanook's numbers every few minutes, almost forgot his excuse for being so far from home. He found it difficult to concentrate but he needed a solid, believable reason – and fast.

Two hours had passed since he had spoken to Walter and hopes of retrieving the letter were fading. He had all but given up on the calls to Tommy and Kanook's cell phones. He tried the business line again. On the second ring, Tommy answered.

"PC repair."

"Tommy? You're there? I've been trying your cell phone forever."

"Battery died. It's on charge and..."

Danny cut him short. "How long you been there?"

"About twenty minutes. Oh, and Danny, I'm really sorry to hear about your wife."

Tommy thought it strange that his words of condolence went unnoticed as Danny badgered him with more questions.

He held the wheel tight as he asked, "Are my in-laws there?"

"Yeah, that's how I found out about your wife. Where are you anyway?"

Danny pulled the car to a lurching halt on the shoulder. "Tommy, listen to me... were you upstairs?"

"Yeah, I had to introduce myself."

Danny cut him short again. "Was there a letter on the kitchen table?"

Tommy thought for a few seconds. "Her father was sitting there by himself when I went up for coffee, but..."

"Listen, I need you to go up there and find a letter. The envelope has "Walter and Alice" written on it."

"Okay, I'll go up right now. I'll take the cordless. Maybe you can direct me to it."

"If Walter is still sitting there give him the phone – I'll talk to him. Don't let him know that you're looking for this letter."

"Okay," Tommy said.

The kitchen was empty. Tommy could hear Alice crying on the bedroom phone to a relative.

"All's clear, Danny."

"The letter – find the letter."

Tommy stood over the table but there was only a magazine on it.

"No letter – wait... yeah, this is it. But it's open on the counter."

Danny's heart sank. He had come so close to the perfect murder.

"I'm picking up the letter... it's out of the envelope. What should I do?"

"Fold it fast and stuff 'em both in your pocket. Get back downstairs. Hurry!"

"Okay I'm down. Now what?"

"Take the metal trash bucket and dump it out. Then put the shredder over it but don't read the letter! Understand? Don't read it!"

"Okay, okay."

Danny could hear the shredder grinding.

"Done, now what?"

"Take it outside right now and burn it. Then stir the ashes up good. You know what? Go do that and I'll call you back in a couple minutes but do it now, okay?"

"Going right now. I'll wait for your call."

Danny felt ill. Having just involved an innocent young man in evidence tampering didn't sit well. He waited a few minutes and called back.

"Tommy, Danny again. You done?"

"Yup."

"You burned it good and stirred the ashes, right?"

"Yeah – do I want to know what was in that?"

"No, you don't and very, very important – if Walter asks you if you've seen it just say no. Maybe help him look for it. I just remembered he's gotten a little forgetful. If he asks say something like maybe he misplaced it."

"You want me to go up again?"

"No, not yet. Stay right by the phone. Wait for my call in a few minutes... and take the wastebasket, rinse it and pour it down the toilet. Wipe it dry, okay?"

"Some day explain all this to me, Danny."

"I'll call you back in a few minutes... wait... go to my Rolodex and find Kanook's work number. Call him and tell him about Cheryl and that I'm coming home." Danny said before hanging up.

Cars whizzed by, shaking the car as he remained on the shoulder. He had to think of all the scenarios. If Walter had read the letter, he would tell the detectives but now the letter was destroyed. They would simply think he lost it. If he hadn't read it, Danny could say it was an apology for leaving without saying anything – but the reason for leaving? He needed that reason. He rolled the car a few feet ahead, pulling it closer to the grass.

What would be so important that I had to leave?

Then he smiled. There could be only one thing more important than his wife in the hospital. The call made by his buddy from the chat room was now about to play a much more significant role. He dialed.

"All right, Tommy, next step. I want you to go on my computer and open up the last Word file that I used. That'll be that letter."

"Wait, let me get there," Tommy said.

"Any rumblings from upstairs?"

"Just hear a lot of crying and talking on the phone."

Tommy no longer needed an explanation for Danny's apathetic attitude toward his wife's death as he searched the computer for the letter. His concern now was how involved was he in the destruction of evidence in a murder.

"Now, Tommy, I know that you're going to want to read this letter – it's human nature. But if you know the contents and the police put you under a polygraph..."

He cut Danny short. "I'm not reading it, trust me. I have it up in front of me."

"I want you to destroy it out of the hard drive. You know what I mean? Delete it so they can never find it. If you have to melt the drive, do it. Got it?"

Tommy's fingers flew through the bowels of the computer tearing out any evidence that the letter ever existed.

"Now, they're going to ask you about the conversations that we had when I called. I was just asking you to make phone calls... asking how her parents were. Stuff like that, okay?"

Tommy said nervously, "No problem."

Danny sighed and readied himself for his explanation to Walter. He could only hope that Walter hadn't read the letter and complicated things more by contacting the police.

"Now... take me back up and hand the phone to Walter. Then head back down and make sure that everything's going right with the deletion. By the way, Tommy, I think we're back in business."

Tommy walked hesitantly up the stairs. Alice still cried on the phone. Tommy, not wanting to disturb her, knocked on the wall outside the master bedroom.

"Danny?" Walter asked Tommy as he took the phone.

He nodded. Walter took the phone to the kitchen before putting it to his ear. Tommy followed but Walter gave a look of needing privacy. Tommy retreated to the downstairs.

Danny could hear the phone being rubbed and banged around as it traveled with Walter. He braced himself for the accusations and was ready with the rebuttals.

"Danny, where the hell are you? Alice is so upset that you're not here."

Danny was thrown for a moment. "Walter, I got a call late last night from someone who said they knew where my father's body was."

"Oh? And?"

"I was supposed to meet this anonymous person in South Carolina. They wanted money but they had info that they could only know if they had seen my father."

"Then why didn't you call the police instead of going yourself?"

"Because the police have screwed up everything so far," Danny said, sounding angry. "I'm coming back as fast as I can. Should be home in a couple hours. Keep Alice calm and tell her I'm coming."

"Okay, Danny. I'll see you soon."

Danny hung up and looked towards heaven. Someone was looking out for him. Walter hadn't even read the letter. He was home free.

Chapter Eight

Danny was only a mile from home when his cell phone rang.

"Hello?"

"Hey, man."

"Kanook," Danny said loudly, "Tommy called you?"

"Yeah, I just got the message – what happened?"

"She died from a blood clot I think. I'm almost back in the neighborhood."

"I'll be there soon as I'm off and Danny," Kanook said getting very serious. "You gotta be real tired. Those detectives are going to want to take advantage of that."

"I know. I'll be careful."

"Lawyer up right away."

"Absolutely. See you in a little while."

Kanook was right, he was exhausted and it took every bit of energy to make it home. Pulling into the driveway, he saw the now familiar unmarked police car out in front. The front door swung open as Danny pulled himself from the front seat. Marone waited with crossed arms. Danny stretched his stiff body, which vibrated a bit from the gallon of coffee he had consumed overnight.

Marone held the storm door open as Danny came up the stairs.

"Took a little trip, huh, Danny," he said.

"Had too," was Danny's reply.

"We know you had to," Marone said.

Danny brushed past him and up the stairs. Alice rushed to him and embraced him.

"Danny, Danny... please say you didn't do this."

Walter and Caloway stood close by, waiting for Danny to speak. He gently moved Alice away. Had the letter been read? He had to play it as if it hadn't - he had nothing to lose.

"These guys have not given me the benefit of the doubt for one second and now I'm sure they're trying to convince you into believing I killed her."

"But Danny, why did you leave us? Walter said you got a call from someone about your father?" Alice asked.

"I'll tell you all about it but for now..." he looked her in the eye. "For now I'm telling you that I didn't do it."

Danny realized with the weariness came lies that flowed much easier and he almost believed himself.

"These detectives are saying that there's no way it could have happened any other way," Walter said, stepping closer.

Alice turned to her husband. "Who do we believe? Family or strangers? We've always believed in family... always. And that's what I'm stickin' to 'til I learn different."

Danny gave Marone a smug look. He stood in front of Walter.

"Who's it going to be, Walter? Them or me?" Danny asked.

Walter started to cry. "I don't know what to believe and no matter what, my daughter is still gone." Alice tried to comfort him as he wiped his nose with a handkerchief. "Now if you gentlemen will excuse us, we have a funeral to plan."

"I'm sorry, Mr. Chambers, but Danny will have to come with us for questioning first," Caloway said.

"Detective, I'm exhausted, I need to use the bathroom really bad and I have to help them with the funeral arrangements. Can't we do this later?"

Caloway glanced at Marone. "I'll give you a couple hours."

Marone took Danny by the arm into the kitchen.

"All right, you got a couple hours but first..." he took out a small pad and pen from his inside jacket pocket. "Tell me real fast about this call you got on your father."

"Got a call from some guy that had info on my father's whereabouts. Said he wanted money and to wait just over the border of South Carolina where he'd call me again."

Caloway joined them. Marone gave him a skeptical look as he pushed on.

"And where were you getting the money and how much?"

Danny pulled the credit card from his pocket. Then he displayed a wad of ten thousand dollars.

"This card has a twenty grand credit limit on it. My name is on it with my father. I took an advance at the bank yesterday to pay bills and stuff."

The portable phone, which sat on the kitchen table, rang. Danny grabbed it fast but covered the mouthpiece before answering.

"Listen, guys, I promise I'll be down in a couple hours. You have a lawyer waiting for me, though. I'm not even going into an interrogation room without one."

He turned his back on the detectives and answered the call. A cousin of Cheryl's gave her condolences. Danny brought the phone to Alice.

"I'll be right back," he said to Walter as he ran downstairs.

Tommy stood quickly as he heard Danny nearing. He had a guilty look on face. Danny stopped short.

"You didn't tell them about the letter," Danny whispered.

"No."

"Walter or the detectives ask about the letter?" Danny asked, cringing while waiting for Tommy's response.

"No, nothing about it. They asked lots of questions about how you and Cheryl got along."

"And you told them..." Danny said sitting and leaning forward, elbows on knees. He motioned for Tommy to sit. Their faces were only feet apart. He glanced toward the stairs to make sure no one was listening.

"I told them you guys had some differences but I just work here and never got involved with your private life"

Danny rubbed his eyes. Tommy continued.

"They asked if I thought you had something to do with her death. I said no. Danny, I'm scared about this letter thing. When I was getting rid of it before I felt like a spy – it was kind of exciting but now I could go to jail. I mean I have information that you killed... her."

"Listen, they're done with you so calm down." Danny caught himself before going on. Marone could've gotten to Tommy and now was recording the conversation. "You don't know that I killed my wife. Did I ever say I did?"

Tommy shook his head.

"Did you read the letter?"

He shook his head again.

"If they really could prove that I killed her, don't you think I'd be under arrest?"

"I guess."

Danny patted him on the shoulder.

"Just stay calm, okay?"

Danny walked a couple of steps away but he had to know. He took a pad from his desk and scribbled down "Are we being recorded?" and held it up for Tommy to read.

"No," Tommy replied.

Danny dropped the paper into the shredder. He again walked toward the stairs.

"Listen, once this is all over we're going to get the business flying again. Right, partner?"

Tommy looked up. "Partner?"

"Once they find my father, I'm going to have a ton of money. I'm making you my partner. How's that sound?" Danny asked.

Tommy looked thrilled. "Great."

"Pssst," Tommy motioned for Danny to come back. "Is this partner thing a bribe?" he whispered.

Danny thought for a second. "Let's just say it's my way of thanking you for your help," he answered nervously. "Is it going to work?"

Tommy realized that he was already in the middle of Danny's mess – there was no reason not to capitalize on the situation. He reached out and shook Danny's hand but Danny knew that more would need to be said. A young man hiding a secret could give cause to many sleepless nights. He gave his leather chair a spin as he passed it and ran up the stairs.

Alice sat with her head laid back on the couch. Tears streamed down both cheeks. Walter was writing on a pad.

"We got lots of family catching planes up here next few hours, Danny. I need a local motel name and we got to git to the funeral parlor."

"We can sleep some of them here if you want, Walter."

"What about your family – cousins and such, Danny," Alice asked.

"I'm not real close with any of my relatives."

In all reality Cheryl had in essence forced him to give up his relations by not allowing him to visit.

"There's no one you have to call?" she asked.

"Just the neighbors and her office."

"Somethin' funny about that there. We may be from the south, Danny, but we ain't stupid. I got a real problem with what those detectives said... and I ain't yet seen you shed a tear."

Danny needed a good speech and fast. Despite being so overexerted, his brain was still functioning well and the words flowed.

"Walter, I'm a hardened man. My father was kidnapped and killed. My business is in ruins from my lack of participation. My wife is dead and I got detectives accusing me of killing her." He walked in front of his father in-law. "I got people calling me in the middle of the night saying they know where my father's body is." He choked up a bit thinking about his dad. "I now have to plan a funeral and then go back to searching for my father. I need to be strong."

"Walter, leave him," Alice said. "The boy's been through enough."

Walter looked down into his coffee. "Maybe so... I'm sorry, Danny."

The front door flew open as Kanook banged on it at the same time.

"Danny," he yelled.

"Up here."

Kanook raced up and embraced his friend. "I'm really sorry to hear... we'll all miss her."

Walter and Alice both stood as the two men held each other for almost a minute. Kanook then approached Alice.

"My deepest sympathies." He hugged her gently. She cried into his shoulder.

"Thank you, Kanook."

"Walter, I'm very sorry for your loss," Kanook said, shaking his hand.

"Thank you."

"If there's anything I can do, just let me know. I'll be taking a couple days off so I'll be here or right next door."

"Thank you... maybe you could help us in getting our relatives set up while we make the funeral arrangements."

"Whatever you need me to do. There's a motel a few miles away. Let me know how many rooms and I'll set it up but I need to take Danny next door and check on the dog. He's actin' a little funny."

"God, I haven't even had a chance to get over there," Danny said.

Steam blew from their mouths as the two men walked across the front yards. They could hear Schmedly scratching the inside door with both paws as Kanook opened the storm door. He moaned and yowled as the two were reunited. Danny's face was wet from ear to ear in seconds as the dog slobbered him.

"What's the game plan?" Kanook asked, pushing past the two. "Bring him in so we can talk."

"C'mon mutt," Danny said.

He smacked his hand on the couch for the dog to jump up. White sheets covered all the furniture to protect it from the new houseguest.

"You know what's really weird?" Kanook asked, sitting in an opposing chair. "Remember when you were sayin' goodbye last night and the dog didn't really care?" He pointed at Schmedly. "He knew you weren't going to be gone for long. He knew."

"Maybe he did," Danny said. "Maybe he did."

Kanook stood up and took off his fatigue jacket. "What's next?"

"I'd love to get some sleep but that's not happening."

Kanook walked into the kitchen. "You want a beer?"

"Little early for a beer, isn't it?

"Never too early."

"How much money do I need for a funeral – I know her parents don't have much."

"I can get some cash – what do ya need?" Kanook asked.

"No, don't worry, Kanook. If I need more money to stay afloat I plan on hocking her jewelry and some of her gowns – the expensive ones. I got ten grand off the credit card and can get ten more. I can't let her parents know that I'm broke. I'm going out of my way to..." Danny continued talking through a yawn, making his words almost indiscernible. "I don't want them to have a clue that their daughter was a witch."

"What about the cops?"

"Oh, I forgot. They were at my house when I got home. Trying to turn the in-laws against me. I have to meet them in a little while but let me take them to the funeral home first." Danny sat back on the couch. "You have no idea what I went through today."

"How far south did you make it?"

"Near Philly. That's when I got the call and tried desperately to call you. I finally got hold of Tommy." Danny sat up straight. "He knows."

Kanook stopped in the middle of a swig of beer. "He knows what?"

"I left a letter of apology for her parents and I had to have him destroy it before they could read it – so he knows."

"You dragged him into this whole thing? Don't you think they'll crack him?"

"I don't know, but I was thinking of killing him just in case," Danny said with great sincerity.

Kanook froze until Danny started laughing.

"I'm kidding, I'm kidding."

"Oh, man, you had me scared. Thought you really went over to the dark side for a second."

Danny got up as Schmedly bounded onto the floor.

"Let me go and get this over with. I'll take the dog. He can stay with Tommy." Danny pulled open the front door and stopped. "You know, Kanook... I had a ton of time to think while I was driving – mostly about my father. I think I have a way – a really far fetched way of finding him."

Kanook took a long sip of beer.

"Can you hook us up with your wife's cousin, Barry, again?"

Kanook looked up slowly from his chair. "You don't mean..."

"Just set up a meeting."

Danny dragged himself up the front stairs. He had only slept two hours in the past thirty. Alice and Walter followed him inside. Tommy was still downstairs tinkering and taking calls. Now that he was a partner, he wanted to put in the hours that were expected of him.

"Hey, Danny," he called up.

"Yeah, I'm comin'." He thumped down the steps. "What's up?"

"The detectives called a couple times. Said they couldn't get you on the cell phone. They're waiting for you."

"I turned it off. I can't see them now. I need some sleep."

He slumped into his recliner. Tommy leaned over and shook his shoulder.

"Danny, if you sit, you're going to fall asleep. You gotta go see them... now. I'll make coffee."

"No, just give me the phone and Marone's number," Danny said, holding out his hand.

Tommy reluctantly obliged. Danny dialed.

"Hi, detective, it's Danny Dillon."

"Where are you, Danny?"

"I just got back from making the funeral arrangements. I'm not going to be able to see you today. I need to get some sleep. I'm so tired that Walter had to drive back."

"We'll send someone for you then."

"No, don't bother. I'm not coming today. I'm not going anywhere. I'm going to sleep. If you want, you can come take my car keys from Tommy and I'll be there first thing in the morning."

Marone wanted him there in that exact state of overexertion.

"Danny... you need to be here now."

"Did you get me a lawyer?" he yawned.

"Yes, he's here."

"Put him on then."

"Hold on and I'll get him."

In a few seconds a young voice came on the line. "Mr. Dillon, this is Stan Bishop your court appointed attorney."

"Listen, Stan," Danny said starting to slur his words. "Stan, do they have the right to drag me down there now. I haven't slept in like thirty hours. I told them to come get my keys if they're afraid I'm gonna run."

"When can you be here then?"

"First thing tomorrow."

The attorney shuffled through a day planner. "I've got nothing planned – it's Saturday. Meet me here at eight o'clock – sharp."

Danny could hear the attorney talking to the detectives.

"My client isn't in any condition to be questioned right now. Do you really want to try and coerce a confession while the man is drowsy and almost passing out? You can go and take his keys. He'll be ready for questioning at nine tomorrow morning."

Marone took the phone back. "Nine tomorrow Danny," he said before slamming the phone down.

* * * * *

Danny sat alone in an interrogation room. He glanced at his watch – his lawyer was late. Hearing voices in the hallway, he stood with anticipation. A young man, tall, clean-cut and no more than twenty-five opened the door while speaking to someone outside. He then turned to Danny, who immediately noticed a couple of razor cuts. Danny's first reaction was that maybe it had been his first time shaving.

"Hi, I'm Stan Bishop." He shook Danny's hand.

"You're kinda young. I don't mean to be rude, but have handled any murder cases before?"

"Is this a murder case? I didn't know it had officially been upped to murder."

He laid his briefcase on the table and then loosened his tie. Bishop could see Danny still wanted an answer.

"No murders – this is my first but no fear – I've gone over the case and I think you'll be out of here very shortly."

Danny sat, as did Bishop. Danny tilted his head slightly and pointed at the attorney.

"You're going to have me out of here shortly?"

"Yep, think so. Let's go over everything to see if I have it straight."

Bishop shuffled through some papers and took out a pen. "Tell me the whole story from the morning 'til the time the paramedics took your wife from your house."

"I don't remember doing much that day but working... at the house – I fix computers in my workshop. There's not much else. I had a few cocktails and then passed out in my chair downstairs. Next thing I know, my friend let himself in and was screaming that my wife was on the floor. Then they took her to the hospital."

Marone opened the door. "You gentlemen ready?"

"Just give me a few more minutes with my client, Detective." He turned back to Danny. "Okay listen – don't answer anything without looking at me first. It'll give me time to object. It'll take a little getting use to but you need to make it second nature, okay?"

Danny began to trust his new caretaker. He admired his confidence and his quick crisp speaking gave him the self-assurance he would need.

"Also, answer everything slowly, very slowly. Don't make mistakes."

Bishop, knowing that the detectives were itching to come in, hit Danny with practice questions. Danny paused after each one and then answered slowly like Bishop had instructed.

Marone and Caloway walked in, both carrying folders. Neither looked friendly.

"Time's up. Let's do this now," Marone said.

"Danny, forensics found a trace of peanut oil in the soup. We checked at the Chinese restaurant and they showed us how they make sure that peanuts can not be accidentally added to someone's food. They're very careful about that," Caloway said.

"Wait a minute," Bishop jumped in. "Are you telling me that there's no way they could've made a mistake?"

"I don't see how," Marone said.

"You don't see how? That's your answer. Great work, Detective," Bishop said jokingly.

Danny's confidence was dashed a bit by his lawyer's cockiness. But within minutes Danny's confidence was restored as Bishop thrashed the detectives.

"All right, Detectives, listen... I'm new to this case and I understand you've had dealings with my client in trying to find his father, right? We'd all like to get to the bottom of what happened to his wife so if you'd oblige, I'd like to go over the details to make sure I'm right in my thinking – okay?" He looked back and forth at the two detectives. "I know it's a breach of etiquette for me to ask this but in all fairness I did just get this dropped in my lap."

Marone leaned back in his chair and crossed his arms. "Go ahead."

"Thank you. Stop me if I'm wrong. Mrs. Dillon stopped at Wang's Chinese restaurant and picked up various food items. What time was that?"

"Danny told us that she got home around six thirty..." Caloway started.

Bishop cut him off but did it courteously. "I didn't ask what time she got home. I want to know when she picked up the food at the restaurant."

Marone leaned forward. "I was trying to be nice by letting you maybe ask a few simple questions to catch up on the case but I'm sure as hell not going to let you interrogate us. You're done."

"But..." Bishop tried to get in a sentence.

"Answer only – don't ask," Marone said.

Bishop retreated but was ready to pounce if either detective tried to trip Danny up.

"Danny, you are the only one who could have put the peanut oil into the soup. Why don't you tell us what you know?" Caloway said.

Bishop touched Danny's arm to keep him from saying anything. "He's the only one who could've put the peanut oil in the soup? Detective, I'm guessing that you don't really know when she left the Chinese restaurant. It could have been an hour. She may have made five stops along the way where any number of people could have had access to that bag of food. Or... maybe someone at the restaurant had it in for her... or maybe she committed suicide."

"You're trying my patience, Mr. Bishop." Marone pointed at Danny. "If you don't let him answer these questions, I'm placing him under arrest for his wife's murder. We'll let a grand jury decide whether to indict – and they will."

Danny got nervous for a moment but Bishop remained cool.

"I'm sorry, Detective. I was just trying to protect my client. Please... proceed."

Caloway stood up. "Now, Danny, you had motive – you weren't getting along and you thought she had something to do with your father's kidnapping."

"Then why would I kill her if I thought she knew where my father was?" Danny asked.

"Anger will do strange things to a man. We've seen it a thousand times. Tell us what happened – maybe you accidentally put the oil in her soup? Maybe your lawyer here gets you tried under an insanity defense. I mean I could see that – you weren't sleeping or eating and she was taunting you. It drove you to kill her," Caloway said.

"Didn't kill her. I told you I heard Kanook yelling for me and I came up. She was on the floor. That's it."

"Detectives, you searched my client's house but found no peanut oil, right?"

"How hard is it to get rid of a bottle of peanut oil?" Caloway asked.

Marone jumped in. "Let's switch gears here. Let's talk about the little ride you took, Danny. You know, the one heading down south to talk to the guy who called you about your father."

"Don't answer that. Sorry, Detective, but I don't know anything about what you're talking about, so I'm advising Mr. Dillon not to respond."

Marone looked angry. Bishop was quick to calm him to avoid the arrest of his client.   "At a later time, I'll have my client describe the trip you mentioned but I don't have all the facts myself," he said.

Marone flipped through some papers. Bishop looked at Danny and winked.

"I also understand that Mr. Dillon's father is still missing and was the subject of a highly publicized kidnapping. They got away with four hundred thousand bucks, didn't they? Are you seeing a pattern here? Maybe someone has it out for Mr. Dillon – an enemy that you haven't been able to find who is determined to destroy Mr. Dillon's family. They kidnap one and kill another."

"I doubt that," Marone said.

"Maybe... but a jury isn't going to convict on what you've got. Unless there's more?"

Caloway gave Bishop a dirty look and turned to Danny. "Here's another question. She carried an alarm in her bag to signal when she was having a reaction. Why didn't she use it?"

Danny glanced at his attorney. He nodded.

"I told you before that maybe she fell before she could get to the alarm."

Marone just shook his head. "Danny, look, I know you did this and I understand why but I still have to do my job. I'm sorry but you had motive and access to the soup. We are going to continue this investigation."

Bishop stood up. "Pursue all you want. My client is innocent and no jury is going to convict on the evidence you have. Hell, you can't honestly say you have grounds to arrest him on what you've got. What was the motive anyway - that he didn't get along with her? If that were the case, we'd have a million murders a day. Was it money? There were no insurance policies - no monetary gain. If you're not going to charge him, let him go. He has a funeral to attend," Bishop said.

"Danny, we understand what you were going through with your wife. Why don't you just tell us what happened? Make it easy on yourself," Caloway said. "We'll see what we can do to make things easier on you."

"I think we're finished here, Detectives," Bishop said.

"Danny, how would you feel about taking a polygraph?" Caloway asked.

"If my client consents to a polygraph and passes it, will it be allowed into evidence as a defense in court if this gets that far?" Bishop asked as he closed his briefcase.

"You know it won't be," Marone said.

"But if for some reason the officer administering the polygraph misinterprets the results and finds that Mr. Dillon had failed the test, it will weigh heavily against him in court. I'm sorry, Gentlemen, but my client will not be taking that test."

With hesitation, Marone stood up. "Danny, you're free but don't go too far."

"How far is too far?" Danny asked.

"Why, Danny? Do you have another trip we should know about?" Caloway asked.

"I may be going on a trip to find my dad after the funeral."

"I don't think that's a good idea right now," Marone said.

"My client isn't charged with anything so he is free to do what he wants. You can't keep him from trying to find his father. Obviously you can't find him so he has to."

"I'll bet if we tried real hard, Counselor, we could keep him here," Marone said, leaning across the table.

Danny held his hands up. He was tired of the bickering. "Look, if I have to go somewhere I'll let you know exactly where I'm going to be, okay?"

"You know something about your father's whereabouts that we should know?" Marone asked. "The call from South Carolina - maybe tell us more about that. We checked and saw the call coming into your phone the other night."

"Again, Gentlemen, I haven't heard anything about this call so it'll have to wait," Bishop said.

"I have one more question, Danny," Caloway said. "If you had a chance of finding your father alive as you say this caller said - why'd you come back? I mean by turning around, you may never hear from them again."

Danny again turned to his lawyer but didn't look for approval. "I can answer this."

He turned back to the detectives. "The last report I got on my wife was she was doing better and expected to make it. She was breathing on her own and opening her eyes - even saying a few words." He pictured Cheryl's face during the brief bedside encounter when she opened her eyes and saw him. He shook his head quickly and continued. "When she recovered, I could see her again when I got back. When I got the call that she had died, I realized that if I continued it would look like I was on the run. That's why I decided to turn around."

Both detectives stared at him. He had an answer for everything. They weren't happy nor were they buying any of it.

"I'll let you know if I get another call... I can only hope the guy was for real. For right now, I just want to get through the wakes and funeral. Can I go?"

Marone waved his hand for the attorney to take him away. Bishop escorted Danny from the room. The detectives remained. Neither had expected to be beaten so badly by the young attorney but Bishop was right - they didn't have enough to go on yet.

"Where do you want to look now?" Marone asked Caloway.

"Don't know. He obviously planned this well." Caloway stood up and walked around the table. "She brought the food home... how did he get the peanut oil in without her knowing?"

"We went through this – she wasn't wearing work clothes when they brought her in."

"Oh yeah, he had time when she changed but would it have been enough?" Caloway said.

The two men sat in silence while they reviewed their notes. Caloway shook his finger in the air and then rubbed his forehead.

"What ya got?" Marone asked.

"We know he killed her but the one thing we never considered... he needed money desperately, right?" Caloway said.

"Yeah... and?"

"Danny is such a nice guy... did we overlook him as a suspect in his father's disappearance because he didn't fit the profile? I mean we didn't – or least I didn't for a minute think of him as a suspect. Now that we know he killed his wife, maybe we should be looking at him for the father too."

Marone raised an eyebrow. "Ya think?"

"He needed money so he has his father killed but the father's will states that he gets nothing if he's still with his wife. He kills her and now maybe he finds his father's body when he goes on this search he talked about. He gets to keep all the money and his wife isn't around to nag the shit out of him," Caloway said.

Marone thought for a moment. "I can see him killing his wife but... I don't know about his father. Funny – I do like the guy even though he whacked his wife. Gonna hate seein' him go away, though. Let's check out your idea – see if we can place him in the kidnapping too."

It was twilight – two days after Cheryl's funeral. Danny stepped from his van carrying a fresh bouquet of flowers. Leaves crunched under his feet as he walked between the rows of graves, coming up to one recently covered plot. It had no headstone but was marked with a bronze plate – he read the name to himself – *Cheryl Ann Dillon.*

He looked around to make sure he was alone before dropping the flowers on the moist dirt, adding them to the piles of other arrangements already left. "I don't really know what to say." His trembling body made it difficult to speak, his words coming out slowly. "Just that I'm sorry." Tears immediately poured down his face. "How did it ever come to this?" His body heaved as he cried and he let out a long moan. He sucked air back into his lungs with short, choppy gasps. "You made me... you made me kill you." He dropped to his knees. "Do you know how hard it is every day to wake up knowing you've killed another human being. Do you?"

He tried to look through his watery eyes but couldn't focus well. He was angry and had more to say but was still conscious of his surroundings – still careful not to be heard.

"Just because you hated me didn't mean I didn't still love you. I don't know why but I did." He remained kneeling; his forehead now pressed against the dirt. "I hope that somehow you can forgive me." He dug his fingers deep into the fresh earth and squeezed it. His face and clothes were now covered in dirt. "Cheryl... Cheryl... please forgive me. I just couldn't go on like that."

Suddenly he felt as if he was being watched. He stood up quickly and spun around but there was no one there.

Chapter Nine

It was early afternoon. Danny and Kanook sat in the same luxurious hotel room where they had met Barry previously. This time Danny was more hesitant, afraid that Cheryl's spirit would come forth and reveal to Barry that he had killed her. Kanook had already raided the bar and he and Danny were drinking twenty-year-old scotch when Barry walked into the room.

"Hello, Gentlemen. Good to see you again so soon."

He hugged Danny and then Kanook.

"Kanook tells me they haven't found your father yet."

"No, not yet. They've exhausted all their leads."

"That's a shame," Barry said, walking to the bar.

"I had another death too," Danny said.

"Yes, Kanook told me about that. My God. You poor man."

Danny stood up. "Please... we didn't really get along. It's hard to say but I'm not really that upset over it."

Barry looked surprised and turned to Kanook.

"Wasn't a fairy tale marriage, Barry," Kanook said.

"I see... and you've come to see if I can contact her? Kanook was very vague on the phone," Barry asked, sounding confused.

"What I'm going to ask... well I'm not sure if it can be done and if it can, I don't know if I can afford you unless we're successful," Danny said.

Barry looked more confused than before. "I'm intrigued," he said, coming to the couch. "What are asking me to do?"

Kanook shook his head. "Barry, just want you to know that I told him I didn't think you could do it but he's my best buddy so here we are."

"Thanks for the lead-in pal," Danny said, turning to Barry. "I need you to help me find my father's body."

Barry's jaw dropped.

"I've never done anything like that before. I have a friend who works with police departments all over the country. She's a psychic. She takes a look at a photo and can sometimes give info on the crime or the whereabouts of a body."

Danny jumped up. "That's who I need then. When can we get her here?"

"Wait, hold on now. She's booked up for years. See, not only do the police use her but families and people like yourself hire her at very high prices to find loved ones."

"But she's a friend of yours. Can't you see if she can fit us in?"

Barry shook his head. "I really hate to ask someone to do that. She'll feel obligated and may have to turn someone else away. Someone who's been waiting a long time – much longer than you. That wouldn't be fair."

Barry saw the dejected look on Danny's face.

"Although there is the fact that you might lose everything you own without the inheritance. Kanook told me the story."

Danny perked up. "Then you'll ask her?"

Barry smiled. "I'll call her now but I can't promise anything." He walked to the bedroom and returned with a black book. He laid it on the bar and flipped through it. "Ah, here it is, Beverly Morgan." He dialed the phone but after getting her answering machine, he tried her cell phone.

Danny grew excited. "What do you think? It's worth a try, right?"

"I guess so," Kanook replied.

Barry took the phone and went back into the bedroom. Danny tried to eavesdrop but Barry was too far away. He sat on pins and needles hoping this would be the miracle that he needed.

"I have good news and bad," Barry said, coming back into the room. "She'll do it but she can't do it right away. She's booked in hotels all over the country for three months."

"Three months," Danny muttered to himself. "I guess I have to wait then."

They watched as Barry sat down without saying another word. He was fidgety – crossing and uncrossing his legs, standing up and pacing behind the couch.

He waved his finger in the air and pursed his lips.

"You know..." he began.

Danny looked at Kanook, who shrugged his shoulders.

"I'm writing another book about my sessions. Id love to be able to do more than just tell people about how their loved ones feel." He sat down next to Danny again. He turned quickly toward him. "I'd like to try and find him."

Danny opened his mouth twice trying to answer but the words weren't there. Finally he spoke. "Yeah, but can you do what she does?"

"I don't know. I've never asked a spirit to guide me... but if I could... it'd make a great chapter in my book." Barry grew excited. "I could detail your whole story - changing the names, of course. From the kidnapping to the time we find him." Barry stopped short. "I'm sorry. I didn't mean to sound upbeat about finding your father's body. I am truly sorry."

"That's okay. I'm as excited as you are but... and it's a big 'but'... can you do it?" Danny pursued.

Kanook walked to the bar. "I need a shot before we go further with this. Anybody else?"

Danny raised his empty glass.

"You can bring me some water, Kanook," Barry said. "Have your drink, Danny. Then we'll see if we can make contact with your father. I don't even really know how to go about this."

Kanook tapped Danny on the shoulder with the bottle of scotch. "Better keep the whole thing over here."

Danny poured a small amount over the remaining ice cubes. He swirled it around to chill it and lifted the glass to his lips. After taking a big gulp, he put the glass down.

Barry was already kneeling in front of him. He put his hands on Danny's knees.

"What if she comes through?" Danny asked.

Barry didn't answer. Kanook shook his head at Danny as to say "keep quiet 'til he makes contact."

Minutes passed without Barry saying a word. Danny looked at Kanook who just shrugged his shoulders again. Barry opened his eyes. "I'm having trouble making any contact."

"Surprised my wife didn't show to curse at me."

"I've yet to see a spirit yell or show any kind of hatred for the living. Usually they are sorry if they led an unhealthy life." Barry got up and shook his head. "I don't understand why I can't contact anyone from your family. Can you guys stick around for an hour or so?

They both nodded.

"I need to go inside and meditate. This will clear my mind and help us. I do this before every show. Didn't think I'd need it now but apparently I do."

He disappeared into the bedroom.

"I didn't get the same feeling this time when he touched me," Danny said.

"Just give him time to do that meditation thing and maybe it'll be different."

Danny took the remote and switched on the big screen. He surfed the channels.

"This satellite TV is great – they got like a thousand channels. Let's see what's on.

Forty-five minutes later, Barry came from the bedroom. Without speaking, he sat on the couch and put his hand on Danny's shoulder. Kanook stepped past them, taking the remote and switching off the TV.

Within minutes Barry was in a trance.

"I believe I have your father. His aura is not as bright as it was the last time... strange. He again puts his hand on his heart showing his love. Now I have to figure out how to ask him a question."

Barry sat with his eyes closed, keeping his hand firmly on Danny's shoulder. He moved his lips but didn't speak. Danny could feel Barry's hand grow very cold, chilling his shoulder down to the bone. His breathing became choppy and made Danny nervous enough to almost pull away.

"I think I have a location," Barry said, falling back in the couch.

"You know where my father is?" Danny asked in amazement.

"No, no, I'm sorry. I didn't mean to get your hopes up like that. But I'm pretty sure that his body is in the South. I was feeling a warm breeze."

"Where?"

"I'm not positive."

Barry looked exhausted from the short session.

"While you were under... or whatever you call it, your hand got really cold – what was that?"

"Very hard to explain all that happened. I've never gotten so wiped out doing this. I mean, this has never happened before and the hand thing – well I have no idea."

Kanook listened intently, finally jumping in. "Your lips were moving. What were you asking him?"

Barry turned to him. "I have no recollection of that at all. I think we should've video-taped this."

"How'd you get the down south thing then?" Danny asked.

"I don't know but I'm sure he's there – very sure."

"He's there where, though? The south is a big place," Kanook said.

"Just south. That's all I got, sorry."

"So, now what?" Danny asked.

"Now we pack and head south," Barry said, dragging a weary body to the bathroom.

"Right now?"

"We leave in four days. Soon as I'm done with my shows here. That okay?"

"Yeah, but there's one thing. I can't afford to pay you unless we actually find him. Then I can get my money from his estate."

"That's okay. I don't have anything planned for the next few weeks so no need to worry. It's on the house if I can't find him – but I think I can."

Barry ran the water in the sink but hadn't closed the door. They watched him splash water in his face.

"Wonder why he got so tired? Oh and I guess I'm dog sittin' while you're gone, huh?"

Danny turned his whole body toward his friend. "Schmed's coming with us. I need him there."

"Better get the okay from the swami first."

"Hey, Barry? How are you with animals?"

"What kind of animals?" Barry asked, now back in the room with them and toweling his face.

"I want to bring my dog, Schmedly. He's a good dog." Danny held his breath waiting for a reaction.

"Sure, bring him along. I love dogs."

Danny gave a long exhale, relieved that he and Schmedly wouldn't be separated for the long period.

"Go ahead home and get ready. This is going to be a new experience for both of us. We'll take my new SUV. It'll fit all our stuff and the dog can lay right behind us."

"I can't ask you to use your car, too. We can use my van."

"Has it got four wheel drive if it snows? We'll be down south but could snow on the way – could be mud somewhere, ya know?"

"Well, no – no four wheel drive."

"Then it's my truck."

Danny shook Barry's hand firmly. "I don't know how I can ever thank you." Danny had a smile on his face and felt happy for the first time in a long while.

"You can thank me – wait 'til you see my bill when we find him."

After two days of interrogation, the detectives were no closer to charging Danny with either the kidnapping of his father or the death of his wife. Early in the inquisition Danny was unnerved by the tape recorder and camera - a mistake would be irreversible but like any good actor, his butterflies faded.

They had bombarded him with hundreds of questions - most of which were the same but just worded differently in order to expose a mistake. In the end, he was free to go but unlike his father's case, the detectives were not giving up so quickly.

Getting permission to go on an extended trip with Barry was another battle but Danny's attorney prevailed. Marone's words of "don't leave town" would now have to be replaced with "stay in close contact."

The detectives were now looking hard at Danny for his father's disappearance. If the trip with Barry were to produce George's body, Danny would get his inheritance - which would be just too coincidental for Marone and Caloway.

Danny sat at the kitchen table, coffee cup in hand. He hadn't slept much from the excitement of the upcoming journey. Although he had some reservations, he had a strong belief in Barry's ability. His one concern was Schmedly. The dog was acting strangely - not as if he were ill but rather more uneasiness about the upcoming trip - that's if a dog could sense that he was about to travel.

A door slammed shut downstairs. *Oh good, he's here.*

"Tommy, I'll be right there."

Schmedly was already getting a rubdown when Danny came down the stairs.

"He's still acting strange to me," Danny said.

"Seems okay to me," Tommy replied.

"Believe it or not, I think it's the trip but that can't be. I know he's got a sixth sense but... I don't know. Anyway, you know the deal. I'll have my cell with me. Just make sure you lock the door when you leave and get caught up on this stuff best you can," Danny said, pointing to the piles of computers and printers with their work order tags hanging.

"Don't worry about a thing. I'll take care of it."

"Let me go back up. He should be here soon and I want to make sure I haven't forgotten anything."

Danny stood over his bags. He opened the video camera case and verified that he had all the accessories. He heard a car door outside and moved his luggage, which partially blocked the front door. As he opened it, he felt a bit queasy – he was about to embark on an adventure many would scoff at, but others would pay good money to join.

Barry came up the walkway, slipping a bit on the shiny cement.

"Little frost," he said as he came inside.

"Hey Barry," Danny said as they shook hands.

"You ready for this?" Barry asked.

"If you are... maybe you better meet Schmedly first. He's been acting weird. See, he didn't even come up to see who you were." Danny turned toward the workshop. "Schmedly, come up here."

Schmedly put his paw on the first step but wouldn't continue.

"Barry, go ahead up and have a seat in the kitchen."

"Right."

"Schmedly, get up here – now."

The dog crept up the stairs. Danny practically had to shove him up the second set.

"C'mon Schmedly," Barry called, bending down while sitting.

Schmedly approached cautiously. Sniffing the air from four feet away. He continued until he was able to sniff Barry's outstretched hand.

"There, see? I'm not a bad guy."

Barry reached slowly to pet the dog on the head. He pulled away at first but after a few minutes of bonding, Schmedly seemed a bit more relaxed, although not entirely comfortable.

"I don't know what's with him. He hasn't eaten much and what's really strange is he doesn't seem to want to be near me," Danny said sadly.

"Dogs are very sensitive to changes in their environment? I'm guessing he knows that we're about to do something involving the supernatural. He's just a little nervous," he said, still petting the dog.

"That makes sense, I suppose," Danny said, "especially considering how close he was with my dad."

"Let's get a move on it."

"Coffee?" Danny lifted the pot. "I got a travel mug for you."

"Sure."

"Barry, do you need to try to contact my father before we go?"

"No... I don't think so. Let's just head south and take it from there. I'm hoping that spending time next to you will make him more easily accessible."

The truck was packed. Schmedly had his own cushioned area on top of the folded down rear seats. From there he was able to lay his nose between the front seats and watch the road. Danny reached back and patted him on the head as the truck rolled down the driveway.

Not even Barry could comprehend the consequences of delving too deeply into the spirit world. He was about to take Danny on the most dangerous and unusual trip of his mundane life.

Chapter Ten

As they slowed to enter a highway, Danny asked, "You got any idea where we're heading?"

"I guess 95 South for starters."

Danny looked confused. "But Barry, the south is a big place. How's my father going to communicate a pinpointed spot?"

"I have no idea. I've given it great thought and my guess is if he can actually lead us, he may take us to a place where someone saw something strange. Maybe they saw someone digging a grave or saw two men leading another. We're going to have to ask a lot of questions in any place we've been led to."

Barry adjusted his rearview mirror for a moment to get a better look at Schmedly, and then returned it.

"You know, Barry, down south, depending on where we are, they might not take too kindly to two Yankees asking strange questions."

"Thought of that too."

"And... what kind of solution did you come up with?"

"Simple – if there's a problem we run like hell."

Danny appreciated the joke and laughed harder. Looking at Barry's belly, he knew he couldn't run more than a hundred feet without passing out.

"No, seriously. We go into some hick town and tell people that my dead father sent us to see if anyone here saw someone burying a corpse. That's not gonna go over too well."

"Danny, I've never done anything like this. I told you that from Day One. I don't know how I'm going to find him – I just think I can. We'll play it by ear."

Danny didn't want to annoy his host too early into the trip but he had thousands of questions. He would have to ask general questions while slipping more direct subjects in at strategic intervals.

"How'd you get into this or should I say when did you find out that you had these powers?"

"When I was a child, very young, I had these visions like I was dreaming but I was awake. It didn't scare me because I was too young – like three years old. I would see spirits... how do I explain this? I would see spirits inside my head."

"You told your parents?"

"No, I just thought that everyone saw it. I didn't know. As I got older... oh wait, here's 95. We have to go south and... there's the sign."

Barry slowed the car and looking over his shoulder, merged into the traffic.

"We're on the drain pipe," Barry announced.

"Drain pipe?"

"Interstate 95 is called the drain pipe because all us northerners use it to get to Florida. It's a joke like we're the dirty water draining into the state of Florida."

"Never heard that before."

"Where was I? When I got older I started talking about what I saw. This was when I was about six or so. My parents took me to doctors. They thought I had a brain tumor or something but all the tests were negative."

Barry tapped Danny on the leg and pointed to the back. Danny turned to see Schmedly standing up wagging his tail. He reached back and scratched under his chin.

"Maybe he has to go out?" Barry asked.

Danny waited to see his next move. The dog circled and flopped back down, his mouth opening wide with a yawn.

"No, he's okay, go ahead. What kind of brain tests did they do back when you were a kid – not that you're that much older than me?" Danny asked.

"I had to hop up and down on one foot while holding a chicken."

It took Danny a second to realize that it was a joke.

"Sorry, Barry, I didn't mean..."

Barry laughed. "Don't worry about it." He took a sip of coffee. "So, when I was about eight I started to put things together. When I saw certain people, I also saw their loved ones who had died. By twelve years old, people were coming to me to act as a medium but – only people close to our family. My parents didn't want the world to know about this. Back then with the Cold War they were afraid the government would take me to be used to see what the Russians were doing."

"That's really wild." Danny thought for a moment. "When did you figure out you could make money doing it?"

"Oh, I made a little money doing it out of the house until my first book came out twenty five years ago. Then demand for my gift went through the roof and the rest is..." He stopped in mid-sentence and took a couple of deep sniffs of the air. Danny did the same, trying to detect what Barry smelled.

"What is it?"

"Peaches, but you won't smell them. I smell them in my mind."

Danny looked confused.

"I think your father is sending me a sign," Barry said as he pulled the truck over.

Danny stayed silent, not wanting to interfere. Barry just stared straight ahead.

"Strange... but I guess things are going to seem different, this being the first time trying to follow a spirit. I'm getting the aroma of peaches but I don't see your father."

"Are you seeing someone else?" Danny asked, having Cheryl in mind.

"No... strange. Very strange. I was getting plain peaches. Now I'm getting the smell of rotting peaches. I think it means Georgia."

"That's right. Georgia is the peach state. And also the state where my wife's family is." Danny waved his index finger in the air. "Hey, Barry, is it possible that my father could take us to his killers instead of where his body is?"

"Hell if I know, Danny. Told you this is a first for me."

"Maybe that was the rotten smell."

Barry shook his head. "I don't know."

Danny had dozed off, giving Barry some time without being peppered with questions. He awakened just as Barry pulled the truck into a travel center.

"Anybody want lunch?"

Schmedly stood and shook himself. Then he stretched on his front paws while yawning with a wide-open mouth. Danny looked around bleary-eyed.

"Where are we?" He sat himself up in the seat.

"Bottom of New Jersey. You were out cold. Snoring up a storm," Barry said.

"I haven't slept in a while."

"Let's grab some food and gas. Let the dog walk around a bit."

"Yeah, I could use a stretch myself."

Barry pulled the truck into a spot in front of the fast food restaurant. Schmedly scratched impatiently at the window. Danny snapped his leash on and he jumped out. The dog had never been on the interstate before. The many people and loud trucks made him cower but Danny's reassurance eventually gave him the confidence to explore.

"Danny, what do you want from inside?" Barry called.

"Couple cheeseburgers – and bring one for Schmed. Here, let me give you money."

Barry waved his hand. "I got it."

Danny followed the "dog walk" signs leading to a dirt lot. Schmedly walked from tree to tree, sniffing and marking each spot.

Back inside the truck, Schmedly had his head stretched as far as he could without falling into the front seats. Danny opened the bag of food while Barry searched through the ice filled chest in the back for a bottle of water.

"I'm surprised – that place was really clean and the food looks pretty good," Barry said, getting back into his seat.

"It's coming, it's coming," Danny said, trying to nudge the dog back.

"Guess he's hungry."

"He loves cheeseburgers," Danny said.

Danny made the dog sit as he handed the cheeseburger back. He threw it in the air to avoid getting his fingers taken off. The burger disappeared quickly.

The men headed south once again – Danny was fidgety, having doubts that this quest could really work. He was used to computer problems where a broken part was tracked down and changed. There was no maybe or could be. It was all tangible.

"What's the matter, Danny? You look preoccupied."

"Just so many questions about... I guess my father... and where he is."

"What do you mean by where he is?"

"Well, just that – where is he?"

Barry looked confused. "You mean his body? That's what we're trying to find."

"No, no," Danny said, shaking his head. Not wanting to pester Barry with any more questions, he stared out the window.

"Danny, I've got nothing better to do here. Ask me whatever you need answered. Let's get it all out now even if it takes hours – we've got the time."

"You asked for it," Danny said.

He turned to Barry. "When someone dies, where does their spirit go?"

"That's a tough one. I can't say that I really know. When I do a reading and I see... say your father. I don't really see what he looked like when he was alive. It's more like a glowing light but I can tell who he is."

"But if you can't see him..."

Barry thought for a moment on how to explain. "I can feel it more than see it. They communicate through senses that most people haven't developed. I get smells and I see pictures of things that they want me to see - like the peaches. Or when they extend their love, I see a hand over a heart but not necessarily their hand. You following?"

Danny answered slowly. "I think so but the question was, 'where are they?'"

"My best guess is they're all around us. I can't give you a location. I don't think it's outer space like we think of heaven being up there." He pointed up.

"If they're all around us... still living or whatever you call what they're doing, what would happen if the earth were gone?"

"Not following."

"Say we're hit by an asteroid and the earth disappeared. I mean there's now empty space where the earth was. Where would they be then or where would we be then?

Barry scratched his head and laughed. "Danny, I've had simpler questions from priests."

"I'm just getting started. You want me to stop?"

"No, I understand your curiosity. I would probably ask some of the same things. Now, let's see. If the earth blew up, where would we be?"

Barry gave the question some thought. "You know Danny, no one has ever asked me that question and I don't have an answer. I'm sorry. I may not sleep tonight thinking about that one."

"I got enough to keep you awake for a week," Danny said with a laugh. "Okay, how about this. How come I can't see them? If they're all around us..."

"That, I might be able to give some insight on. That's a question that I've been asked before and the best answer is... you've heard of ultra-violet light? And infrared light?"

"Sure."

"Ever see either?"

"Maybe but I wouldn't have known it if I saw it."

"Trust me when I tell you that you can't see it with your eyes. It is possible the spirits are just an energy form... a form of light that we can't see."

Danny took a sip of water. "I'll buy that. Sounds reasonable. But..."

Barry cringed and waited for Danny's objection.

"Don't scientists have instruments that can see the different light forms?"

"Oh, absolutely, but they haven't invented the one yet that can see spirits. I hope they don't - I may be out of a job."

They looked at each other and laughed.

"I've got a few more and then you're off the hook... 'Til I think of something else," Danny said.

Barry took a deep breath. "Okay, I'm ready. Shoot."

"Heaven... when you see or feel the spirits... this kind of goes back to the where they are thing but follow me here. We're taught by our religion that if we're good we go to heaven. If we kill or steal we might go to hell. Have you ever spoken to a spirit in hell?"

"I told you before that the brighter the light of the spirit, as far as I can tell, means the better a person they were in life. I have done readings where the spirit aura was dull."

"Any idea if that person had committed a murder in life?"

"I didn't ask that."

"If you didn't ask that, how do you know you can speak to someone who is in hell? I mean have you thought about having a session with the families of murderers to see if you can reach them?"

Barry opened his mouth and then shut it quickly.

"You've really thought these questions out. Although I must say it's is an interesting idea." Barry waved his finger in the air. "I'm going to try that. Matter of fact, I'm going to call my assistant and have her look into that." He grew excited and yelled "wow", startling Schmedly.

Barry picked up his phone. "Kelly, it's Barry. Listen – I want you to find ten families of men killed by the death penalty after being accused of murder. We're going to do a show to see if I can contact them."

After a short conversation, Barry hung up. He looked at Danny with the face of a man who had just hit the lottery.

"Danny, that idea is excellent. I'll have that show on from coast to coast. It'll be a huge hit. Talking to dead murderers. I love it. What else you got?"

"One problem though."

"What's that?"

"What if there is a hell and you can't contact any of these guys? You now have a bunch of people sitting around crying."

Barry pushed a button on the GPS screen to enlarge the picture.

"No, someone else in their family will show. There's always a spirit wanting to be heard and if none of the murderers show up I can still air the piece. Might put the fear into the viewers' eyes – if the murderers don't show up, people will really believe in hell."

Danny just nodded and pondered the conversation. He felt sleepy again.

"Barry, do me a favor? Later when we stop for the night, can you try to reach my wife? Maybe this'll be your first try at reaching someone in hell."

He nodded off.

The last rays of the sun illuminated the drifting clouds in reds and purples. Sunset far off in the west gave reason for the men to stop for the night.

The exit ramp was well lit, making it easy to read the large signs with the directions and distances to the various motels and restaurants.

"There... one mile to The Richmond Inn. Hang a right," Danny said.

Both sides of the roadway were lined with fast food restaurants and truck stops. Schmedly, feeling the truck slow and make a turn, stood up and peered out the window.

"Oh, look who's up."

Schmedly gave a couple of sleepy wags of his tail and a yawn as they pulled into a truck stop for the evening's rations.

Up ahead between the lights of the restaurants and the lights of the motel far in the distance was an incredibly steep hill. Barry dropped the truck into a lower gear to tackle the incline. Once over the hump, the motel showed itself.

Danny closed the door and started for the office but stopped and turned back. Barry brought down the passenger window.

"Hey, Barry, we never discussed the sleeping thing. Do you want your own room? I mean I know you're used to fancy..."

"One room's good but make sure there're two beds," Barry said, winking.

Danny returned carrying the red motel key. "Room one eleven. Down there."

Only a few cars were parked in the lot of the horseshoe shaped building. Barry backed the truck to their room. The door stuck a bit but Danny gave it a shove. The room smelled like cigarette smoke but the odor soon dissipated as Danny sprayed a can of deodorant.

"Hope you don't mind later, Danny, I've got a cigar I'd like to take a couple puffs of," Barry said.

Danny hated the smell of cigars but there was no way he could complain. He kept an uncaring face. "No, I don't mind."

"You want one, I've got extras."

"No, thanks. I never was a smoker."

He opened the food bag, which he had laid on a small square table just big enough for two people. A glass fixture hung low over the table. Danny banged his head repeatedly as he tried to set the table to look presentable.

Barry sat on one of the two queen size beds and removed his shoes. He reached into his bag and, taking out a pair of slippers, slid them on.

Danny surveyed the evening's accommodations. A large mirror sat behind the television. From where Danny sat in front of the window, he could see the reflection of a clown painting on the wall behind him.

Danny laughed. "Nice place – I think that's a Picasso." He pointed to the clown.

Barry smiled through a mouthful of food. Danny watched Schmedly devour his food, which was served out of a plastic bowl on top of a place mat carrying the NY Mets logo. The dog looked up once at Danny, food falling from both sides of his mouth back into the bowl. Danny smiled and took a sip of beer.

"So what's next?" Danny asked.

"I'm going to do a reading and see who shows up. Hopefully I'll get some kind of clue – at least more than the peaches. God I hope this works."

Both men lay on their beds, pants unbuttoned, watching the news. Danny held a beer on his stomach while Schmedly lay next to him with all four paws in the air.

"Think I'll light that cigar now – it'll relax me – maybe help with the reading."

Danny jumped up. "I'll put the exhaust fan on in the bathroom. It'll suck out some of the smoke."

Barry puffed the cigar, unintentionally sending a big cloud of smoke in Danny's direction. Schmedly stood on the bed and went into a sneezing fit.

"Is he allergic to the smoke?" Barry asked.

"I don't know. Thinking about it, I don't know that he's ever smelled a cigar."

"I only need a few puffs just to get the taste and some nicotine. Start setting up for the reading," he said, pointing toward the table.

Danny jumped up.

"Make sure those drapes are closed tight. Last thing we need is someone walking by seeing me holding your hand across the table," Barry joked.

Danny pulled the plastic rod to draw the curtains tightly together.

They sat across from each other. Barry took both of Danny's hands and closed his eyes. After a short period of dead silence, Barry opened his eyes slightly.

"I think I have him... but his light isn't as strong as it was."

"What does that mean?" Danny asked.

Barry shook his head for Danny not to talk.

"I'm feeling something – almost like sadness... strange. He's showing me – I feel like I'm skiing and I'm feeling pain in my leg. But I'm also still feeling a warm breeze. It's like I'm being pulled around." He paused. "This is weird. I'm getting a name of... mister but mister who?"

Danny had perked up. He knew what the ski vision meant. He wanted to explain but knew to wait until Barry was finished.

Barry opened his eyes. "Who had the red hair?"

Danny didn't know whether to answer.

"No, it's okay. Do you know who the redhead is?"

"No, but I had a friend who skied with us when I was a boy."

Barry sat back in the chair and rubbed his eyes.

"He only lived in our neighborhood for a little while. His name was Lester. You heard mister. Lester, mister – kinda sound the same, no?"

Barry moved his head from shoulder to shoulder. "Could be. I'll keep the name in my log. Tell me more about him and the ski trip."

"He went down the bunny trail for the first time and wound up in the trees – he broke his leg. He just kept saying he couldn't stop. Died a few years after that from cancer."

Barry sat with a blank stare, trying to piece together the clues. He finally broke the silence. "It's hard for me to tell if we should be looking for these things or doing them. Everything was cloudy when I did this reading. I think we still need to head south and find a guy with red hair."

They sat in silence for a few more minutes.

"Was my father the only one there?" Danny asked nervously.

"I didn't feel your wife if that's what you're asking. But... your father's aura wasn't as bright. Keep in mind that most of the people I read for – I never see again. So I don't know if it's normal for a spirit to lose brightness. I've only done multiple readings on a handful of people because I travel around so much. And of course I've seen family members many times... but again, they've never shown a faded aura like that."

"There was nothing else from my father?"

"No, but I really believe we're on the right path. It feels right."

Barry got up and switched on the TV. He walked between the two beds and sat on Danny's next to Schmedly. He patted the dog's belly.

"I hope they get a lot of channels here," Danny said, picking up the remote. "I don't think I can sleep tonight."

"It's too early to be sleepy. Plus we didn't really do much but sit and drive."

"You know what? I better call Kanook and tell him what's up. I'm sure he's dying to know where we are."

Barry laid his laptop on the table. "I'll start the log for a chapter in my next book and if I can get an Internet connection after, I'll check the weather for where we're going."

Barry took his duffel bag into the bathroom and closed the door.

The alarm went off at six o'clock. Danny, being unfamiliar with the clock radio, fumbled with it as he tried to hit the snooze button. He felt for the remote and turned on the TV.

"You asleep?" he asked Barry.

"Yeah, not too bad considering I'm used to better conditions," he said, yawning. "Put the Weather Station on."

"I'm starving. What's for breakfast? I could go for some home fries and eggs."

"I bet at that truck stop we won't have a hard time finding that."

Schmedly stood on the bed and shook himself. He gave Danny a quick lick in the face and then fell back into a lying position.

"Let's get a move on," Barry said.

"You don't believe in hitting the snooze button a few times?"

Danny crawled out of bed. He leashed Schmedly and took him outside. It was cold – the sunrise was way off to the east while the stars were still visible to the west. Schmedly led him to a grassy area. On the return they walked back across the parking lot, where Danny slipped a couple of times. He looked closely at the pavement, unable to determine whether he had slipped on an icy surface or just a wet one.

"Cold out," he said as he entered the motel room.

"I'm just watching the weather now – lower thirties out. It gets nicer later on today as we make our way south. Let's pack it up."

The truck was loaded and the engine running to warm it up.

"Okay Schmed, let's go."

The dog didn't move. He laid on the bed calmly as though Danny wasn't talking to him. Danny walked up within an inch of the dog's nose.

"Let's go. What's wrong with you?"

"Maybe he's not feeling well?" Barry asked.

"I don't know. He's acting weird."

Danny put his hand under Schmedly's belly and lifted. After tugging as hard as he could, he finally got the stubborn dog off the bed.

"Now get in that truck. What the hell is this all about?"

Once outside, another struggle began. Danny had to force Schmedly into the vehicle. The dog didn't seem to be in pain but was very reluctant to get in. After the brief struggle, Schmedly laid down in the back.

"Barry, I have to tell you, this dog doesn't want to be in this truck. He knows something."

Barry looked at Danny in disbelief.

"You think he can tell something's wrong? That's silly."

"As silly as you talking to the dead."

"Touché."

"Just be careful driving, that's all."

Barry stopped at the front desk. Danny ran out with the key, dropping it in the pan of the night window and rushing back into the warmth.

"And we're off," Barry said.

He turned onto the road. It was only a hundred feet to where the road dropped out of sight. Barry took the truck over the hump. They could now see the bright lights of bustling truck stops below. Barry's mind was on eggs. Danny's was on why Schmedly didn't want to be in the truck. Half way down it became apparent.

Barry stepped lightly on the brakes as the truck picked up speed. A slight fishtail of the vehicle made Danny grab tightly to the hand strap over his door.

"What was that?" he asked, sitting up straight.

"We're on ice - black ice," Barry yelled.

He stepped harder on the brake pedal but even with the antilock system the hill was too steep. The truck skidded slightly and started sliding down the hill sideways. Barry turned the wheel from one side to the other but that only exacerbated the truck's now swaying motion as it left the roadway.

The truck was now traveling at better than thirty miles an hour in the dirt along side the road. He stood on the brake pedal as the truck slowed slightly. For a moment it seemed the worst was over as Barry had the truck facing forward again, but a sharp turn of the wheel to avoid a boulder sealed their fate.

Both men yelled as the truck flipped on its side and slid for a few yards before hitting a small gully, sending it tumbling over and over. It came to rest standing upright. Danny was semi-conscious. He felt no pain. Blood trickled from his forehead and dripped into his lap. He spit out pieces of glass.

He tried to turn to Barry but his seat had twisted out of position and now faced more toward the door. He fumbled with the seat belt but couldn't find the release. He was almost paralyzed - all he could do was wait.

It took only minutes before Danny could hear garbled voices coming toward him. Everything was in slow motion.

"Get an ambulance and police here now," a man screamed into his cell phone.

He shined a flashlight into Barry's window. Seeing no movement, he ran to Danny's side. The passenger door was crumpled but the man tugged until it opened half way.

Danny was still dazed and was making a feeble attempt to release the seatbelt.

"Are you hurt?"

"I don't know. Where's my dog?"

The man undid the seatbelt. Danny started to pull himself out.

"Whoa there. Just stay put 'til the paramedics get here. I'm gonna check on your friend over there."

"Wait... where's my dog?"

The man was already by the hood but turned and came back. He shined his light into the back of the truck. Reaching in behind Danny's seat, he moved the piles of disrupted luggage.

"I don't see no dog back here, Mister."

"I need to get out. Help me out."

"Mister, please don't move. You might hurt yourself."

Danny glanced over at Barry, who was just regaining consciousness. The man moved the side air bag out of the way for a better look. He shined the light in. "You okay?"

Barry moved his arms and legs one at a time. He felt his head but found no holes. He turned to Danny. "You all right?"

"Where's Schmedly?"

Barry turned to the back. "I don't know. Maybe he's buried under all the stuff."

Barry was able to exit the vehicle against the pleas of the Good Samaritan.

"Danny, you stay where you are and I'll find Schmedly."

Danny made another attempt to get out but as he regained his faculties, the pain in his head and right arm pounded, rendering him helpless. He could feel the truck being moved as Barry dug feverishly to find Schmedly.

Sirens blared as the first police car pulled up. The man who had gotten there first ran to the officer and pointed in Danny's direction. Together they came to his window.

"How you feelin'?" the officer asked.

"Not so good. Just find my dog."

The officer put a flashlight up close to Danny's head to see where the blood was coming from.

"You just sit tight, Son, we'll find him."

By now, Barry had almost everything out of the truck through the back door.

"Danny, he's not in here," Barry called.

"Then find him. He must've fallen out."

Danny, fearing the worst, started to cry. The physical agony that gripped his body was nothing compared to the emotional pain he began to feel.

"All right, spread out. We're looking for a dog," one of the officers yelled.

The paramedics had just arrived. One had to practically drag Barry away from the search party. The other came to Danny's window. An officer who had been asking Danny questions moved to the side.

"Where do you hurt?"

"My head. My arm."

Another ambulance pulled up. The paramedic waved his hands for them to get as close as possible. They rushed out with the stretcher. With the help of the officer, the paramedic eased Danny from the wreck.

"I'm not going anywhere 'til they find my dog."

Danny was out of the truck and being helped onto the stretcher. The officer motioned to the paramedics to take him.

"We'll find your dog, Sir. We'll contact you at the hospital."

Danny was being wheeled over the uneven ground. Every bump felt like a baseball bat to the head. He tried to turn to see the police who were searching for Schmedly but his head was tight to the backboard. As he was being lifted into the ambulance, he heard yelling from a distance. One of the paramedics took off in that direction.

"Please, can we wait to see if he's okay? And how's Barry?"

The paramedic shook his head. "If I don't get you right to the hospital, it's my ass if you die. They'll find him. Your friend is going to the same hospital in the other ambulance."

The doors were closed and the ambulance started to pull out. The driver stopped abruptly when one of the officers banged on the back door. Danny held his breath as the paramedic opened it.

"We found him. He's in pretty bad shape. We're going to take in the patrol car to a vet. I'll come to the hospital myself when I have news – I promise."

Danny's exhaled deeply. He felt so helpless. His best friend was dying or even worse – maybe already dead and he wasn't there for him. Danny sobbed; his world was falling apart.

Chapter Eleven

Paramedics flew Danny through the emergency room doors, almost hitting them before they had the chance to open automatically.

"MVA," the paramedic yelled.

A doctor ran alongside the gurney as the paramedic wheeled Danny down the hall and into a room.

"What we got?"

"Head trauma – he's been goin' in and out."

The doctor leaned over Danny and shined a pen light into each eye.

"Can you tell me your name, sir?" the doctor asked.

"Danny, Danny Dillon. Can you find out how my dog is?"

"Let's get you taken care of first. Then we'll see about your dog, okay?"

The doctor turned to an orderly who waited behind them. "Once we get the IV in him, run him up for a CAT scan. I wanna see what's happening inside."

Everything was happening so fast. Nurses running around him. Four different conversations going on. They rolled him from side to side to cut off his clothes. Doctors barked orders. His head hurt and he began to black out again.

* * * * *

Danny felt the vibration and low hum of a motor as he glided into the CAT Scan. A soothing voice came over the intercom.

"Just relax and try not to move, Mr. Dillon."

Once completed, Danny was wheeled back to the emergency room. The doctor followed him in.

"Mr. Dillon? I'm Dr. Muller. I saw you when you first came in. Are you in pain?"

"My head hurts... and my arm."

"Your head should hurt – you have a nasty concussion. I'm going to send someone in to sew your head up."

The doctor leaned over to examine the gash. "Should take twenty stitches or so."

"My dog, Schmedly. Can we find out if he's okay? And the guy I was riding with – Barry, is he all right?"

"I've seen your friend. He's banged up but functional. No breaks or major problems. We'll keep him overnight. As for your dog, the paramedics said the police took him to a vet fifteen miles from here. I'll have one of the nurses call over and see if we can find out for you."

"Thank you."

"The pain in your arm is a slight fracture and we're going to set it in a soft cast. You'll only have to wear it for two weeks."

Danny wasn't really listening. The doctor hung the chart on the end of the bed. "I'll have the nurse check on your dog."

Danny waited patiently for over an hour. A young doctor finally appeared.
Danny tried to sit up.

"Stay there. I'm going to sew you up."

"You don't know about my dog?"

"No, what about him?"

"He was in the accident. The doctor told me a nurse would call the vet and ask about him." Danny broke down crying. "Please, I need to know."

The man looked shocked. He put down the medical kit. "I'll be right back."

Danny stared at the door and waited for him to return. Thankfully this time his wait was short.

"Mr. Dillon, I spoke to the nurse who spoke to the vet. They weren't able to give her any news when she called so I just called now. He's going to be okay..."

Danny's body sunk into the bed with relief. The doctor continued.

"He's got a broken leg and some cuts and bruises. He was unconscious but he's awake now and he's asking for you."

Danny smiled. "If you knew Schmedly, you'd know that might not be very far fetched."

The man laughed. "They're going to keep him in for a couple days though. Get your wallet out – I know they charge a small fortune at that place."

"Doesn't matter. As long as he's okay."

"Okay, now can I close you up? I have other patients to tend to. After this we'll have a cast thrown on your arm."

He braced himself as the doctor came at him with a large needle.

Danny lay dozing as he waited to be moved out of the temporary room. It was lonely. There were six other beds but all empty and no TV. He felt someone watching him.

"How you feeling?"

"Barry – it's good to see you," Danny said, trying to sit up. "You all right?"

Danny looked over his friend's face. There were no cuts but a couple of lumps and bruises.

"Yeah, I feel okay. Those air bags really do work. I'm going to have some nice colors all over my body but believe it or not there's nothing broke or cut."

"Should you be out of bed though?"

"I convinced them to let me see you if I stayed in this wheelchair," he looked both ways. "Tell the truth I did a reading for one of the doctors who saw me on TV once. He let me out of the bed. So how are you feeling?"

"My head's throbbing and my arm hurts a little." He lifted the dark blue fiberglass cast on his right arm.

Barry feared asking the next question. "Anything on Schmedly? They wouldn't tell me anything."

"Yeah, he's going to be all right. He's banged up but the guy said he would make it. Did they tell you when you're getting out because I'm going to be here a couple days at least. Someone's got to go see Schmed."

Barry patted Danny's wrist. "Don't you worry – I'll go to see him as soon as I get out. Maybe tomorrow."

A nurse came into the room. "We're going to move you in a few minutes." She turned to Barry. "Weren't you in the accident with him?"

"Yes."

"Who let you out of bed?"

Not wanting to get anyone in trouble, Barry turned the chair quickly.

"Hey nurse, can you put us in the same room overnight?" Barry asked.

"I'm guessing he's going to a different unit than you but I'll ask," she said.

Barry flipped through the channels of the TV in his semiprivate room. A nurse walked in.

"You have a guest," she announced.

Two orderlies wheeled Danny's bed into the room.

"Hey, they got you in here. That's great," Barry said.

"Glad to be out of the room down there. They brought some guy in who was high on something and wouldn't shut up. He was screaming and yelling something about rats."

Danny's bed was positioned and the curtain between the beds pushed back to the wall so the two men could see each other.

"Are you definitely getting out tomorrow?" Danny asked.

"Pretty sure." Barry reached over to a table between the beds. "Here's the number where Schmedly's at. You can call them."

The nurse put the phone on Danny's lap. He dialed, his hand shaking a bit. The conversation was short and to the point. Danny looked relieved as he hung up.

"He's hurting but he's okay. He's going to hobble around a bit because of the cast on his leg. Hey, like father, like son," Danny said, laughing and holding up his cast.

"God, I'm glad to hear he's okay. When's he getting out?"

"The vet didn't say but I think it sounds like he's in for a while." Danny paused. "You know, Barry, if this is going to take too long with all this, we can go back."

"Nonsense, I'm in this 'til we find him. Don't worry about the money thing. Remember, if I can find him - and I think I can - I'll make a fortune looking for other dead people. Hell maybe I can find Jimmy Hoffa."

Danny laughed but stopped and grabbed his throbbing head. "Remind me not to laugh again, will you?"

Both men lay quietly watching TV for a few minutes before Danny broke the ice.

"You feel like talking about the accident?"

Barry muted the TV and sighed deeply.

"I don't know what happened, Danny. It's not all clear to me right now either. I've been going over it in my mind."

"Schmedly knew something was wrong. You have to be able to see that, Barry."

He reluctantly agreed. "Animals can sometimes tell when earthquakes are imminent but how could a dog know that we were going to be in an accident?"

"He knew something. He never acts that way."

A nurse walked in, carrying a tray of medicine. "Mr. Dillon, I have some pills for you to take."

"What am I taking?"

"Just something for your head."

"Nurse, could you close the door on your way out?" Barry asked.

"I'm really not supposed to do that. We need to be able to hear."

"Just for ten, fifteen minutes."

"Ten minutes," she said, pulling the door closed.

Danny gave Barry a questioning look.

"I want to try to contact your father." He wiggled his way out of the bed and into a wheelchair. With a couple of moans, he wheeled himself to Danny's bed. He took Danny's hand, careful not to pull on the IV. He closed his eyes but within seconds his eyes popped opened quickly in surprise. "Wow, I've got him."

Barry, still in the chair, put his forehead down on the bed.

"I'm having trouble interpreting his message. It's like a caution sign but I'm also getting pictures of trees – I guess he means a forest."

Danny didn't want to speak but the urge to question was too strong.

"Maybe his body's in a forest?"

Barry didn't answer right away but shook his head while lifting it off the bed.

"I don't know what it means, Danny. I'm still seeing like... red hair but way off in the distance."

A doctor opened the door but stopped short upon seeing Barry holding Danny's hand. "I'm sorry, am I interrupting anything?" he asked, looking embarrassed.

Barry pushed away from the bed. "No; I was just doing a reading."

"Oh, that's right, you're that guy." He reached out to shake Barry's hand. "I heard you were here."

"Yeah, that's me – I'm that guy."

"I'm Dr. Simpson." He picked up Barry's chart. "Mr. Leonard, could you do me a favor and stay in bed at least 'til the morning?"

"Sorry, Doc."

"I know you feel fine but just humor me."

"No problem."

"And you are... Mr. Dillon," he said, picking up Danny's chart. "How are you feeling? You took a pretty good knock to the head I see. Any discomfort?"

"Just a never-ending headache and some nausea. The arm's not too bad. Some other little pains but nothing too bad."

"The nausea is normal and your head is going to pound. The important thing is you're both going to be fine. Mr.

Leonard, you're most likely going to be discharged tomorrow barring any problems. Mr. Dillon, on the other hand, will be with us for at least two days - maybe three. We want to monitor your head - make sure that you're healing."

A police officer gave a light tap on the open door. Danny sat up straight, letting out a loud moan from the pain.

"They're all yours, Officer," the doctor said. "I'll be around if you guys need me. Get some rest."

The officer walked in. "Do you remember me?" he asked Danny.

"Vaguely - you have something to do with my dog."

"I'm the officer who took him to the vet."

Danny threw a line of questions at the officer. "How is he? Were they telling me the truth? Will he be okay? When was the last time you saw him...?"

"Whoa, slow down. I'll tell you everything," the officer said. "When we brought him in, he didn't look good. He was breathing funny and he was bleeding but I couldn't really tell where the blood was coming from. Couldn't stick around and wait so I went back just now when my shift ended. He's okay but I think he's going to be in for a while."

"Did you see him?"

"No, just talked to the vet's assistant. She's real nice and she'll be there all night."

"I talked to the vet but he didn't have a lot of time," Danny said.

"Yeah, she said he lost some blood but they got him in time so he should make a full recovery. You know he's got a broken leg,   right?"

"Yeah, they told me. Thanks for taking the time to come here. It means a lot."

He reached out his uninjured hand to the officer but the man was hesitant to come forward. He then approached between the two beds, the reason for his reluctance now evident. Under the white fluorescent light, brownish stains stood out on both his hands.

"I didn't want you to see this."

It took a second for Danny to figure out what it was as he shook the officer's left hand.

"Blood – Schmed's blood?"

The officer nodded. "It doesn't come off easy when it dries and I haven't had time to really clean them."

Danny stared up at the ceiling. "Maybe this whole thing was a bad idea."

"I have to be going. Hope everything turns out okay. Oh – your truck is at the impound. A bunch of your stuff was ejected from the vehicle. We picked up as much as we could in the dark. Anything of value will be kept inside and locked."

"Thanks again, Officer," Barry said.

He tipped his hat and began to walk out. "Mr. Leonard, when you do your next show, could you give us a mention – the Virginia Police?"

"Consider it done." He turned to Danny. "You feel any better knowing he's okay?"

Danny's mouth was wide open in mid-yawn.

"I'm so tired," he mumbled. "Poor Schmedly, my poor Schmedly."

Barry smiled. "Good night my friend." He turned down the TV. "Better call Kelly and maybe Kanook. Let them know what happened."

By ten o'clock the next morning, Barry had been discharged. Kelly made arrangements for a rental minivan to be ready and waiting outside the hospital. An orderly wheeled him through the front doors.

He hadn't anticipated the soreness that he was experiencing. Both his legs were stiff, as was his back. His sternum hurt every time he took a breath – the seat belt being the culprit there. He took a few steps toward the parking lot and stopped. The cane that was offered and denied now sounded like a smart idea.

He hobbled back inside and in minutes returned to the lot with the cane. He eased himself into the minivan. He placed a piece of paper with the directions on the passenger seat and took off – the vet being the first stop.

* * * * *

Barry walked into the vet's office. A woman sat with her fidgety, moaning German Shepherd who obviously preferred to be elsewhere.

He winced in pain as he reached the counter.

"Are you all right?" the girl asked.

"Yes, I'll be fine. I'm Dr. Barry Leonard. I'd like to see how Schmedly is doing. We were in an accident last night."

"Oh yes, he's recovery. Are you his owner?"

"No, his owner is still in the hospital."

She stood up. "Wait here for a sec. I'll get the doctor."

Barry decided to sit down. He kept a good distance from the shepherd who had now urinated on the floor.

"Nice dog," he said.

"Not a dog today. Today he's a big chicken," the lady said.

The vet came out. "You're here to see Schmedly?"

Barry stood up with the help of the cane.

"Guess you were in the accident too, huh?" the vet asked.

"Yes, unfortunately."

"Wait, you look familiar," the vet said as his eyes opened wide. "You're the guy who speaks to the dead." He reached out his hand.

"Yes, that's me."

"Wow, it's great to meet you. I'm Dr. Christian. C'mon back and you can see the dog." The vet kept talking as Barry followed him down a hallway. About halfway to the door, the doctor stopped and with a soulful look he asked, "Can you really speak with the dead?"

"Yes, I can."

"I wish I had more time to talk to you about it now. Anyway, he had a rough time last night. Lost a lotta blood. He was very lucky. I understand he's not your dog."

"No - Danny his - owner is still in the hospital. He'll be in for another day or two."

The vet opened another door. Cages were stacked from floor to ceiling along the walls. Barry spun slowly, meeting the eyes of each unhappy critter behind the bars of their cages. He scratched the nose of a rabbit that lay listless. As he continued following, he waved his hand in front of his face – the smell of the animals wasn't pleasant. In the far corner past an examining table, Schmedly lay with his nose up against the bars of the bottom cage. His tail wagged upon seeing Barry.

"Ah, the poor thing," Barry said. "Looks like he's in jail."

Schmedly made a feeble attempt to stand but the hours of inactivity and the aches from the accident made him fall back down. Barry bent down with a couple of moans and put his finger through the bars, scratching Schmedly behind the ear.

"How you feeling, Boy?"

An IV line was taped tightly to his front left leg while the other was in a cast. A bandage covered his back left leg completely.

"Can you let him out?"

"Rather not just yet. He's got some mending to do. He's got no internal injuries but he lost some blood from a couple different gashes. One on his back leg and one under his belly. We stitched him up."

"I'm glad Danny can't see him now. I think he'd lose it."

Schmedly rolled his body so Barry could rub his back.

"How long's he going to be in for?"

"Hard to say. We can take the IV out maybe tomorrow. That big bandage in back isn't as bad as it seems. We overdo it so he can't chew it off. That can be removed in three days – the cast in three weeks. He's gonna have trouble walking on that leg for a while. Unfortunately I can't let you stay. I don't want him getting too excited. He needs rest."

The men stood up. Schmedly's big brown eyes looked up at them, pleading for Barry to stay – he was lonely. Barry wiped a tear from his eye.

"Is there any way I can stay with him? Even if you just put a chair here so I can sit and talk to him for a while."

"No, I'm sorry. I really want him to stay calm and rest, you know? Come back tomorrow and we'll see maybe then."

* * * * *

An officer opened the gate to the impound lot. Barry pulled the minivan in and followed the officer, who was still on foot. He waved Barry ahead and pointed to where his truck was. Barry's jaw dropped at the destruction of the vehicle. The officer walked up behind.

"Back up to the other vehicle and we'll unload it," the officer said.

Once in position, Barry got out and walked around his truck. There was not a square inch of unscratched paint and only one rear window was still intact.

"If this had happened years ago, we'd all have been killed. The air bags and belts saved us," Barry said.

"We've got some of your stuff inside, Mr. Leonard. Laptop and camera."

"Are they still in one piece?"

"I don't know. I didn't really look at them."

Barry, with the help of the officer, dragged the strewn luggage from the back of his demolished truck. Each piece had to be shaken to remove the thousands of broken glass fragments. Water from the cooler had spilled and soaked Schmedly's dry dog food, swelling it to twice its normal size.

"By the way, Mr. Leonard, we sent some guys over to the crash site and recovered a few things. It's clean now but you're welcome to go over and check it yourself."

"I do, thank you. I won't be going over there for a couple of days. I'm quite stiff and right now I'm exhausted. Just want to lie down."

"I understand. Just don't forget to stop at the office for the rest of your stuff."

Barry sat in a handicapped spot in the hospital parking lot. His body had stiffened and his ability to maneuver had greatly decreased. He took out a bottle of painkillers the doctor had prescribed. Hours before he had scoffed at needing them but now he couldn't swallow them quickly enough.

Hope these things work fast.

An orderly wheeled Barry into Danny's room.

"What happened? You wanted to jog out of here this morning..."

"The doctor was right. It caught up with me. I hurt all over. How about you?" Barry asked.

"My head's a little better but I'm still nauseous. Tell me about Schmed."

"He's going to be fine." Barry wheeled himself between the two beds. "He's going to be in for a few days and the cast has to stay on. He licked my hand and I scratched him behind the ear. They wouldn't let him out of his cage and I wasn't allowed to stay long. They want him to rest."

"You sure he's all right? I mean you would tell me if something was wrong, right?"

"The vet thinks so."

"Will you go back tomorrow?" Danny asked, trying to sit up.

"Of course I will, but right now Danny, I hope you don't mind if I don't stick around. I'm in a lot of pain. My joints hurt and even my hair is starting to throb."

"Hop back in," Danny said, motioning to Barry's former bed.

"I would if they'd let me. I got a nice hotel room down the road. Had a bellman empty the minivan I rented. Oh I forgot. I saw my truck and emptied it. Everything's back in the room."

"How'd it look – the truck I mean."

Barry shook his head. "Surprised we're alive. It's totaled."

"Barry, I can see you're in pain. Go ahead back and call me later. Now that I got the update on Schmed, I'm going to call Kanook. You speak to him?"

"I tried him last night but didn't get an answer. Maybe he was working. Didn't have time yet today but you call him."

Barry wheeled himself toward the door. "I'll call you later."

"Okay."

Danny reached for the phone and started to dial but stopped. He thought for a moment and decided to lie about Schmedly's condition to save his friend the torment that he himself was going through. He dialed.

"Kanook, it's Danny."

"Hey man, what happened to you? I tried both your cell phones and couldn't get through."

"We're okay but we did have a car accident. I'm in the hospital and Barry was discharged. Schmed's at the vet's."

"No way. What happened?"

Danny explained the entire ordeal, including the messages Barry was receiving. He told Kanook that Schmedly had a broken leg but didn't mention any of the other wounds.

"So what's next?" Kanook asked.

"We keep going south when we're all healed."

After calling Danny the following morning, Barry headed to the veterinary hospital. He was moving around a bit better with the aid of the painkillers, which he now took regularly.

Remembering the look of anguish on the vet's face upon realizing who Barry was, he had a plan to barter a reading for some extra time with Schmedly.

Barry's assumption was dead on. With his unique ability came perks and special treatment and within an hour of arriving at the vet's office, Schmedly had an unused examining room all to himself. The doctor in return got a message from his son, who was lost while very young.

Barry kneeled over the dog and petted his head. The IV had been removed but he was still very tired.

"Danny should be able to come see you tomorrow. He misses you."

Schmedly gave a wag of the tail in recognition of Danny's name. He was soon drifting in and out of sleep, checking to see if Barry was still with him.

Barry sat reading a book. He dozed on occasion also, but had to be careful not to fall asleep and risk an added lump to the body if he fell off the metal folding chair.

He was wide-awake in an instant when Schmedly let out a loud growl.

"What's the matter with you? Trying to scare me to death? You hear another dog outside?" Barry said, his heart beating a bit faster for a moment.

He then felt warmth over his body. He was being contacted. He closed his eyes and again had the vision of a redheaded man in a woodsy setting. He could see Danny's father, his aura dimmer than before.

What does that mean?

The doctor opened the door, breaking Barry's concentration.

"Damn," Barry muttered.

"I'm sorry. Did I interrupt something? I need to give Schmedly his meds."

"No... go ahead."

Danny had been discharged but still hadn't seen Schmedly. The dog needed calm to heal his wounds and the excitement of seeing Danny could tear stitches.

Staying in a high-class hotel made the two long days of moping around more bearable but both men were still bored. They were healed to the point of easy mobility but the cast on Danny's arm made him itch uncontrollably.

Barry had many contacts with Danny's father during the period they spent together but most were the same – a redheaded man and the woods.

Danny jammed an opened wire coat hanger inside the cast to scratch.

"Does that work?" Barry asked.

"Absolutely." he said, moving the hanger up and down quickly. "What's the game plan? How do we sneak Schmed in here for the night?"

"No sneaking needed. I spoke to the manager and we can bring him in. Matter of fact, it's three o'clock; let's go get him."

"But you told me five o'clock," Danny said, standing up quickly.

"I didn't want you to go nuts as the time approached, so I lied. Let's go."

* * * * *

They stood in the waiting room. The door opened and the vet walked Schmedly out on his leash. Danny kneeled down with his arms open.

"Where's my buddy?"

Schmedly let out a loud yowl and ran toward Danny on three legs, holding the broken leg up high. Danny cried and hugged the dog tightly. Schmedly licked his face.

"Oh, he looks great doesn't he, Barry?"

Barry bent down to pet the dog, but instead Schmedly jumped up and suck his nose into Barry's mouth. Barry stood up, spitting. The other people in the waiting in the room laughed – they had all been there before.

"Mr. Dillon," the vet said. "He's all ready. Just keep him quiet for a few more days."

"Can he go in the car? We still have a long trip ahead."

"I don't see a problem with that. But you'll have to stop at another vet in a week or so to have his stitches removed."

"No problem, we'll find a vet along the way."

"That's it – just see the girl for the paperwork."

The vet shook their hands.

"And thank you very much, Mr. Leonard," he whispered to Barry. "Hearing from my son was the greatest gift that anyone has ever given me."

"You're very welcome."

Barry had the minivan pulled up in front of the door when Danny walked Schmedly outside. Coming down the stairs was tricky but Schmedly made it without a problem and hopped into the back where his bed was waiting.

"We better find my father," Danny said, handing the bill over to Barry to read.

He whistled. "I don't think our stay at the hospital cost that much. The reading I did for the vet only got us the private room for him but no discount."

"That's for sure – three grand – what kind of tests did they do?"

Danny read the long list attached to the bill as Barry drove them to the hotel.

Once back in the room, Schmedly made a beeline for the bed. Sleeping in a cage and on the floor wasn't meant for a spoiled dog. He surveyed the situation deciding how he would make his first attempt at a jump with only three working legs.

"Wait," Danny called. "I'll help you."

Schmedly shook himself and backed up. Danny used his good arm under Schmedly's back legs and in one motion the dog was standing on the bed barking in victory.

"No barking," Barry said, sternly. "We get one complaint from the neighbors and we're out."

Danny took out a pen and signed Schmedly's cast. He held it up for Barry who gave a look of *are you kidding?*

"C'mon Barry," Danny coaxed.

"All right, give me the pen."

They were checked out and the minivan loaded. In minutes they were back on the highway, off chasing spirits once again.

"So next time when Schmedly says not to go, we don't go, right?" Danny said.

"I'll definitely ask his advice before I do anything from now on."

"Good, now, we had a ton of time together but we never decided where we're heading to."

"South. I still think it's Georgia. Get the peaches smell once in a while."

Barry's cell phone rang. He answered it on the speaker.

"Hello."

"Hi, Barry? It's Beverly."

"Hi Bev, it's great to hear your voice."

"One of the cases I was supposed to work got solved so I'm going to Connecticut early. I'll be there tomorrow."

"Oh, that's great, my dear. I really do appreciate it."

"I've already spoken to the detective and he's expecting me. He didn't sound all too happy to have a psychic leading them around, but when I mentioned that I can sometimes see how people died, he seemed more interested."

"I'm sure you're used to that, Bev. Danny and I are just leaving Virginia. We had a little accident but we're back on track now."

"Everyone okay?" she asked.

"Oh yeah, we're fine - a little banged up but fine," Barry replied.

Danny looked at him like he was nuts. "We're fine?" he muttered.

Barry put his finger up.

"I'll call you when I get there, Barry."

"Very good, Bev."

Barry hung up the phone. "I had to tell her we were fine or she'd keep me on the phone for an hour wanting the details. She can talk forever."

"Got it," Danny said. "Glad she's going to be there early. We can attack this on two fronts."

"You know - I'm really glad she's going tomorrow. Tell the truth, I was getting nervous on where to go once we hit Georgia. It's a big place and unless I get a vision... with her there, maybe she can give us an idea."

"Sounds good. So what do we do 'til she calls us?"

"We can be in Savannah by tonight. Let's check out the town tomorrow. It's one place I've never been. It's warm enough to walk around and it's supposed to be beautiful."

"What about Schmed?"

"I'll Kelly get us a nice room. He can stay there by himself for a couple hours here and there. We can even get one of the hotel staff to look in on him."

"Sounds good and speaking of making phone calls, I better call Tommy. He'll worry now if I don't call every day."

"And Kanook too," Barry added.

With not much else to do, Danny went over in his mind the clues that they had. The friend who had broken his leg skiing stuck in his mind and after great thought he came to a revelation.

"Hey, Barry? You know the contact you had with my father in the first hotel room? We were concentrating on the red haired guy but remember, I told you we took my friend skiing?"

"Yeah."

"He went down the hill and couldn't stop. The next day we went down the hill and couldn't stop. Could that have been a warning?"

Barry thought for a moment. "I never gave it much thought. A warning instead of a clue. Don't know why we didn't think of that right after the accident."

"Now what if the red haired guy or the peaches are a warning?"

Barry looked at Danny and shrugged his shoulders. "Don't know."

They came into Savannah. Despite their pain, they noticed the city's beautiful hanging moss and its historic old houses.

Barry laughed to himself – by this time the next day, the detectives would be drinking heavily after a day with Beverly Morgan.

Chapter Twelve

T he doors to the station house swung open.

"Hello, my dear, I'm here to see Detectives Marone and Caloway."

Beverly Morgan had arrived. The desk sergeant didn't know what to make of this woman. She was a loud speaker with poorly applied makeup and big jewelry. She appeared much like an elderly gypsy.

"Are they expecting you, ma'am?"

"Yes, they are. I'm the one and only Beverly Morgan."

The officer picked up the phone with skepticism and dialed. He ducked down so as not to be heard.

"Listen, Caloway, there's some lady here, Beverly something, acting like I should know who she is. She's like something from a sideshow."

"Send her back," Caloway, said.

"Ms... "

"Morgan."

"Right. Ms. Morgan, please go through those doors and they'll meet you."

Caloway and Marone greeted her. Thanks to the heads up from the front desk, they were not overly shocked by her appearance.

"Mrs. Morgan, it's a pleasure to meet you," Caloway said. "This is my partner, Detective Marone. Come this way."

"It's *Ms.* Morgan and it's a pleasure to meet you both."

"Please have a seat. Can I get you something – coffee, tea?" Caloway said, as they entered his office.

"Nothing; thank you."

"I've looked at your website and I called some of the detectives that you've done work for. They were very impressed," Caloway said.

"I have worked with many. What I'm doing here is very important to me. I'm helping my good friend Barry Leonard. He's on a trip right now, as I'm sure you know, to find the same man that I'm here trying to find."

"That would be George Dillon. We're not sure if he's dead or alive. Officially we have him listed as missing. Your friend Mr. Leonard seems to think he's dead but I hope you understand that we can't go by a medium's say-so to declare a man dead."

"Yes, I understand. Do you have a picture of the man for me?"

Caloway opened his drawer and took out a manila envelope. He poured the contents onto his desk, spreading them around until the pictures surfaced.

"Here you go Ms. Morgan. These are of George and this is him with his son Danny, who is traveling with Mr. Leonard."

She took one of the pictures of George alone and held it between her hands as if praying. "I think I can read this man. Let's go to the scene."

She stood up. Caloway looked toward Marone.

"There's another case that we'd like you to look at as well but first... like I said, I've done some reading on you but can you tell us what exactly it is that you look for? What do you expect to be able to tell us?"

"Each case is different but mostly what I see is... how do I explain? I see flashbacks of what happened. I don't get names and only sometimes do I see the perpetrator's faces clearly enough to help a sketch artist."

"You mean you can see back to when the attack or abduction took place?" Marone asked.

"That's right. I've actually been able to lead officers to a body or at least within a few hundred yards."

"Tell me more about what you can see. Can you see what took place before a crime?" Caloway asked.

"I don't follow," she said.

"For example, say someone set a trap for someone else... maybe a guy opens a door and a shotgun is rigged to kill him. Would you be able to see who rigged the gun?"

"Maybe; but wasn't this a kidnapping and ransom case? Barry didn't mention anything like that."

"You're right, but we had another case in mind and needed to know what to expect," Caloway said. "We'll work on that later if it's okay with you. Both cases are sorta connected."

"Shall we go, Detectives? I've been traveling quite a bit of late and I'm not as young as I once was. I'm feeling a little tired."

"All right, let's get out there right now," Marone said. "I'll grab the keys."

Marone pulled the car in front of George Dillon's house. Yellow barrier tape still encircled the entire property. Beverly wrapped her arms around herself and ducked under the tape held up for her by Marone. Caloway searched through the keys to find the right one.

"Here we go," he said, opening the door.

"Please give me absolute silence for a moment," she said.

Caloway closed the door gently and watched as Beverly walked through the living room, looking up and down the walls and rubbing her hands on the furniture.

"There was a slight struggle," she mumbled.

Caloway and Marone exchanged glances, but neither knew whether she was talking to them or to herself.

She continued to the kitchen where she sat at the table, sliding her hands along the top. She took the pictures of George from her purse and laid them out. One at a time she picked them up and passed her right index and middle fingers in a circular motion across the photos. She became almost entranced and on occasion would suck in a deep breath of air.

The detectives remained in the living room but were able to observe through the open doorway. Caloway came up behind Marone and whispered in his ear. "Kinda reminds me of a witch doctor."

Marone cracked a smile but contained any laughter. He cupped his hand and turned to whisper back. "Witch doctors don't look that scary."

"Gentlemen, I see you're finding this amusing," she called.

"Ah, no ma'am. We were discussing something else," Caloway said.

"Don't think you're the first to laugh at what I do – but I'm getting a strong feeling here. We'll see later who's laughing."

"Ma'am, I'd like nothing better than to congratulate you on anything you find here," Marone said.

"Let me walk around the rest of the house. Where's his bedroom?"

Marone pointed to the hallway. She motioned for them to wait.

Beverly returned from the bedroom clutching a framed photo of George and his wife against her chest.

"There was a struggle here and great fear. What I'm saying is that Mr. Dillon was taken against his will. I don't believe he knew his abductors."

"Is there any way you can see if his son Danny was involved with this?" Marone asked.

"I don't sense that." She stood still for a second. "Take me to where the money was dropped off. I might be able to tell you more."

"No offense, Ms. Morgan, but you haven't told us anything that we didn't already figure ourselves," Caloway said.

"I'm not finished yet, young man. You're very fresh."

She turned in a huff for the door.

"Now look what you did," Marone said, shoving Caloway toward the door.

"What I say? I said no offense intended."

"Just go... apologize to her."

They sat in the car. Caloway turned to the back seat. "Ms. Morgan, I meant no disrespect."

"In my line of work you get used to non-believers. Apology accepted... but be careful or I'll put a spell on you."

Caloway stared out the windshield, his eyes wide open. Marone burst into laughter.

"You wouldn't do that to my partner, Ms. Morgan, would you?"

"Of course not. I'm not a witch but I scared the pants off the fresh one, didn't I?"

"You sure did," Marone said, as he watched Caloway let out a sigh of relief.

As they approached the ransom drop site, Beverly took out a pad and jotted down notes.

"You know, boys, I have a lot more information for you. I just want to see what I get when we arrive at the spot where the money was dropped."

"What else you got?" Caloway asked.

"Just wait 'til we're finished there. Oh, you brought that file? Where's the picture of Danny Dillon."

Caloway handed it back to her.

"Looks like a nice boy," she remarked.

"Maybe, but we're not so sure," Marone said. "Do you know the rest of this story – about his wife?"

"No, Barry didn't mention anything to me." She reapplied her lipstick. "I'm actually coming into this case earlier than planned and we didn't have time to go over anything."

"I don't want to tell you about it then. Let's see what you can tell us first."

"Drive slow. Take the same path that he did to the spot," she said.

"He was alone –" Caloway started.

Marone cut in, "No, he had the dog."

"Oh, that's right. But none of us were here so we don't know exactly what path he took. Probably just went straight to the trail head sign."

They pulled up next to the sign; they all got out.

"He dropped it here," Marone said. "We swept the whole area for clues – not just right here, but we also had teams with dogs scour the whole park. We found nothing, but it is a big park."

"You didn't look in the right spot," Beverly said, as she walked a few feet up the trail.

Marone and Caloway looked at each other.

"Where should we look?" Marone called to her.

"Be patient," she called back.

The cold wind forced her back to the car quickly. "Brrr, these old bones get cold fast," she said.

Caloway and Marone were now both turned and hanging over the seat waiting for what she had seen.

"First, I feel great fear here. Great fear. Danny was extremely fearful for his father's safety and for his own as he dropped the money. As far as I can see he had nothing to do with his father's disappearance – and I'd stake my life on it."

"What did you mean when…

"When I said you didn't look in the right place?"

"Yes," Marone said.

"When I was back at the house I could feel rock all around me. The house felt like it had walls of solid rock."

"Like a cave?" Caloway asked.

"I guess they didn't make you a detective for nothing. You get a gold star. Yes; a cave. The cave doesn't necessarily have to be in this park. Find it and I believe you'll find some evidence."

"Can you give us any idea where to look? I mean, it's not a big state until you try to cover every square inch," Marone said.

"I'm so very tired." She yawned. "I don't believe the cave is very far. I'm sorry, but I have to ask you gentlemen to take me back. I need to get some rest. We can start again tomorrow, okay?"

"Sure, Ms. Morgan. You've given us a place to start at least," Marone said.

* * * * *

Marone dropped Beverly off at her hotel, which was not far from the station house. Both men were relieved to see her go, for she liked to talk.

"We do appreciate the help. We'll pick you up tomorrow say around noon, okay?" Caloway said.

"That'll be fine. I'll see you then."

They drove off, both silent. Now they were able to concentrate on what she had told them.

"Whata you think? You believe Danny's clean in this?" Marone asked Caloway.

"Yeah, I think so but we still can't rule anything out. Let's find this cave she's talking about – if it exists."

"You don't think it does?"

Caloway could tell by the tone of Marone's question that there was more behind it.

"No, I don't think we find a cave," Caloway announced after a minute of contemplation.

"The usual twenty bucks?"

"You're on – twenty says we don't find it. And we still got one problem – is the boss gonna let us spend more money searching on the say so of a psychic?"

"Let's hope so. At least he didn't meet her or all bets would be off," Marone said.

"For sure. I mean she's a nice lady and all but she never stops. I really didn't need to know about her bunions."

"I'd be happy to listen to her everyday if she could help us solve some of these cases. We might even get home for dinner for once."

Barry and Danny sat in recliners on opposite sides of a couch in the living room area of the mini suite. Schmedly lay between them. Both men were tired from two hours of very slowly walking through the town, mostly to kill time awaiting Beverly's call.

The phone rang. Barry sat his drink down and lifted the receiver.

"Hello?" He looked at Danny and nodded. "Beverly, we've been on the edge of our seats waiting for you."

"I'm sorry it took so long to get back to you, Barry, dear. I'm falling asleep on my feet from all the traveling and the cold."

"So how did it go?"

Danny brought his chair to the upright position and put his hand on Schmedly's back.

"The two detectives were non-believers at first but I think they'll come around. One was a bit fresh but I put some fear into him. As far as Danny's father, I was able to gather that he was held in a cave but I was too tired to see much more. I'm going back first thing in the morning."

"He was held in a cave? I didn't get anything like that... but that's probably something I would never see."

"I got an impression of stone walls. They're going to search the area for caves tomorrow."

"Any idea of how he died, Bev?"

"Maybe tomorrow when I'm rested. Oh, they also took me to the ransom drop site. They were asking if Danny was in on the kidnapping."

"Really. I don't know why they're asking about that – I have no doubts that he wasn't," Barry said, sounding stunned.

"Neither do I, and that's what I told them."

"Thank you for the fine work, Bev. Let us know tomorrow what happens."

"Will do – oh, any luck on your end?"

"No, haven't had any contact from Danny's father today. Maybe later. I guess we'll just drive and see what we find. Go get some rest, Bev."

Danny was about to burst by the time Barry hung up. "Well?"

"She was really tired but was able to give the detectives some insight into the place where your father may have been held or may be now. She's going to try again tomorrow to pinpoint it."

Danny sat back in the chair but after going over the conversation in his head, he sat up straight again.

"Barry, what were you talking about when you said something like, 'Why were the detectives asking questions about that?' About what?"

"They wanted to know whether you were involved with his kidnapping."

"Guess stranger things have happened – a son gets rid of his father for the inheritance. You believe that I had nothing to do with it, right?"

Barry stood up to refill his glass. "We wouldn't be here, Danny, if I for one second believed that."

Danny looked relieved. "What next?"

"Like I told Beverly – we drive on and see where your father leads us. I would like to try and contact him later before we go to bed," Barry said from behind the small bar.

"Okay. Barry, listen, we really need to decide if we want to head right for where Cheryl's family is. Besides her parents, they don't care for me too much – it's the New York thing, I think. If someone in her family – a cousin or whoever, is involved with my father's disappearance, they're not going to take too kindly to us poking around. They're a big clan and that area is a perfect place for people like us to disappear, real rural."

"Or people like your father," Barry said. "If we're led close to the clan's location, I'll call in a couple of bodyguards."

"I don't have that kind of money and I can't ask you..."

"Danny, if I have to bring in bodyguards, people who read books will be dying to know why. It adds danger and sells books. Don't worry about the expense."

Danny sat back in the chair. He ran his fingers over Schmedly's head. "Wish I'd left you home with Kanook where it's safe."

Danny assumed the position of hands across the table as Barry closed his eyes and attempted to make contact with the spirit world. After ten minutes of dead silence, Barry sat back.

"Nothing. I got nothing from your father, but I did connect with the cat."

"Jonesy?" Danny asked, smiling." I've got such fond memories of him. Did he say anything?"

"Animals don't really communicate thoughts as much as who they're with, but he was hunched up, from what I could make of it."

"I think you're wrong there, Barry. If Jonesy was hunched up, he was conveying a message – a message of danger. That cat was smarter than I was and if any animal could figure a way to get a message over – it's Jonesy."

"Well, I guess there's always a first." He stood up. "Let's look at the map and figure a course. Show me Cheryl's family location again."

Caloway and Marone poured coffee outside a meeting room. Inside were officers and volunteers outfitted in heavy hiking gear. The detectives looked at each other, nodded and walked in.

"Listen up, guys... first... I thank the volunteers for showing up on such short notice," Marone said.

Caloway stood in front of a wall map.

"Many of you have already been out looking for George Dillon. We have new evidence that he was kept in a cave but we don't know exactly where." He moved a laser pointer in a circular motion over the map. "Does anyone here know of any caves in the vicinity?"

A man sitting in the back of the room slowly raised his hand.

"Yes," Marone said, pointing to the man. "Your name?"

"I'm Daniel. There are some caves... they are important to us, the Native Americans. They are not well known to you. We would like to keep them secret. Can you do that for us even if you find some evidence there?"

"We'll send a small group of officers. The civilians will stay behind. It will stay secret – I promise," Marone said.

The man stood up. "I knew George Dillon and that's why I'm here. He was a good man. I'll take you there now."

* * * * *

Caloway and Marone, uncharacteristically out of their suits and wearing jeans and hiking boots, led a small team through the unexplored back country. Five men carrying forensic kits trudged up a small mountain. Two miles into the trip, Daniel turned to find his followers far behind.

Marone yelled up to him. "We're coming. How much further?"

"Another mile or so," he called back.

"If there's a place to land a chopper, you're a dead man."

"You'll see – nothing but trees."

Marone stopped and waited for Caloway who came to him breathing deeply. Puffs of steam were taken away in the light breeze.

"Man, I hope there's something up there," Caloway said.

"Tough it out – remember, we still have to go back," Marone said, laughing.

The last mile was long and tiring. They came to a group of white birch, whose leaves had turned but had refused to fall.

"Just a little ways ahead," Daniel yelled back.

"Okay, wait then. Let us catch up," Marone said.

Marone approached him. "We want to be careful of where we step in case of footprints. If this is a crime scene, we need every spec of evidence."

Caloway walked a bit ahead of Marone as they came to a cluster of three caves hidden by large maples.

"Let's take one at a time," Caloway said, as he turned to the others. "You guys wait here while we go inside."

"Detective," Daniel called. "You might want to go in with guns drawn."

Marone looked at Caloway. "Why, I'm sure they're not still sticking around here."

"They may not be but there are bears here."

Both detectives had their weapons drawn faster than a western gunfighter could. Their footsteps echoed as they entered. There was more than enough headroom to accommodate both men but they still walked hunched over, shining lights above, fearing bats. Caloway shined his flashlight to the back of the cave while taking a deep breath of the stagnant air. The bones of a small animal lay to the side near the back.

"Maybe a rabbit," Caloway said.

Marone got down on his hands and knees and combed the floor. He swept every inch with his light.

"We're not going to find anything here," Caloway said.

"I agree. Are these the right caves?"

The two men emerged from the cave. The others perked up upon seeing them but the dejected look on their faces said it all. The men outside continued to search the immediate area for any clues.

"Which one next?" Marone asked Caloway.

"I don't care." He headed for the cave opposite the first.

They were almost inside when one of the other officers shouted for them. They hustled to his call. In a gully adjacent the caves he pointed to a piece of paper.

"What is it?" Marone asked.

"It's a candy wrapper."

"Bag it," Marone said, turning to Caloway. "Maybe we'll get lucky."

They continued back and hurried inside, the wrapper now giving them some inspiration. After only seconds inside, another officer called out. They went back out to investigate.

"Over here," the officer yelled.

Caloway and Marone followed a rock path that led to the backside of the first cave. The rock here was dark - almost black. An officer stood in front of the opening of the third cave and pointed to the ground. Caloway kneeled down and sifted through the ashes of an abandoned campfire.

"Doesn't look new," he said.

By now all the men were crowded around.

"All right, boys, take samples and everyone please make sure you don't damage any evidence. Watch where you walk - don't destroy any footprints," Marone said.

"Go back to the other one or go in here?" Caloway said, pointing to the opening.

"Fire's here. Let's check out this one."

The entrance to this cave was different. It was only large enough for one man at a time to squeeze through. Caloway went first, shining his flashlight.

Together they searched every inch of the floor. For more than an hour they swept the flashlights back and forth. Caloway made a final pass of a corner area when something caught his eye. He bent down close to where the wall met the floor.

"Holy shit," he exclaimed.

Marone ran to his side. "What do ya got?"

Caloway shined the light on the wall about two inches from the floor. The initials GD were scratched lightly into the stone.

"George Dillon – I don't believe it," Marone said.

Searching the area immediately around the find, Caloway discover a small triangle shaped rock the size of a dime.

"This is what he used to carve them," Caloway said, dropping it into an evidence bag.

Marone went outside. "Listen up. We got some stuff inside. This is officially a crime scene." He turned to Daniel. "I have to notify my superiors. They may send more men."

Caloway called from inside.

"Everyone in. Dust everything that can be dusted."

Caloway called to Marone again.

"Got something else?" Marone asked, coming back in.

"A thread with what looks like glue on it."

Another officer set up a light stand and connected the battery. He flipped the switch, lighting up the entire cave. The next officer came in and looked over the two detectives' shoulders as Caloway carefully lifted the single strand into his hand.

"That's duct tape glue on a piece of the reinforcing threads that run through the tape."

"Nice job. Here, bag it," Caloway said.

"All right guys, me and Caloway are headin' back. We got some other things to attend to this morning. There'll be a bunch more men coming up to help search the entire area. We're a step closer to catching these clowns," Marone said.

Marone and Caloway moved as fast as gravity would permit without falling down the hillside. Their conversation was choppy as they spoke in between heavy breaths.

"Even if she does... say he did it... how do we prove it to a judge?" Caloway asked.

Marone put his hand up to stop for a brief rest. His lungs were on fire.

"We'll know if it's worth... draggin' him back in again. We can't keep bringin him back... without a good reason. I just hope she can give us something we missed."

Their heavy breathing returned to normal as both men sat on a long flat rock.

"I don't know how you're going to tell her," Marone said.

"Tell her what?"

"How you're going to tell Ms. Morgan you're sorry."

Caloway gave a dumb smile. "Sorry for what?"

"For doubting her."

"Oh, yeah, I forgot," Caloway said, staring at the ground.

"Bullshit you forgot – you're the fresh one, remember? "Never mind that. Let's move; we're gonna be late picking her up."

By noon they were showered and back into their suits. They sat waiting outside Beverly's hotel.

"There she is," Marone said. "You ready to eat crow?"

"Yup."

Beverly climbed into the back of the unmarked car.

"Morning, boys."

"Morning, Ms. Morgan, you all rested?" Marone asked.

"Yes, I am. Ready to take on another day. So you started saying on the phone before that you found the cave where Mr. Dillon was held?"

"Yes we did. We found the initials GD scratched into the wall near the floor. We have no real proof that he was the one who left them there but the odds of someone else doing it ... well you know – we think it was him," Marone said.

Beverly leaned up in between the two officers. Caloway could almost feel her breathing. She tapped him on the shoulder.

"Don't you have something to say to me?"

"Yes ma'am. I'm sorry I doubted you and we really appreciate your help."

Marone looked out the driver's window to hide his smirk.

"Now that wasn't so hard was it?" she asked, sitting back in the seat. "Today I'm going to try and locate the area where the body is. That will take a lot out of me. You know... if I can't get anything more from the house, the best thing would be for me to see the cave."

"Let's hope we can avoid that. There's no way other than to hike to it and it's far up a mountainside," Marone said.

"I see."

"Like we mentioned, we'd like you to look at something else for us today. Will you have the strength?" Caloway asked.

"I'm sure I will. You haven't told me anything about that one yet or how it has to do with this case."

"Let's wait on it 'til we're finished at Mr. Dillon's residence," Caloway said.

"Have you called Barry to tell him about finding the cave?"

"No ma'am, we haven't called him yet. We'd rather wait 'til later," Marone said.

"I spoke to him this morning and they're going to wait 'til they hear from me this afternoon before pressing on," she said.

Beverly paced through George Dillon's home once again. Caloway and Marone sat on the living room couch and observed her strange behavior. She alternated clenching her fists at her sides and rubbing her cheeks very hard, and on occasion, darted around the room with energy that surprised both men. After half an hour, she collapsed into a chair across from the men. They both rushed to her.

"I'm okay," she said. "I forgot to warn you that I may look a bit pale and get very weak after doing this."

"Can we get you anything... water?" Marone asked.

"Water would be good," she replied.

Caloway was back quickly with a glass of water. As she sipped, both men watched and waited for the results of her reading.

"I don't know what Barry is searching for. I think his body is still around here. I got the feeling of cold and wet, not warm like where they are."

Marone helped her stand.

"Cold and wet?" he said.

"He's deep... deep down but I don't think he's buried. Maybe in a well or something... I'm not sure. But I am pretty sure he's not far from your caves. I need to discuss this with Barry right away," she said as she walked toward the phone.

"We'd appreciate if you could wait on calling him," Marone said. "We need you to check out this other thing for us first, if you could. We'll explain later."

She gave them an untrusting look.

"What are you two up to?"

"Please, let's just go and we'll explain on the way," Marone said.

"Explain it now." She sat back down. "Have a seat, gentlemen."

They complied and Marone went into the details of Cheryl's death. After giving her the shortest version of the story, both men waited for her reaction.

"You don't want me to mention this to Barry? Why?"

"He's friends with Danny and we thought he might ask you not to help us with this," Caloway said.

"Nonsense. Barry would want the truth... and justice if Danny were involved. Let's go see if that nice boy Danny had anything to do with it."

"He's got a helper that works with him fixing computers in the workshop downstairs. I think that's his car," Caloway said.

"Let's go around back and knock. We won't need the key," Marone said.

Marone knocked on the door. Tommy peaked through the blind. Recognizing the detectives, he opened the door.

"Hi, what's up?"

"Tommy, we need to look at the kitchen again," Marone said.

"Sure, go right ahead."

"Oh, Tommy, this is Ms. Morgan."

"Pleasure to meet you," Tommy said, confused about who she was and why she was there.

"Tommy, if you don't mind staying down here..." Caloway said.

"Sure." He sat at the bench and screwed a cover on a computer. Once the visitors were out of earshot, he picked up the phone and called Danny.

"Hi, Danny, it's Tommy. You told me to call if the detectives asked... well they're here."

"Now?" Danny asked. He turned to Barry, "it's Tommy – the detectives are at my house."

"Yeah, and they brought some old woman," Tommy said.

Danny's blood pressure spiked as he realized the reason for the detectives' visit.

"Beverly Morgan is there with them?" Danny asked in a panicked voice. "Don't let them in. Don't let them in."

"I'm sorry, Danny, but they're already upstairs."

"Oh, no, they're in the kitchen?" Danny asked.

Barry's idea of using Beverly was backfiring. Danny couldn't believe they were using her to find evidence against him. He held the phone at his side. Tommy's voice could still be heard asking, "Danny, are you there?"

Was there anything that a psychic could lead them to that he could not have foreseen? He put the phone back to his ear.

"Okay Tommy, thanks for the call."

Danny put the phone back in his pocket and turned to find Barry staring at him.

"My, God, you killed her," Barry said. "I had my suspicions and I wanted to ask..."

"No..."

"Don't tell me 'no', Danny. I heard that conversation. You were petrified that Beverly was there. You're afraid she's going to tell them that you killed her. Maybe that's why your wife hasn't tried to contact you."

"Barry, you don't understand. I had to find my father and she knew where he was." Danny sat in a chair and cried. "Barry, you have to believe me - I'm not a killer but it was the only way to find him."

"Danny, Kanook told me what kind of life you led because of Cheryl. I didn't understand why he thought it important to tell me all the details. I understand now - he knew I would probably find out that you killed her. Although I don't believe in a murder going unpunished, I'm not going to tell anyone anything, okay? Because of you being..." he made quotation marks in the air. "Under my care as a psychiatrist, I'm not obligated to tell anyone anything. If I did, I might not be trusted as a doctor - you know the confidentiality thing."

Danny sniffled. "Thanks, Barry." He thought for a moment. "You're not scared to stay with me now or..."

"I'm not happy about what you did, but I know that sometimes a human being can be pushed to the edge and do things totally out of character."

Schmedly came over and put his head in Danny's lap.

"Barry, what if she tells them something that I didn't figure on? What's going to happen to Schmed if I go to jail?"

"I can't answer that, but my guess is Kanook would make a good father," Barry said.

"Yeah, we talked about that before. Kanook said he would take him. Ya know... Wait," he yelled. "Can't you call Beverly and tell her not to..."

Barry was already shaking his head.

"She's going to do her job. I can't tell her to lie."

Danny held his head in his hands.

Marone and Caloway waited in the living room as Beverly read the kitchen. For fifteen minutes she stood over the spot where Cheryl's body was found, swaying back and forth. The detectives could hear her mumble words from time to time. She came from the room.

"I don't have much to tell, but it's what you want, I'm sure. I must sit first."

Caloway brought her a glass of water as she caught her breath.

"It's so exhausting," she said.

"What did you see?" Marone asked.

"What happened to her was no accident."

Caloway jumped up. "I knew it."

Marone put his hand up. "Wait now – can you tell us who was involved?"

She lowered her head. "I'm sorry to say that I could see someone standing over her while she laid there. The only other thing that I got was that she was very, very angry while on the floor."

"He was there watching her die," Caloway said. "He was watching her die. She was angry with him for not helping."

"Sounds good, but how do we get an indictment? We'll be laughed at if we bring this in as our only evidence... and wait a second. We don't know if it's Danny or our friend Kanook standing over her. Could've been either one of them. They had both been in that kitchen."

"You're in a bit of a pickle here, gentlemen."

"Our intuition was right but we can't really prove it. What do we do?" Caloway asked Marone.

"We wait 'til Danny gets back and question him again. See if we can't guilt him into a confession."

"Gentlemen, if you don't mind, can I call Barry now and tell him about George Dillon?"

"By all means. Use the phone in the kitchen."

"Hello, Barry, it's Beverly."

"Hi, Bev."

"You're never going to guess where I am."

"Already know, Bev. Tommy, the young man that works downstairs there, called Danny."

"I don't have good news from here, I have to tell you."

"I know Bev, but I'm more interested in George Dillon," Barry said.

"I understand. The detectives did find a cave..."

"Wait, hold on, Bev." He motioned for Danny to go into the bedroom. "I'm going to put Danny on with us." Danny picked up the extension phone.

"Hello, Ms. Morgan," Danny said nervously.

"Hello, Danny," she replied. Danny could tell from her voice that she knew his secret. "Danny, the detectives found a cave where your father was held. He scratched his initials into the wall as a signal. I'm afraid though, that after going back to his house, I did envision his body."

"Where...where is it?" Danny asked.

"I see it as being around here. When I say 'here', I mean in the Connecticut area. Barry, I don't see him being down there," she said.

Barry thought for a moment. "Guess you're not going to be any help in directing us here."

"Sorry, no."

"Is it possible that he died there and was moved here? Because I'm still getting communications that I should be looking here."

"Hmmm, that is possible, I guess. Let me tell you where I see him. He's down deep and it's wet. Like a well or something. Danny, do you know anything like that around here?"

"No, nothing I can think of off hand... Ms. Morgan... can you tell me how he died?" Danny asked.

"No, couldn't get that, but you know what? I think maybe I'll go back to the house once more. Maybe I can find something I missed," she said.

"Thanks so much for your help with this, Bev." Barry said.

"And thanks from me, too," Danny said.

She didn't answer. Barry jumped in with one last question.

"Bev, one more thing. Did you see anything having to do with a redhead?"

"A redhead... no, not at all. Why?"

"I've been seeing a redheaded person - maybe one of the kidnappers - I don't know. Let us know if you go back. We're going to take off and look some more here."

"Okay, Barry. Talk to you later."

Danny came out from the bedroom.

"I could hear in her voice that she knows something."

"She does, but don't worry about it. It'll be tough for the police to make a case on her say-so."

"So I guess we drive on."

"Yup, let's pack it up and move out. C'mon, Schmedly dog. Up and at 'em," Barry said, helping him off the couch.

A light rain fell as they drove.

"Supposed to get drizzle for a couple days before turning to torrential downpours and flooding. That'll hold us up I'm sure," Barry said.

Danny had lost much of his ambition for the trip. The forecast of rain would make their journey more uncomfortable and they really had no idea what they were even looking for. "You want to turn back?" he asked.

"No way. We've come this far. Why turn back now?"

"Yeah, I guess. Plus, what do I have to look forward to back home? The detectives are going to be all over me again."

"I can't tell you what's going to happen, but my instincts say they don't have enough to arrest you – or they would have taken the phone from Beverly and asked you to return."

Danny stared out the window without replying. For almost an hour the only sound that was heard was the consistent thumping of the windshield wipers.

"I've got to make this call. I'm afraid to ask him, but I have to," Danny said.

"You mean Kanook – about taking care of Schmedly?"

"Yeah, how'd you know that?"

"That's what's been on your mind, hasn't it? Ever since you found out that Beverly was at your house, the idea of jail has haunted you."

"Kanook, it's Danny. Call me on the cell as soon as you get this."

It was almost dusk as the two men drove west through Georgia. A billboard for a restaurant caught Barry's eye.

"Hungry?" Barry asked.

"I could eat and I'm sure Schmed's ready for something."

Barry pulled off the exit and stopped at the intersection. He did not proceed. Danny peered at him. "You all right?"

"Yeah, I'm just feeling something from your father I think."

Danny looked behind them to see if they were blocking any traffic but they were alone.

"He's gone. I'm noticing that his communications are shorter every time." He turned the minivan. "Really strange."

"What'd you see?"

"I don't know. I think he showed me your kitchen but that was it."

"My kitchen? Why the hell would he show you my kitchen?"

"I have no idea, Danny."

They pulled into the restaurant parking lot. Schmedly poked his head between the seats at the first scent of food.

"Barry, why is it that my father comes sometimes when you don't expect him and other times when you're trying to contact him, he doesn't show up at all?"

Barry opened his door. "Danny, you should know by now that I don't have answers for questions like that. They just show up."

Danny patted Schmedly on the head and closed the door. He took two steps.

Schmedly barked three times.

Danny turned. "Okay, how many?"

The dog barked again.

"Okay," Danny said.

"What was that?"

"He wants two cheeseburgers – didn't you get that?" Danny asked with a grin.

"I talk to the dead and you talk to dogs. If we could only put that together somehow." Barry stopped and looked at Schmedly sitting in the passenger seat. "He's getting around pretty good for all his bumps and bruises. Doesn't seem to be in much pain."

They sat at a table and discussed the last clue from Danny's father. Neither could put a meaning to it other than Cheryl had laid near death in that kitchen. Barry was halfway through his meal when Danny had finished his. He got up immediately to deliver the cheeseburger to Schmedly.

"Meet you outside." He threw a twenty on the table and walked out.

The rain was coming down harder now; Barry put a newspaper over his head while walking quickly back to the minivan.

"Hi, Schmed. How was your cheeseburger?" Barry asked. "Where to now?"

"With the storm brewing, maybe we just find a place 'til the morning."

By morning the rain came down steadily. They just stared from the doorway of the motel room, ducking and backing away with every loud clap of thunder.

"Let's just go. We're not going to find anything here, that's for sure," Barry said.

Danny ran out, opened the sliding side door, and then ran back inside. Fearing that Schmedly would hurt himself running to get out of the rain, he carried him, placing him gently in the minivan. Barry threw a bag in from the other side and climbed in.

"This oughta be fun."

"Listen, Barry, if we don't find anything in the next couple days, let's head back."

"Let's just play it by ear," Barry said.

By noon his optimism had dwindled. The driving rain was almost impossible to drive through. They pulled into a diner parking lot just off the main route.

They procrastinated as long as possible, looking up at the sky as if that would make the rain subside. They both had umbrellas ready but the will to exit was just not there.

A beat up pick-up truck pulled in four spots down from them. Three men hopped out, talking and laughing as if it weren't raining at all. They walked past the truck. Barry and Danny's mouths dropped open.

"You see that?" Danny asked.

"You mean the guy with red hair?"

They looked at each other.

"What's the odds that's the guy we want?" Danny asked.

"One way to find out. Let's get a table as close to them as possible."

As the three men neared the steps to the front door, Barry and Danny made a mad dash after them. Closing their umbrellas, they rushed in to find themselves standing behind the trio, who were waiting to be seated.

Barry whispered into Danny's ear. "Follow me."

The hostess picked up menus. "How many?" she asked the men.

"Three."

"Follow me," she said.

Barry motioned for Danny to stay close behind. They followed the men until they got to the table and were seated. The hostess looked at Barry. "I'm sorry, I thought there were three."

"No, you're right. We're not with them but we'll take this table right here," Barry said.

"I'll be right back with menus for you."

The three men were now sitting only five feet away at a window booth. Listening to conversations would be easy but understanding the heavy southern accents would take some concentration.

Danny glanced over at the men. One of them had already put his menu down.

Barry seized the opportunity to get a conversation going. "Mind if I take a look at that menu? I think the waitress forgot about us."

"Sure," the man said.

The man with the red hair perked up upon hearing Barry's accent. "Where you all from anyhow?"

"Connecticut. Just passing through. Maybe you can tell us what's good to eat," Barry said.

"They make great pork chops – and you gotta have grits."

Barry tossed his menu on the table. "Pork chops and grits it is."

The waitress came to the three men's table. "You all ready to order? Special on fried chicken today, boys."

She took their order and turned to Danny. "You ready too?"

"We'll both have pork chops and... grits?" Danny said.

"That's right," one of the men called over, "grits."

She took the menus and passed the orders to the cook over the counter.

"Okay, when the food gets here we compliment it and get another conversation going," Barry said.

"About what?"

"Just let me handle that."

While waiting for the food to arrive, Barry continued idle chitchat with the men about the weather and driving conditions.

A few minutes later, their food arrived. Thick gravy covered the pork chops. Grits sat on the side. The waitress put a big basket of biscuits on the table.

"You use them biscuits to soak up the gravy," the red-headed man said to Barry.

Barry dunked the biscuit and brought it to his mouth, gravy dripping all over. He then took a fork full of grits.

"This isn't bad. Thank you for the idea."

"Anytime Mister."

"Hey, let me ask you – you're from around here, right?"

"Sure ain't from up north."

They all laughed again.

"Can you tell us where we can find a decent place to stay tonight?" Barry asked.

"Hell yeah. By the way, my name's Andy and I work the front desk of a little place right down the road. We'd be glad to have ya."

Danny stopped chewing.

"That's great. Oh, and we have a dog with us – any problem?"

"Mister, you'll need the dog to keep the coons away. This place is mostly for hunters and fisherman. It's back in the woods a bit."

Danny was getting nervous. How ironic was it when the radio speakers overhead played a banjo tune.

Chapter Thirteen

Barry plugged the address of the motel into the GPS, which had survived the earlier crash and was held to the dash with Velcro.

"This is about five, maybe six, miles into the back woods from what I can see," Barry said. "There's a big lake right near it for fishing."

"Like I said, I'm not comfortable with this."

"We'll be fine. I'm going to let everyone know where we'll be and make sure that anyone at or near that motel knows we're being accounted for."

They drove along a winding road. A red neon sign with the words "Hunters Paradise Inn" appeared. Barry pulled in. The red pickup truck they had seen at the diner was parked in front of the office. Danny looked into the forest where individual cabins were spaced at fifty feet apart. "Oh man, this looks like a nightmare," he said.

Schmedly let out a growl when Andy came out from inside the office on the way to his truck. He stopped upon seeing Barry creeping toward him.

"Barry, Schmed doesn't like this guy. Let's stay someplace else."

Andy waved them into a spot next to the pickup. Schmedly let out another growl.

"Barry, remember last time what happened when we didn't pay attention to Schmedly's warning? We did hospital time."

"Danny, we came all the way here to find... at least I think it's this guy we're looking for. We have to go through with this."

"Can't we just call the police?"

"And tell them what? We need evidence."

The sky had brightened. The cold rain had for the moment waned. Barry got out and followed Andy inside. Danny opened his door and then the slider for Schmedly to hop out. Danny could see that his dog was not comfortable with the surroundings.

A few short minutes later, Barry came from the office carrying two keys and a receipt. He looked into the woods. "I think that one's ours. Let's just go. We'll find it."

A narrow dirt road wound through the campsite-like grounds.

"Here it is; number six," Danny said, matching the number on the plastic key ring.

The cabin sat on half buried cinderblocks and had its own little porch. Two rocking chairs made from tree branches and vines sat on either side of the door. Danny walked past the iron fireplace in front of the cabin and climbed the three steps to the porch. Wooden posts held up a slightly sagging overhang. Danny shook one but stopped quickly, realizing it could come down on him.

"Hey Barry, I don't think this is what you're used to at all," he said, as he opened the door.

"Is it that bad?"

"Is it that bad? You mean you couldn't tell when we pulled in that it was going to be a nightmare?"

Danny walked inside. The musty smell knocked him back a few feet. He shooed Schmedly back outside while he opened and closed the door to fan some fresh air in.

He flipped up the light switch. To his amazement it worked, though it only turned on a lamp on the table between the two beds.

Barry walked in behind him. Danny opened the door to the bathroom.

"They've got plumbing and it actually looks clean. But Barry, let's not spend a whole lotta time here."

"Ah, so we rough it for a couple days. Let's just find out what we can."

"Hey, where's Schmed?"

Both men walked back outside.

"Schmedly," both men yelled.

"There he is," Barry said, pointing to the minivan.

The dog had climbed back inside and lay down on his blanket.

"Barry, I'm getting a real bad feeling about this place. He doesn't want to be inside."

"C'mon Schmed. Come inside with us," Barry begged.

The dog reluctantly followed. He sniffed the whole room, and then jumped up on the bed.

"See, he's fine," Barry said.

"He's not fine, Barry. I'm telling you that he knows things. You promised to listen when he warned us."

"Yes and now that he warned us, we know to be extra careful."

"Terrific. Now that we're here, what do we do?" Danny asked.

"We can hope for a sign from your father, but meantime we can drive around the area. I don't have a feel yet if we're supposed to question this guy Andy or just find this motel. I think we're on the right track though," Barry said.

"Let's get unpacked. Then we'll head back to the office and see what we can find out. We're going to tell him that we want to do some fishing in a couple days when the rain stops. We'll mention your wife's name and where she's from and see what we get."

Danny stiffened. "I don't think you should mention her name. If this guy had something to do with my father's death, he's gonna know who I am. That's just asking for trouble."

Barry nodded. "Agreed."

Danny ducked when they heard gunshots in the distance. "Yeah, we're real safe here, Barry."

Barry laughed. "Just hunters. Tell you what. You get unpacked. Call Kanook and Tommy and the detectives – see if they found anything more, and I'll go talk to Andy."

"Okay."

Danny tossed a suitcase on the bed next to Schmedly. The dog barely moved as it hit the bed.

"Why so sad, buddy?"

Schmedly looked up at him without lifting his head.

"You know something, don't you?"

Danny, fearing they would never be seen again, called Tommy and Kanook to give them the motel address and fill them in on the most recent developments. He thought about calling the detectives to leave his whereabouts, but didn't want to get into a conversation about Beverly's visit to his house.

Barry pushed open the sticking door, startling Danny. Schmedly didn't move.

"Barry, Schmedly's acting weird. We need to get out of here."

"Okay, let's give it today and tomorrow. If we get nothing – we leave either for home or to a different area of Georgia, agreed?"

Danny looked relieved. "Yup, find anything out?"

"No. I spoke to him for a bit but he didn't flinch when I mentioned different things. Maybe we're supposed to find something in the area. Let's get out for a ride. Tomorrow is supposed to be nasty. An inch an hour of rain."

"Great. Do me a favor and call Beverly."

Barry dialed his cell phone but only got her voice mail. "Bev, it's Barry. Give us a call when you can talk freely. Bye dear."

Hours of driving through the nearby hick towns provided the men with no clues to George's whereabouts. Conversations with the locals only made Danny more nervous – especially the gentleman cooking a squirrel on a stick.

The rain had been coming down steadily for hours. Danny was almost happy returning to the cabin to get some dry clothes. Once inside, both men tired and wet, stopped short, both raising their eyes to the pointed ceiling. A steady stream of droplets fell from a beam and landed in between the beds. The thin carpet, which didn't cover the entire floor, was wet but there wasn't a puddle. The floorboards, visible around the edge of the room, had gaps allowing the water to run underneath.

"I'll call Andy and see if there's anything he can do," Barry said.

"You want him in here?"

"You want the leak?"

Andy was there quickly. Danny watched his every move.

"Damn, I thought I fixed that. Only leaks in the middle so just throw a bucket under it and I'll tend to it in the mornin'," Andy said, going to the bathroom and returning with a five gallon pail.

"How are you going to fix it in the rain?" Danny asked.

"I'll just get up there and throw a tarp over 'til the weather dries."

"Thanks Andy," Barry said, closing the door.

"You know, Barry, Andy doesn't seem like a bad guy."

"I see that but 'til we know for sure, he's a suspect or whatever you want to call him."

A knock on the door froze both men.

"Who is it?" Barry called.

"Andy."

Barry let him back in.

"Forgot to mention to you fellas. There's a week-long fair under a big tent startin' tomorra. Might be somethin' for you to do while you're waitin' for the rain to break."

"That sounds like fun, Andy. Thanks, we'll stop by the office first thing for directions."

"Okay."

"Danny, that's got to be it. There's something at this fair."

Danny sat up attentively. "Why, did you see something about a fair?"

"No, but I just think this could be why we're here. We needed Andy to lead us to it."

"I guess it'll be better than just sitting around here or trying to strike up conversations with the locals," Danny said, as he rubbed Schmedly with a towel. "Glad it's warm enough down here to be outside, too."

Barry's cell phone rang.

"Hello?"

"Barry, it's Bev."

"We've been waiting for your call," Barry said, then mouthed the name Bev to Danny. "Find anything new?"

"I'm sorry to say that I still think his body is up here. I spent an hour in his house and I'm as sure as I've ever been that he's here."

"Listen, Bev, you're the expert in this area. I don't know what I'm following... maybe you're onto the body and we're going to find the kidnappers themselves."

"Whatever the case, Barry, please be careful."

"Thanks again for your help, Bev. You going back home tomorrow?"

"Yes, I have a morning flight, dear."

Danny could see the conversation was coming to an end but without all the information that he wanted from her. He quickly grabbed Barry's pad and wrote "Cheryl" on it. Danny tapped Barry on the shoulder with the pad. He took it and whispered, "Oh, yeah."

"Say, Bev, when you were in Danny's kitchen with the officers, what did you see?"

Danny held his breath, waiting for the answer.

"By the way you're asking, I'm guessing that you already know. I saw the woman was very angry in the kitchen – unusual for a person dying."

"Were you able to give them any specifics to help in their investigation?"

Danny paced the small area in front of his bed. Schmedly followed him with his eyes.

"Barry, by the tone of your voice, I'd say you were sympathetic to Danny."

"It's a long story Bev – but a good one. When we see each other again I'll fill you in."

"And to answer your question... I didn't give them anything that they could use in court."

"Okay, Bev, thanks again for everything – safe flight home. Let's meet up over the next month," Barry said.

"Will do and good luck."

Danny waited for his findings, but instead Barry flipped
through a road atlas on the bed.

"Barry..."

"Oh, you want to know what she said." He laughed. "She
didn't give them anything they could use in court."

Danny fell back on the bed, coming face to face with
Schmedly. Barry turned on the TV.

"Look we even have a remote... and cable – wow."

He turned the TV off after a minute.

"Danny, let's try to contact your dad now. I've gone over
this country fair thing in my mind and want to see if I get anything
on it."

Barry picked up the only chair in the room and placed it at
the foot of Danny's bed. He pointed for Danny to sit on the
edge. Barry took Danny's hand but with the water dripping into
the bucket every four or five seconds, he couldn't concentrate.

"Hold on," Barry said, going into the bathroom. He brought
out a towel and dropped it inside the bucket. He played with it
until the water hit the towel and made no sound.

"Better, let's try again," he said, sitting down.

Barry's face strained as he attempted to make contact, but
within minutes he threw Danny's hand down in disgust.

"I can't get him. It's like he's right there but I can't read him.
So frustrating."

"Could it mean that maybe Beverly is right and he's back
there?"

"No; this would have nothing to do with that. I'm not getting
anyone coming through for you. I don't know, Danny. Let's
just hit the fair and see what we find."

Barry flipped open his laptop and typed some notes into his
log.

The next morning the rain came down like nothing either
man had ever seen. Umbrellas were of no use as the rain came
from every direction in the blowing wind. Barry made the first
mad dash to the van, opening the side door. Danny carried

Schmedly with both arms. As he ran toward the van, he watched the umbrella that he had attempted to carry, cartwheel away.

"Get him in," Barry yelled.

They closed the doors and looked at each other. Water dripped from their noses and chins. Schmedly shook himself in the back, spraying the windshield.

"This is going to be a long day," Barry said.

It was late afternoon. They had seen everything at the fair twice. They were even desperate enough to show George's picture around hoping for a clue. Barry started to doubt his ability to analyze what he was seeing in his readings.

Both men were soaked to the bone. Walking in the dirt parking lot was strenuous – the mud sucked their feet in, making a long walk longer. They were both sore and exhausted. They looked at each with surrender in their eyes.

Danny could hear Schmedly barking as they approached him. The windows were all fogged except for a few spots where Schmedly's nose had made imprints in the condensation.

Danny reached back and grabbed dry towels, handing one to Barry.

"That was not a fun day," Barry said.

"I'm even looking forward to getting inside the cabin. Wonder if Andy fixed our leak."

"God, I'm cold, I'm wet... I'm too old for this," Barry said. "Let's get something to eat and then head back."

Schmedly barked.

"Yes, yes, we'll get you a cheeseburger," Barry said.

"See, now you're starting to understand him."

Back at the cabin, Danny again had to wrestle Schmedly out of the van.

"Barry, I'm telling you – he's still not comfortable here. Promise we leave here tomorrow?" Danny asked, pushing Schmedly in from behind.

"We're out of here first thing," Barry said, peeling off his wet clothes.

* * * * *

It was midnight. A window in the clouds had slowed the rain. All three were asleep. The television remained on but at low volume.

Underneath the cabin and out of sight, a small trickle of water ran down a set of badly taped electrical wires, shorting them out. Sparks fell on dry brush, which had somehow eluded the torrents of water running past both sides of the cabin. The smoldering pile sent out small puffs of smoke, filling the crawl space until a gust of wind blew through, giving the fire its first flame. In minutes, toxic fumes were rushing up through the floorboards. The smoke detectors remained silent for the batteries were years old.

A small twig cracked as it burned. Schmedly, who slept on the floor, was the only one to hear it. He sprang up, barking his warning but neither man moved. They had already succumbed to the smoke. Schmedly jumped up on Danny's bed, barking and scratching with his broken leg.

Barry began to wake. He coughed and choked. His first instinct was to get out. He fell to the floor and crawled, stopping only for a second to consider pulling Danny out as well but in his weakened state, only had the strength for one. As he reached up and opened the door, he heard Danny cough over Schmedly's barking, which was quickly becoming strained and hoarse.

Barry made it outside, still on his knees. He drew in a long breath of fresh air but choked and gagged on the fluid that had built up in his lungs. He continued to crawl off the front porch and into the muddy parking area - his goal was in sight. He continued to cough - the sound coming from deep down in his burning lungs.

"Help...fire," he screamed, but his yells were merely raspy whispers.

He made it to the van. With mud dripping from his body, he lifted himself to his knees and opened the door. He reached for the steering wheel, pulling himself in just enough to hold down the horn.

Smoke poured from the open cabin door. Schmedly's barking had subsided. Barry feared the worst, but he could do nothing to help them. He turned his head toward the office, still holding steady on the horn. Andy and another man had come out and were now running in his direction. They were still a good ways off. Barry feared for the two inside. He had used all his strength and now fell to all fours and gasped for air.

"Fire, fire," the men yelled as they came closer.

Barry heard what sounded like scratching. He raised his head. From under the smoke, he could see Schmedly's tail in the air and his back legs straining as he tugged on Danny's shirt. Barry thought that he caught a slight movement in Danny's arms. As Danny was pulled to the edge of the porch, Barry could see that he was holding a rag to his nose and mouth. He rolled off the porch and landed two feet below with a thud.

Barry was amazed at the determination of the little dog. He continued to pull Danny until he was only a few feet from Barry. The dog, now exhausted, breathed and coughed while holding his broken leg in the air.

Danny looked at Barry, who gave a nod that he was all right. Both men's eyes were bloodshot from the smoke. Danny got on all fours and retched while trying to reach out and touch the choking dog but he was too far away.

The two men from the office reached the cabin, coming first to Danny and then to Barry.

"Anyone else inside?" Andy asked.

Barry shook his head as saliva strung from his mouth. The two men ran back toward the office to call 9-1-1 and retrieve a fire extinguisher, which they had forgotten to do in their haste to reach the cabin.

Danny panicked when he was unable to draw a breath, but after a hard cough, he was able to inhale once again. It took all his strength just to hold himself on his hands and knees.

Schmedly came to Danny's side. His breathing was labored, but he appeared in better shape than the men did.

"Good boy. You saved us," Danny managed.

Schmedly gave Danny a sad look and licked his face. He then turned and hobbled on his broken leg toward the cabin door. Danny watched but didn't understand. He looked at Barry – who else was inside to be saved? Was he in a dream? Why was the dog going back inside?

Schmedly disappeared into the billowing gray smoke. Danny tried to stand but barely had enough strength to crawl. For every foot he moved, he needed ten deep breaths – one more painful than the next.

Danny collapsed face down in the mud as Andy ran back with a fire extinguisher, dropping it upon seeing Danny's position. He flipped him over. Barry watched as Andy checked for breathing, and then put his lips to Danny's and blew fresh air into his lungs. After five breaths, Danny's head lifted as he coughed. He stared up at Andy, realizing that his life had been saved once again.

"My dog," Danny whispered, as he pointed inside.

"Your dog? I saw him out here," Andy said.

"He went back in," Barry croaked.

Andy jumped up and took a step toward the cabin, but flames had engulfed the curtains and poured out the windows. They heard a siren in the distance.

The other man who had accompanied Andy ran up with a hose that he had connected nearby. Andy covered his mouth with the same rag Danny had used and stepped onto the porch. He blasted the hose inside and crawled in. He took a deep breath and entered the cabin on all fours, feeling his way around. On the floor between the beds he felt Schmedly's soft fur. He grabbed the dog by the tail, dragging him outside. He laid him next to Danny.

"Is he all right?" Danny whispered.

"He's in bad shape," Andy said through his coughs. "He's not breathin'."

Andy closed Schmedly's mouth and puffed small breaths into his nose. They could only watch in disbelief, as Schmedly didn't respond.

A crowd of men from the other cabins had now gathered around the scene.

"We need to get these men to the hospital right now. We can't wait. Load 'em in whateva vehicle you can."

Danny heard a man's voice giving commands but his field of vision narrowed until he was almost out. He felt himself being lifted.

The next thing he saw was the nurse standing next to his bed.

"You comin' 'round?" she asked. "You 'member me? You fought me when I was puttin' the oxygen mask on you."

Danny shook his head. "I don't remember... oh, my God – my dog. Where's my dog?" he coughed heavily into the oxygen mask.

"Now jest calm down. Your friend is in the next room and he's in better shape than you. I'll go ask him."

Danny thought hard – had he really seen Schmedly go back inside the cabin? Did he watch Andy attempt to revive him? Or was he delusional from smoke inhalation?

The nurse wheeled Barry in without making eye contact with Danny. Barry didn't have to say a word – Danny knew immediately that it was all real. The nurse left them alone.

"Is he all right, Barry?"

Barry looked to the floor and removed his mask. "They couldn't save him, Danny, I'm sorry."

Danny sobbed. "Why did he go back in? There was nobody left in there to save."

Barry had no answers. Tears streamed down his cheeks as well.

"Where is he?" Danny asked, as he pushed the button to summon the nurse.

"I asked Andy if someone could take him to a vet. They were going to take him to an all night emergency clinic about forty miles away," Barry replied.

Danny played with the buttons that controlled the bed positions and attempted to raise himself.

"Barry, what started that fire? I mean we're thinking this Andy's a nice guy but maybe we asked too many questions and he really did have a connection to my father. Maybe he started the fire?"

"Danny, he saved you... and went back in for Schmedly, remember? They'll do an investigation and we'll find out. We're certainly not staying anywhere near here once we get out. All our stuff that was saved is in the office, and we'll get that on the way to..."

A different nurse answered the call. "Everything all right?" she stopped short upon seeing both men crying. "What's going on?"

"When can we leave?" Danny asked.

"The doctor has to answer that, but my guess is you're here for the night. You can't play games with carbon monoxide poisoning even if yours was a mild case."

"You want to be alone?" Barry asked.

Danny just stared into space.

The nurse turned Barry's wheelchair. He stopped her at the door.

"Danny, you want to go home or do you want to continue on?"

"I don't know."

She wheeled Barry out but Danny called him back.

"Barry, have you seen him?"

Barry knew what he was asking.

"I haven't, Danny, but I'm sure he's with your father now."

"When you get a chance, maybe you can try to contact him?" Danny pleaded.

Barry felt great pity for his friend. Never was there a tighter bond between a man and his dog. "Danny, I'll do whatever I can to contact him – I promise."

Within a few short weeks Danny had lost his father, his wife albeit of his own doing, and his dog. He was alone. He had no money and bills that he could never pay unless they could find his father's body.

Maybe if Barry's right and there is an after life; maybe I belong there. Anything is better than this.

Chapter Fourteen

The men made a quick stop at the office to retrieve what was left of their belongings. The air smelled of smoke.

"Andy around?" Barry asked the man behind the counter.

"Nope. He's gone 'til tomorra. Anythin' I can help you boys with?"

"We're the guys who were in the fire," Danny said.

"Oh, we got your stuff here in the back."

"Can we check to see if anything is still inside the cabin?" Barry asked.

"Nope. Fire chief don't want no one goin' in 'til they done 'vestigatin'."

Danny went behind the counter and rummaged through their bags.

"Hey, Barry, our stuff doesn't look too bad but it reeks of smoke."

"Let's get it packed," Barry said as he lifted a duffel bag.

Danny's body trembled as they approached the bright lights of the upcoming city. Although Schmedly was gone, he needed to see him. Barry flipped on the inside light and fumbled with the directions to the clinic. He noticed Danny continuously turning to the back of the van hoping that Schmedly would some how miraculously reappear.

"I'm really sorry, Danny. This was my fault. I got so caught up in finding your father that I dismissed Schmedly's premonitions."

"Wasn't your fault that he ran back into a burning cabin." He raised his hand in the air and dropped it back onto his thigh. "Makes no sense," he said, half-crying.

"No... no, it doesn't, Danny"

Barry turned up the heat up as the wind howled through the half-open windows. The smoky smell had permeated so deeply into their duffel bags and clothes, that without fresh air neither man would be able to endure the ride.

"Here, read this to me," Barry said, handing Danny the directions. "Damn GPS wouldn't take the address."

Danny guided Barry to the parking lot. They sat in silence as Danny stared at the building, dreading the inevitable.

"You want me to come in with you?" Barry asked.

"Yeah, would you?"

Neither was in a rush to go inside. Barry held the door open.

"Can I help you?" the girl behind the counter asked.

"I believe you have our dog here. Died in a fire," Barry said.

"Oh, I'm so sorry. Yes, he's the one that came in last night, right?"

"Yes."

"Do you want to take him... or..."

"We don't really know what to do," Barry said. "We're traveling back to Connecticut."

"May I suggest that he be cremated," she said, handing them a brochure. "It's what most people do. You'd have to wait a couple of days."

Barry looked at Danny for any clues of what he was feeling.

"Can I see him now?" Danny asked.

"Oh, surely. If you'll wait for just one minute. Let me..." she picked up the phone and then put it back down. "Let me run to the back."

A few minutes later, the girl opened the door and waved Danny in.

"You want me to come?" Barry asked.

"No."

Danny followed the girl down a hallway.

"We brought him out of the cold for you," she said.

As they passed through the next door, Schmedly's body came into view. Danny stopped short for a second. Tears poured down his cheeks. The girl, seeing Danny's emotion, turned away for fear of crying herself. She walked into a back room and without turning toward him said, "call me when you're ready. My name is Carol."

Schmedly's eyes were closed and his mouth open slightly. Danny took his cold paw in his hand and lifted it a couple of inches.

"I'm so sorry, Schmed." Danny shook his head back and forth. "I didn't know this would happen. Why did you go back in..." he burst out crying as he laid his head on the dog's shoulder. His fur was still soft although his body was frozen. Danny felt faint. The room blurred and for an instant he felt as though he was in a dream but with Schmedly's cold body under his head, he knew this was all real.

"Why did you go back? There was no one left inside to save."

The girl had heard Danny's outburst and was concerned. She waved for Barry, who sat on the far side of the room, to come over. "I think your friend may need your help," she said, leading him back. She opened the door for Barry and returned to the front desk.

Barry watched and waited for an appropriate time to speak but there was no right time here. He scraped his shoe along the ground to let Danny know that he was there. Danny turned; his eyes were puffy and wet.

"Why did he have to do that, Barry?"

Barry walked over and ran his hand down Schmedly's body.

"I don't know, Danny... but if it makes you feel better... you'll see him again. You believe in what I see, don't you?"

Danny sniffled, "Yeah."

"Then you have to know that you'll see him again."

Barry knew there were no words to ease the pain; a bond so strong would not easily be broken.

"I'll wait outside. Take as long as you need." He put his hand on Danny's shoulder. "I mean it – take as long as you need."

Barry entered the hallway. He took out a tissue from his pocket that he had forgotten to give Danny and wiped his own eyes. His cell phone rang. He continued down the hall and answered once back in the main waiting room.

"Hello?"

"Mr. Leonard? This is Detective Marone."

"Yes, Detective."

"We tried Danny's cell phone but couldn't get him. Is he with you?"

"Not right this second. We had some problems."

"Everything okay?" Marone asked.

"Well... yeah, everything's fine. Can I pass along a message?"

"We found his father's body."

"Really," Barry said in amazement.

"Kind of where your friend Ms. Morgan led us – deep in an old well."

Barry was silent for a moment.

"Mr. Leonard, you still there?"

"Oh, yeah. Just trying to figure out what the hell I'm chasing down here."

"I don't know but we've made positive ID on him. When are you heading back?"

"We'll be leaving very shortly. Thank you Detective."

Even though Danny believed that his father was dead, hearing that the body was found would just add heartache to the recent events. Barry went to the girl at the counter.

"How is your friend?" she asked.

"He couldn't be worse. Listen, you mentioned that it could take days to get the dog cremated. Is there any way of speeding that up?"

"If you want to transport the dog yourself, that would save some time but there's always a wait at the crematorium."

"What time do they open?"

"Nine, I guess."

"Good. Is there a good hotel nearby?"

Barry sat in the waiting room for almost half an hour. Danny finally opened the door and came out.

"Sorry I took so long, Barry."

"Doesn't matter, Danny."

"What's the plan now?"

"I got us a room a mile down the road." Barry paused. "Danny, you given any thought to the cremation idea?"

"Yeah, I think it's the way to go. I can keep him close at least. What do you think?"

"I agree. What we can do is come back here in the morning and pick him up and take him to the crematorium. Then we head to Atlanta and catch a flight back. They can ship his ashes back home in a couple days."

"Couple days – no way. I'll stay and wait for him. I'm not taking any chances that they might lose him. You can head back, Barry. We'll catch up when I get back."

Barry thought for a moment. "We've gone through hell together here, Danny. I won't leave without you and Schmedly. Please forgive me for being so inconsiderate."

Before Danny could ask any more questions, Barry led him to the van. Danny could see there was something more on his friend's mind. He got in the van and waited.

"Danny, they found your father's body. I was going to wait but there wasn't going to be a better time to tell you."

Danny, already numb and traumatized, just sat without saying a word or shedding a tear.

"They called you?"

"The detective did. They couldn't get you on your phone."

Danny pulled his phone from its holster. "Had it turned off." He slipped it back. "Where'd they find him?"

"In a well back in Connecticut. Danny, I'm really sorry. I don't know what I was seeing to bring us here."

"So Beverly was right."

"Yes, I'm afraid so."

"God, then why are we here? Don't get me wrong Barry. I'm not blaming you but something told you to come here."

Barry didn't have an answer. "Let's just get to the room and try and get some rest. Maybe I can sort this out there."

Both men collapsed onto the beds. The grief that Danny was feeling was immeasurable and the emotional stress so great that he passed out almost immediately. Barry wasn't too far behind.

The ringing phone in the morning barely woke them. Barry coughed as he picked up the receiver only to hear the recorded wake-up call he had requested.

"You awake?" he asked Danny.

"Yeah... what's that noise?"

Barry sat up holding his head, as it pounded like a fierce hangover. He gazed out the window but could see no more than a few inches in front of him. Rain came down so hard, it sounded like a passing train.

"Another lovely day," Barry said. "Never saw so much rain."

"Like I don't have enough crap to take care of. I have to pick up Schmedly from the morgue, have him cremated, wait days for his ashes, catch a flight home and have a funeral for my... my father." Danny broke down and cried. "I've got no reason to get out of this bed, Barry."

"I know it's hard and I hate to say what everyone else says – life goes on. You have to be strong. Remember, like I keep telling you – you'll see them again."

Danny believed in what Barry was saying and it did give him a bit of comfort but the thought of seeing Schmedly again was saddening.

"I hate to rush you, Danny, but we need to get done what we have to," Barry said.

"Barry..." Danny started.

"Sorry Danny – he hasn't come to me yet. I'll keep trying though. I told you that sometimes they don't come for a while after they die."

* * * * *

Danny filled out papers at the vet's office. Barry got the ear of one of the vets.

"How can I get a cremation done in a hurry? We need to get home today." He pointed at Danny. "That gentleman's father was murdered and they found his body yesterday. His dog – the one we're here to pick up today – died saving us from a fire."

The vet appeared shocked and saddened. "I'll make a call," he said. "Come with me."

Barry was given the name of the man at the crematorium who would expedite matters from days to hours. Danny looked up from signing a credit card receipt.

"We're taken care of," Barry said.

"If you'll just bring your car to the double doors, we'll help with your pet," the vet said.

"Thank you," Barry said. "You ready?"

"As ready as I'm going to be."

Barry ran to the van while Danny waited under the awning that covered the walkway from the main door to the double doors. A teenager pushed the gurney holding the black bag with Schmedly's remains to the rear of the minivan as Barry backed into place. Danny tried not to think about what was happening. Barry came up behind him.

"Hop inside, Danny. I'll help him," he said, opening the back door of the van.

"Nope, I got him."

Danny scooped up the bag and lifted it gently. He carried it the few feet and laid it down behind the rear seat.

"Wait, no... I want him right behind me where he belongs."

He picked up the bag again. Barry ran ahead of him and opened the side door. Both men were now exposed to the torrential rain and were soaked to the skin within seconds. Barry climbed in and helped Danny situate the body. Danny slid the door shut and they both took their seats.

* * * * *

The short half-hour trip to the crematorium turned into a two-hour ordeal with flooded roads and zero visibility. On approaching, a tall smokestack belched thin black smoke – an eerie reminder of what went on at the facility. They pulled into the lot and followed a sign that read "drop offs".

"Drop offs?" Danny said. "You think they could have used some etiquette when wording that sign."

"I imagine most of the deliveries here aren't by the family. It's usually the funeral home or the vets van."

"Right."

Barry backed the van up to a garage door in the rear of the building. A man opened the door and Barry continued in. Getting out, both men sniffed the air expecting a horrible odor but there was none.

"You..." Barry pulled a piece of paper from his pocket. "You Carl?"

"That's me."

"I believe the vet spoke to you," Barry said, inconspicuously rubbing a fifty-dollar bill between his fingers at his side.

"Yes, he did." Carl put up his hand, "The money won't be necessary. I'll take care of you immediately, sir."

He followed Barry to the side door of the van where he lifted Schmedly onto a gurney.

"Can I see him once more?" Danny asked.

"Of course. I'll be right over there. You just holler when you're ready."

Danny unzipped the bag, exposing Schmedly's head. He stroked his cheek.

Barry put his hand on Danny's shoulder. "He was a good dog."

"God, I'm going to miss him so much," Danny said, choking back tears. "I'm so used to having him next to me."

"I'll be in the van. Take your time."

Danny stared at his friend. As he started to zip the bag closed, reality set in – this would be the last time he would ever see his dog. He cried as Schmedly's face disappeared into the plastic bag.

Barry came out and waved Carl over.

"How long will it take?" Barry asked.

"'Bout two and half hours or so."

"Okay, we'll see you later."

"Wait, there's one more thing," Carl said. "I'll be right back."

He wheeled the gurney out of sight and returned with a catalogue.

"What type of urn do you want?"

Danny flipped through the pages, surprised at the many styles. Into the fourth page he stopped and put his finger on the page.

"That one."

Barry came to Danny's side to view the picture – a golden box, the front panel with an etching of a man kneeling and holding the paw of a sitting dog.

"That's the one," Barry said.

The men returned to the hospital for their follow-up as the doctor had requested. After x-rays and a review both men were given the okay to leave. The stitches Danny had received in the first accident were not ready to come out, but a fresh bandage was applied.

Barry and Danny flapped umbrellas, shaking off the water as they reentered the crematorium.

"May I help you?" the woman asked.

"Last name Dillon," Danny said.

"I'll be right back."

She returned carrying a plastic bag. She laid it down and flattened the plastic to the counter, revealing the beautifully etched urn. Danny picked it up expecting it to be lightweight, but to his surprise it weighed about two pounds.

"Awful heavy," he said. "Thought ashes would be lighter."

"Everyone says that," the woman responded.

He pulled the plastic bag up and carried the urn in both hands to the van. Barry patted Danny on the knee.

"I'm so very sorry for your loss, Danny."

"Yeah, he was a good dog. Let's go home."

Barry drove through the relentless downpour. He had mapped out the fastest way to Atlanta but it encompassed many miles of smaller, less traveled roads before a major highway could be reached.

Danny held the urn on his lap. He played Schmedly's life over in his mind – from the little ball of fur as a puppy to the barking for cheeseburgers on the trip. The one vision that haunted him was of Schmedly lowering his head and running back into the smoky cabin.

Barry stopped the van.

"What's wrong?" Danny asked, searching for something ahead in the road.

"I don't know. I just saw something."

"In the road?"

"No... I don't know." He shook his head. "It was a quick vision but... I think I just need some rest after this whole ordeal."

He continued on, driving on a never-ending, two-lane winding road. Finally a straightaway – a tree lined highway where he could make up some time through the rain.

Unforeseen to the weary men, a small stream ahead had become a flash flood. The hundred-year-old bridge that spanned it creaked and moaned as the rushing water smashed its panels.

Barry leaned far forward in his seat pressing his eyes to see more than thirty feet ahead but the heavy rain engulfed them like a thick fog. They approached within a mile of the distressed bridge, which swayed in the massive rapids. Finally it could hold no longer and in an instant was snapped into kindling and swept like a toy downriver.

Barry pushed the limit, knowing that he was driving too fast for the weather but the race to catch their flight was on. Now only a short distance from certain death, Barry yelled out and jammed the brake pedal to the floor with both feet. Skidding sideways, both men screamed. With one hand, Danny held tight to Schmedly's urn, the other jammed against the dashboard. The van came to rest off the road in the mud. Neither man could really see the explosion of water ahead but Barry knew it was there.

He gunned the engine, dragging the van from the pull of the sticky mud and back onto the roadway. He rolled ahead twenty feet – the raging river was now in view. Trees from the banks were torn down and dragged into the tumult – its water brown with silt.

Danny's mouth dropped open. His body shook. "I'm real glad... real glad that you saw that coming, Barry."

"I didn't see it – I felt it."

Barry held back tears. "My God, he knew... he just couldn't tell us. How sad for that poor dog. He must've been exploding inside like a person in a coma who can hear the voices but can't communicate."

Danny looked at the river ahead and back at Barry. "You gonna let me in on this? What about the poor dog and the coma?"

Barry sat silent; his chest heaved as drew in a few deep breaths. Danny waited. Barry finally continued.

"You know how we've been following your father?"

"Yeah."

"We haven't been. We've been following her."

"Her who?" Danny eyes then opened wide.

Barry smacked the steering wheel while speaking excitedly. "Cheryl, we've been following Cheryl. She's been leading us into places of danger."

"But you saw my father. I don't get it."

"She suppressed your father's spirit and assumed his identity. Her strong will in life must've followed her over. She was able to overpower him in the spirit world. She's been trying to kill us – well, you anyway."

"How come you're only seeing this now?"

"It was Schmedly. He must've sensed it. He knew we were following her – just couldn't tell us."

Danny shook his head in confusion. "What?"

"Danny, you told me that Cheryl feared Schmedly, right?"

"Yeah."

"Apparently he was able to scare her off and allow me to see the true spirit of your father. That's why I stopped short. Your father showed me danger," Barry said, pointing to the screaming water. "Danny, do you understand what I'm saying?"

"I... I think so," Danny said, still with a puzzled look.

"The only way Schmedly could've saved you was by going back into that fire."

Barry waited for Danny to put it all together. It took just seconds. He looked at the urn still on his lap and ran his hands over it.

"Barry... you mean to tell me that he committed suicide?"

Barry nodded. "It was the only way to scare off the... the demon, I guess you would call her."

Danny began to weep. "Did you see him? Schmedly, I mean."

"No, but when I had visions flashing in my mind, I smelled wet dog fur – like Schmedly after the rain. I also saw your father's true spirit. A very, very bright aura."

"How do you know about him," Danny looked down at the urn. "Chasing Cheryl?"

"Can't really explain it. I just felt a deep fear like Cheryl would've had for Schmedly and knew your father's soul was being set free." Barry looked confused. "Never felt fear from the other side before... usually just happiness."

Danny continued to cry. Barry rested his hand on Danny's shoulder. "Danny, he'll be there for you when you leave this life."

"I guess this is where I'm supposed to say, Barry, someday explain all this to me."

"It's over – all the unanswered questions that were driving me insane are now put to rest. Let's go home."

Barry pushed buttons on the GPS, plotting a new course to the airport. He turned the van around and drove away.

It had been a year since George's murder and Schmedly's death. Two carpenters who had done work for George were convicted of his kidnapping and murder and were sentenced to life in prison. Much of the ransom money was recovered.

Danny was free of all charges in Cheryl's death. The detectives were never able to collect enough evidence for a conviction. Although free from jail for his crime, emotionally he was imprisoned with the knowledge that he had killed an innocent human being – Cheryl had no hand in George's disappearance.

Danny sat in his father's house, which was now his. The memories of Schmedly in the old house made it unbearable to remain – at least that's the story he told. In reality, it was the haunting memory of his act against Cheryl and the constant feeling of someone lightly grasping his ankle while in the kitchen. That house and business were sold to Tommy, whom Danny now worked for a couple of days a week just to keep busy.

Kanook popped a beer in the kitchen and sipped it as he carried another for Danny. A football game played on the big screen TV that was only a glance away from the fireplace, its mantle holding Danny's treasures. Three urns sat side by side accompanied by a picture of his parents and a larger photo of Schmedly. Cheryl's picture was not among them.

Kanook handed Danny the beer and stared at the pictures. "I miss that dog – he was the best."

"I miss him too, but I know that I'll see him again one day. Gives me something to look forward to."

"Looking forward to dying?"

"It doesn't really matter. I'm happy in life right now and I'll be happy when I'm with them again," he said, pointing to the pictures. "A wise man once said 'Death is but the beginning'."

"Here's to that wise man," Kanook said.

They raised their bottles and took a sip.

Ken Myler lives on Long Island, New York. He is an avid boater who enjoys navigating the Great South Bay but his passion for hiking and cycling draw him to the unexplored arches and spires of the American West. His admiration of nature is surpassed only by his love for animals.

He is an admitted daydreamer having a wandering mind rivaling that of the fictitious character – Walter Mitty. Many of his stories have been maturing secretly since childhood and only recently did he put them to paper. Discovering the calming affects of Native American flute music, he uses it to focus on the many twists and turns that he writes into his stories.

He is the author of the IPPY award-winning book, *The Will to Defy*.